A Daughter's Courage

Books by Misty Beller

HEARTS OF MONTANA

Hope's Highest Mountain
Love's Mountain Quest
Faith's Mountain Home

BRIDES OF LAURENT

A Warrior's Heart
A Healer's Promise
A Daughter's Courage

BRIDES of LAURENT

A DAUGHTER'S COURAGE

MISTY M. BELLER

BETHANY HOUSE

a division of Baker Publishing Group
Minneapolis, Minnesota

© 2022 by Misty M. Beller

Published by Bethany House Publishers
11400 Hampshire Avenue South
Minneapolis, Minnesota 55438
www.bethanyhouse.com

Bethany House Publishers is a division of
Baker Publishing Group, Grand Rapids, Michigan

Printed in the United States of America

Library of Congress Cataloging-in-Publication Data
Names: Beller, Misty M., author.
Title: A daughter's courage / Misty M. Beller.
Description: Minneapolis, Minnesota : Bethany House, a division of Baker
   Publishing Group, 2022. | Series: Brides of Laurent ; 3
Identifiers: LCCN 2022015493 | ISBN 9780764238062 (paperback) | ISBN
   9780764240782 (casebound) | ISBN 9781493439003 (ebook)
Classification: LCC PS3602.E45755 F35 2022 | DDC 813/.6--dc23
LC record available at https://lccn.loc.gov/2022015493

Scripture quotations are from the King James Version of the Bible.

This is a work of fiction. Names, characters, incidents, and dialogues are products of the author's imagination and are not to be construed as real. Any resemblance to actual events or persons, living or dead, is entirely coincidental.

Cover design by LOOK Design Studio
Cover photography by Aimee Christenson

Author is represented by Books & Such Literary Agency.

22 23 24 25 26 27 28   7 6 5 4 3 2 1

To my mastermind group:
Christy, Erin, Laura, and Robin.
You ladies have meant the world to me.
Thank you for your support, your wisdom, your prayers,
and your unconditional love.

And we know that all things work together for good to them that love God, to them who are the called according to his purpose.

Romans 8:28

1

Cooking fulfilled Charlotte Durand like little else did.

Maybe not the act of slicing meat and stirring stew over a hot fire, but the steps required to ensure each morsel she prepared would bring her family pleasure. That her food would nourish and strengthen. And, in this case, furnish the setting for a celebration.

The trading party had returned from Fort Versailles.

Laurent's council had finally opened their solitary village to a small bit of trade with the fort located two days' ride to the east, but only a couple men went at a time. For this journey, Erik and Monsieur Rochette had been gone five days, returning this afternoon with heaping packs of supplies.

Tonight, their table would be overflowing just like the traders' packs, and she had so many final preparations to finish. In less than an hour, both men would sup at the Durand table to share news. Who knew what fascinating tidings they'd bring this time? So many people passed in and out of the fort's log walls. . . . . Charlotte couldn't imagine meeting so many strangers every day.

The rear door of their apartment opened, and her father stepped in, brushing something from his hands. Probably rock dust, if he'd been visiting the new homes being cut into the mountainside. "Smells wonderful in here."

She smiled at him. She was no great chef, not like her good friend Audrey Masters and some of the older women in the village. Her skill had been completely self-taught through testing and watching others and tweaking her own methods based on the results. That had always made her outcome a little different from the rest. But she loved working in the background to make things happen as they should and to keep their home running seamlessly.

And this meal had to be perfect.

Papa had asked her to prepare *ragoût d'ours*, and thankfully the fatty bear meat was almost impossible to scorch.

Papa approached the fire where she stirred the ragoût and inhaled deeply. "Ah, wonderful. Hugo will be pleased."

She stiffened and glanced at him. "Hugo Lemaire? I thought Erik and Monsieur Rochette were dining with us."

The chagrin on her father's face tugged her middle into a knot. "I invited Hugo also. He was interested in hearing news from the fort, and he'll be trading some of the supplies when our Dinee friends come in a few days." Papa's eyes turned hopeful. "He really is such a good man, Charlotte. And he thinks highly of you."

The knot tightened into a thick coil. Papa had taken the young man under his wing. At first, she'd thought her father's efforts were simply for Hugo's benefit, to help him return to a better path after the mistakes he made in his youth—especially the debacle with Gerald that nearly took her sister's life.

But Papa had clearly seen something he liked in the fellow, and the more time they spent together, the more her father spoke his praises specifically to *her* when Hugo wasn't around. She'd finally come to terms with the truth: Her father thought Hugo should be her match. Hugo had made his interest clear, too, even in his shy way.

Could he really think she was interested in the man? Had he not seen the times she'd gone out of her way to avoid Hugo's presence or turned the conversation when Papa droned on about the fellow's growing list of good qualities? Hugo had come far in the past few years, exchanging his slothful ways for a trade where he worked hard. He'd even stopped mumbling, as he'd once been known for, though now his shyness kept him even quieter than before.

Still, he wasn't the man for her. Every part of her cringed at the thought.

The look on Papa's face now was almost sappy, as though he was caught up in the possibility of budding amour. He resembled more a meddling mother than the wise chief of Laurent she'd always considered him.

She had to stop this. If she didn't speak plainly now, he would keep on with this matchmaking until he went too far. Once he knew exactly how she felt about the man, Papa would leave it alone. Surely. He cared about his children's happiness. He'd always been the best of fathers.

Rising so she could face him, she steeled herself to speak the hard words. She hated confrontation, but getting this over with would stop the situation from growing worse. She never raised a stir if she could help it. Hopefully all those times she'd passively given in to his requests would help him do the same for her now.

Her father lifted his brows, waiting for her to speak. Probably expecting a simple request, like for him to bring an extra pot of water or to borrow Audrey's larger stewpot.

She let out a breath. "Papa. I need to talk with you about Hugo."

His brows rose even higher, and a hint of a hopeful smile played at his mouth. "Yes?"

She steeled her nerves and started in. "You've made it clear you like him and feel he would be a good match for me. I've not been straightforward with my feelings on the matter, but it's time I do so. I'm glad Hugo has come so far under your tutelage. I'm glad he's become a respectable citizen now." *Instead of the lazy vagabond he was only a few years ago.* "But I don't want to marry him. I feel no attraction toward him. No deeper sentiment."

None of the fiery sparks that lit between her sister Brielle and her husband, even two years after their marriage. Watching the pair together had shown Charlotte a passion she wanted for herself. If she were ever to marry, she wanted that depth of connection with her husband.

And Hugo Lemaire inspired no such reaction.

"Charlotte, *mon chou*." Papa's voice took on that coddling tone he'd used back when she was a girl and he urged her to eat one of Brielle's scorched attempts at biscuits. "You've grown up alongside Hugo, so I understand how you might think of him as only a friend, not a potential husband. But I think if you work to adjust your thinking, you'll find him the perfect match for your personality. He's quiet and thoughtful, just like you. He's become such a hard worker,

MISTY M. BELLER

taking pride in everything he does. The two of you would have a pleasant, productive home."

Pleasant. Productive. Not her primary goals in a marriage.

She squeezed her eyes shut as she scrambled to find the words to show him just how impossible it would be for her to find happiness with Hugo.

But before she could manage them, a knock sounded on the front door. Papa clapped a hand on her shoulder. "Our guests have arrived. And please, Charlotte, give Hugo a chance. I really think he would make a good match."

She couldn't speak past the roiling in her belly as her father stepped around her to answer the door. She turned back to the stewpot hanging over the fire, sinking to her knees on the stone floor as the strength in her legs gave way.

Her father wouldn't force her to marry Hugo, would he? He had the right. Often marriages in Laurent were planned by the parents. But the potential bride and groom were usually allowed a voice in the process.

Yet even if Papa finally let go of this ridiculous notion that she should marry Hugo, what other man lived in Laurent whom she could possibly love? Their little village had been separated from the rest of the world for so many years—more than a century. Brielle's and Audrey's husbands were the only two strangers who'd joined their numbers during that entire time, and that had only happened in the last two years.

"Charlotte, whatever you're cooking smells good enough to bring a weary traveler home."

She turned to smile at Erik, one of her father's good friends and a leading member of the council. "You returned a day sooner than we expected. I'd like to think it's my ragoût,

11

but I suspect your haste has more to do with your sweet wife." Erik was nearly her father's age, so he didn't often go on the trading journeys to the fort. There must have been a particular reason he'd left Madeline and their warm home just as winter's chill had begun to set in.

He sent her a wink. "You know me well."

Erik turned to speak with her father, and Charlotte slipped into the background, placing bread and dried fruit on the table, then filling bowls with the stew and mugs with tea. With so much to do, she managed to avoid catching Hugo's eye, though she could feel the weight of his gaze at times.

When everything was ready, she nodded to Papa.

He sent her a smile of thanks, then motioned to the neatly spread table. "Please, my friends. Be seated and fill your hungry bellies before we hear the news from the fort."

She stayed by the fire, perched on a stool to scrub the utensils she'd used in cooking. But mostly she listened to the sounds of pleasure as the men ate. At last, as she polished the grooves in the fir trees Papa had engraved on her cooking spoons, he sat back in his chair. "Now that we're warmed from that wonderful meal, what news have you learned?"

Erik wiped his mouth on the cloth and placed it on the table. "Not much seems to have changed since Thayer and Gaume went in the spring. Most of the trappers have already set out for the winter season, but a few stayed behind to work on the fort. I heard there were some skilled artisans in the group—metalworkers and carpenters, mostly—but we didn't get to meet them. The North West company is sending an assistant for the factor, and it's said he'll be bringing his wife with him."

Charlotte paused in her cleaning. A white woman? Dinee

bands that included women and children sometimes camped outside the fort for trading, but this was the first time she'd heard of a white woman coming to the area. Would she be from the Canadas or the United States?

As much as she wanted to ask these questions now, this conversation was Papa's to lead. She could ask him or Erik for more details later. Besides, the last thing she wanted was to draw Hugo's attention—more than he already looked at her, anyway. Had Papa told him she would be interested if he made an effort for them to spend time together?

A twinge niggled in her chest. She didn't want to hurt Hugo. He really seemed to have changed from who he had been as a lad.

But there was no way she could marry him. She'd rather die as the favorite spinster auntie to Brielle's children, whenever they came, and even to those her younger brother Andre would produce when he grew of age to find his own bride.

That would be far better than sacrificing her life to a man she didn't love.

❧

Damien Levette's mule rocked back on its haunches as they plunged down the slope. Gulliver had done this so many times the past few months that the mount no longer balked at going straight down an incline. If he weren't so surefooted, Damien would never ask the mule to charge down a mountainside like this. He didn't mind risking his own life, but he had no desire to jeopardize his faithful friend—the only companion he had left.

But Gulliver seemed to enjoy the challenge as much as

Damien did. And the rush that came when Damien's body dropped before his middle could catch up, when the base of the mountain loomed far below, made him finally feel alive. For a few moments, at least.

Then the truth would catch up with him. He had no right to feel so vibrant. Not when Michelle, his other half, the twin who'd always brought out the best in him, lay buried under six feet of mud and a block of carved stone.

He slowed Gulliver partway down the slope, guiding him to the left so he could descend the rest of the incline at a safer angle. If something happened to him because of Damien's recklessness, well . . . he already couldn't live with himself.

For now, though, he had to keep pushing on. That's what Michelle would have wanted. One day at a time. One hour at a time. These next few weeks would be the worst as he passed the first anniversary of her death, but at least he'd come far enough into the mountain wilderness that his misery wouldn't affect anyone else.

Gulliver didn't seem to mind his ill humor. Just stayed by his side faithfully. Exactly like Michelle had done for all those years.

A glance up at the sky showed the dark clouds descending lower than they'd been earlier. A few snow flurries had fallen yesterday but not enough to stick to the ground. The first real snow looked ready to fall soon, though. That might make tracking easier, but he needed to set some beaver snares before the rivers iced over.

Now that he'd left the main trapping party, it was up to him to find the best locations. No seasoned trapper like Arsenault was there to glance around and say a particular region seemed promising. But he also didn't have anyone telling him when he had to pull up his snares and move on. He would be making his own decisions, then living with the consequences.

A bark jerked his attention to the base of the mountain. A doglike animal trotted from rock to rock, sniffing, then it raised its snout in the air and loosed a short yip. Coyote. Not big enough to be a wolf, even a lean one. Though this animal certainly was skinny. Bones poked up at its hips and shoulders, and very little flesh covered its ribs. Did that mean there wasn't much game in this area? The meat-eaters should be at their healthiest this time of year, having scarfed down plenty to prepare for the winter.

As the slope began to level out, Damien aimed the mule toward a line of trees that signaled water. A small creek, probably, but it might lead to a larger river prime for trapping.

When he rode past the coyote, the animal eyed him but didn't leap away. Daring fellow. They had that in common.

The creek contained only a small stream of water, but he turned Gulliver to follow it downstream. The larger rivers and lakes were fed by many such trickles.

The farther they rode, the banks on either side of the water grew deeper until they were nearly cliffs, twice the height of a man. For the most part, the ground dropped straight down to the stream, except for a few places where the animals had trod shallower paths down to drink.

At last, the sound of a distant rustle rose above the gentle murmur of the creek. Through the growth of trees ahead, he caught a glimpse of water—a great deal of it, as large as a lake. Relief eased the tension in his shoulders.

He did know what he was doing. Arsenault's scant teaching had taken root.

When he reined in Gulliver at the edge of the trees surrounding the larger body of water, he finally saw the full extent of what lay before him. A lake, yes, though not as large as he'd first thought. On the opposite shore, the grass met the lapping waves in a muddy cluster of underbrush and reeds. A prime place to set traps for otter and muskrat.

In front of him, the bank dropped in a steep rocky cliff to finally meet the water's surface far below. He should simply ride around to the shallow part of the lake, the place where the trapping would be best. Yet the lure of the cliffs drew his focus there. He could at least take a few minutes to study the landscape.

Dismounting, he stepped closer to the edge, grasping a thick sapling as he leaned over to better see the layers of stone that made up the bank. Where the creek fed into the river, it created a small waterfall, dropping about two arm-lengths to meet the surface of the lake. That accounted for the rustling sound.

He'd heard many a story about caves tucked behind falls, but this scant bit of liquid couldn't hide much. The stone behind the falling water looked solid enough.

But to the left of the falls . . . What was that dark place in the rock? Merely an indentation shadowed by an overhang? It looked too deep for that.

Moving over so he could get a better view from a different angle, he peered at the spot. Now it looked even more like a cave. The opening was small, but probably large enough for him to crawl into.

Did he dare?

A rush of anticipation surged through him. Yes, if he could get to the spot, he wanted to see what lay within. Besides, with the snow coming, he would need shelter. Hopefully this nook would be deep enough to provide cover.

His gaze tracked a possible path along the cliff wall to reach the cave. There looked to be footholds he could manage. And they were deep enough that he could use them to climb back up.

Turning back to Gulliver, he dug through his pack to find one of the few candles he carried, along with his tinderbox to create a flame. The moon and his campfire usually gave enough light to see at night, but if the cave went very deep, he'd need something to illuminate the darkness.

Of course, it was probably only a shallow opening. Where the hole was positioned in the center of the cliff, only birds would have easy access. With his tinderbox and candle tucked in his waistband, he trekked along the bank to the place he'd identified to begin his descent.

Maybe he should have tied a rope around his middle and secured it to a tree before going down, but if he slipped from the cliff, he'd only hit water. He could swim as well as the next lad who'd grown up in the land of many lakes.

The rough ground scraped his belly as he dangled his feet over the ledge, feeling along the wall with his boots for the foothold he'd seen. There. From one perch to the next, he moved sideways and downward. When he descended far enough that there were no saplings left to hold, he clutched the edges of stone jutting from the cliff, his fingers aching. The leather soles of his shoes flexed enough that he could use his feet to help grip.

At last, he stretched the final distance to place his foot

on the floor of the cave. Before leaning much weight on it, he shifted his toes farther into the opening, searching for a rear wall. Nothing.

With one foot on the secure surface, he pulled the other into the cave opening, then worked his upper body down so he could kneel just inside the entrance. He finally took in a full breath as he reached for the candle and tinderbox. The murky darkness inside the cave gave no sign of how deep it went or what lay within.

After two tries with the flint and steel, he built enough spark in the tinder to light the candlewick. Snuffing out the tinder, he peered into the darkness as he extended the candle.

The light flickered off the cave sides, which were narrower than the span of his arms in either direction, but he still couldn't see how deep the opening went. He crawled forward, holding the candle in front of him.

He'd only gone a few strides in when a distant rumble sounded. As the noise grew louder, it seemed to shake the air, vibrating in his chest and stirring alarm through every part of him.

An earthquake? The roar of a bear?

He dropped low, tucking against the wall on his left, preparing for whatever threat came. This time, his recklessness might have finally taken him too far.

2

Charlotte slipped inside to escape the bustle in the courtyard. Their Dinee friends had come for trading, as they usually did after the Laurent men returned from a trip to the fort. With the first winter snow looming, she'd been surprised to see that two women had accompanied the three men. She would have expected the women to stay home to finish any final preparations before winter kept them bound mostly to their homes.

Speaking of final preparations, she had much to do herself. Brielle had brought back a host of caribou meat from a hunting trip that still needed to be smoked, and that would be done easiest with an outside fire. They should have plenty of food for the next few months at least—a relief for sure.

She placed the bundles she'd traded for on the table and paused to survey the room. Andre had cleaned the chimney yesterday, and he'd left a sooty mess all around the hearth. She'd swept the ashes already, but grimy handprints still marred the mantle. A thin layer of black covered many of the decorations on the wood piece—proof the chimney's cleaning had been long overdue.

Her gaze caught on the brass chalice reigning atop the mantle. It held an honored place in their home and among their entire village as the special heirloom passed down from Louis Curtois, the leader of the group that first founded Laurent. Each of the village chiefs through the years had held charge of the cup, and Papa had made a special metal mount to hold it in place on their mantel.

The intricate engraving of Jesus at the Last Supper possessed such detail that it was hard to believe the etching had been done by a man and not by the Lord himself. She'd always loved studying the portrayal of Jesus's face. The mixture of love and sorrow made her chest ache, even back when she'd been a young girl.

She reached for the chalice, easing it out of the base. With the annual Discovery Day celebration in just over a fortnight, this treasure needed a thorough cleaning. It would be moved to a place of honor in the assembly room for the feast as the story was told and retold of the day their ancestors discovered the web of caves within this mountain.

After grabbing the tin of cleaning mixture from her supply shelf, she moved to her chair by the fire. Her toe stubbed on a rough place in the stone floor, a bump she'd stepped over hundreds—no, thousands—of times.

But the momentum of her movements, maybe even the unrest in her spirit, knocked her off-balance, pitching her forward. She threw her hands out to catch herself. One knee struck the ground at the same time her palms did. The cup and cleaning mixture flew through the air, clattering across the stone.

Pain burned through her hands and up her wrists. She dropped to her elbows to take the weight from her hands as fire seemed to sear them. A groan slipped out, and she struggled to take in steady breaths.

Little by little, she pulled herself up to sitting. The agony in her hands and knee had dulled to throbbing, and her wrists ached, but nothing seemed broken. She eased out a long breath and glanced around.

The chalice.

She scanned the floor around her feet, her heart hammering. If she'd caused even a scratch to the heirloom, a treasure that had been kept safe for over a century . . . Her gaze caught the glimmer of brass, and her heartbeat stalled completely.

The fire. How could the cup have landed in the flame?

She crawled to the blaze and reached in, tapping at the chalice to roll it away from the burning logs. But the cup had landed directly in the center of a leaping flame, and she would have to submerge her hand in the orange glow to reach it. Heat already singed the skin of her palm.

Ignoring the burn, she reached for the metal poker and used it to roll the cup from the blaze.

With the heirloom finally on the cold stone floor, she eased out a breath, though the tension remained in her shoulders. She couldn't rest easy until she saw for sure no damage had been done to the village's favorite treasure.

The cup was much too hot to pick up with her hands—her first try proved as much—so she reached for the rag she'd planned to use to buff out a shine on the chalice. Lifting the cup by its long thin neck, she held her breath as she examined the engraving. Smoke had darkened much of the image of the Last Supper on one side, but she should be able to clean that off.

As she turned the cup, though, her middle cinched, burning as though the fire that had melted the face of Jesus now seared her insides. The brim itself had melted into a *U*, with the metal seeping down to completely cover the image of the Lord at the final meal before his death.

She squeezed her eyes shut. That chunk of meat and bread she'd eaten at midday might have been her own last supper if her father and the council—the entire village, really—found out what she'd done to this treasure.

Panic welled in her throat, clawing and suffocating. She worked the drooping brass with her fingers, doing her best to massage it back into shape. But the metal had cooled too much to be pliable. Her efforts managed only the faint impression of a fingerprint. *Lord, no.*

Frantically, she used the cloth to scrub the soot-blackened surface. The dark texture began to rub onto the rag. Her belly turned as she worked on the metal, using more of her cleaning mixture and grabbing a clean cloth when the other grew too grimy. This time, though, she kept the chalice nestled safely in her lap as she worked.

She scrubbed until her hands ached, then finally straightened and lifted the cup to examine it. The brass didn't hold the same shine, but at least it didn't show black any longer. She would probably be able to bring out the full luster with more effort.

But when she turned the chalice to view the melted side, the churning in her belly rose into her throat. This was so much worse than she'd first thought. Not even Papa, master metalworker that he was, would be able to repair this part, not without melting down the entire cup.

And would he be able to re-carve such an elaborate picture? The first one had been done by Titus Trouvé, a master engraver, as part of a set. The other chalice had been given to Louis Curtois's brother as an heirloom to pass down among his own family. It wasn't likely the two cups would ever be reunited. Perhaps differences in technique could be overlooked, should another artisan attempt to fix the damage.

Still, this loss would be a blow to the village.

Voices outside the rear door warned her just before it opened. Papa stepped in first, Andre on his heels chattering on about one of his friends.

She did her best not to look guilty as she sent them a quick welcoming smile, then lifted the cup back into its holder on the mantel. If she turned the melted section to the back, its flaws weren't immediately obvious. How long before someone noticed?

For now, she needed to build the smoking fire outside, all the while pretending she'd not just destroyed the village's most precious treasure. And then, she had to figure out how to repair the damage . . . before the Discovery Day celebration.

∽⟨𝒳⟩↝

The rumble in the cave's depths turned into a horrendous screech as Damien pressed himself against the stone side. His bulk filled most of the small opening, no matter how low he crouched.

The awful noise echoed from within the cave, closer and louder, til it thundered through his heart.

Then a *woosh* raced past him. His candle flame sputtered out, so he couldn't see the creature in the darkness. Yet it kept coming and coming. How long was this beast?

As the sound finally faded, he spun to see the source of the noise in the daylight outside the cave.

Bats. The horde of tiny black creatures separated in the dusky light, swooping in all directions.

He struggled to rein in the pounding in his chest, gulping deep breaths of icy air. He should've expected bats, but he'd only seen a couple of caves since he'd begun trapping at the end of summer. None had held a colony of bats.

Rising to his knees again, he fumbled for the tinderbox. Did he really want to see what else lived here? He'd heard the bats long before he saw them, so this passage must extend a great deal farther into the mountain.

The thought sent a wave of curiosity through him. He touched the handle of the knife hanging around his neck, then reached to make sure his pistol was still tucked securely in his waistband. It wouldn't be enough to kill a bear, but between the two weapons, he should be able to handle any other animal. Besides, a bear couldn't maneuver the cliff down to this cave. Unless there was another opening, no such creature would be inside.

Maybe he should set up camp before exploring, since full dark would be on him soon, but it shouldn't take too long to hike down this corridor. He would have a great deal more trouble finding his footholds on the cliff if he waited much longer. Thankfully, the moon should be bright tonight, which would help him make camp later.

Once he managed to light the candle again, he moved the taper around the cave walls. But once more, all he could see were the narrow sides and the yawning darkness ahead.

He began crawling once more, attuning himself to every detail his senses noticed. The passage seemed to continue straight in, perhaps moving a little downward. It grew larger also, and finally he could stand stooped over. He could move faster now.

Leaves and sticks littered the stone floor. Though he kept watch on the walls, there didn't appear to be any tunnels forking to one side or the other. As he continued, the air grew colder. A glance back showed the opening as a tiny pinprick of light, much higher than his current position.

At last, the passageway turned to the left, then opened into a wide cavern. A thrill swept through him as he raised the candle high to see as far up and around as he could. The ceiling rose beyond the reach of his light, so he focused on the walls nearest him.

Moving to the left, he followed the curve of the stone as it spread in a large circle. A faint rustling pricked his ears, growing louder the farther he went. From the sound, he realized there must be a small stream running through this chamber.

Markings on the walls slowed him, and he stepped nearer to see them. Drawings, maybe painted by the natives in the area. He'd heard of such art but had never seen an example. This meant others had explored this cave before him. Did they still come here?

His mind scrambled through the materials that might have been used for each color, the detail added in some areas that accentuated the story being told. He wanted to examine the wall more, but for now he needed to scope out the full area, then get back out to set up camp.

Moving onward, he found the trickle of water he'd heard. It seemed to run toward the lake, so the stream likely fed into the larger body. A few steps farther exposed exactly where the bats had roosted. Thick, squishy dung layered the floor, and after a single step he moved backward away from the place. The candle helped him skirt the area, and he tried to scrape the mess off his boots. Even dipping the leather in water did nothing to cleanse it.

As he finished his loop around the edge of the chamber, a few more drawings came into view on the walls. These looked to be made by a different artist than those in the other area, as the style was less ornate. He would definitely return to examine them more closely.

There seemed to be the sooty remains of a long-ago campfire just past that place. Most of the ash had been swept away, leaving only a dark spot and a few charred sticks.

Might this make a good campsite for him? It would certainly be out of the weather, though he'd have to find another place for Gulliver to graze. Would the mule be safe out on his own, especially with that lean coyote on the prowl? Maybe once he knew the area better, he could decide for sure.

For now, it was best he return to his faithful companion before darkness took over completely.

3

Charlotte opened her eyes in the premorning darkness, casting her gaze to the fire. Only coals glimmered in the hearth. It was time.

Easing the covers off, she sat upright and glanced toward her father's bed, where gentle snoring sounded, then to Andre's. It was hard to hear the lad's breathing over Papa's noises, but Andre usually slept like a hibernating bear, so she should have nothing to worry about from him.

The Dinee trading party would be leaving at first light, and this was her one chance to slip out without worrying her father and the others. She had to take the chalice to the fort and find an engraver skilled enough to repair the damage.

Creeping around the room, she gathered her winter gear in case it snowed. And the nights would be cold. The first snowfall had yet to come but might be on them any day. The early snows rarely fell deep, so she shouldn't need snowshoes.

She'd need food, too—at least three days' worth. And the meat knife she usually kept tied at the top of her tall moccasins. The men from Laurent could reach the trading post in two days, but it may take her longer. Perhaps she'd better pack for a fourth day, in case she had trouble locating the place. Best bring a few medicines in case something unexpected arose on the journey. Or she could use them for bartering at the fort.

Using both hands, she eased the mangled chalice from its base, then tucked it in a soft sack. This she rolled inside of five furs she'd recently finished tanning for Brielle. These would give her something to trade for food, lodging, and payment to a metalworker—as well as an excuse to be at the fort at all. Would people there think it odd that a woman brought trading furs? Perhaps, but she could be vague in her answers.

She paused in rolling the furs and inhaled a breath of the cool early morning air. Was she really going to do this? Leave home without forewarning and travel to a fort full of men? It wasn't *such* a big thing. She'd simply trade a few furs, look around the place, and hopefully meet a few new people.

Lord, let me find a skilled metalworker there. Please. If one of the artisans at the fort Erik had spoken of could repair the melted cup, she would never have to tell Papa about the damage. And if she could find no such man existed, she would bring the chalice back and beg for her father's help. He would do what he could, no doubt. But she wanted to at least try to get out of this mess she had created.

Then she'd return home. Several days before Discovery Day, if all went according to plan. And this would give her a look at the outside world, a chance to see if she really was missing anything here in Laurent. Perhaps she'd realize that Hugo was a far better catch than she thought. This trip might make her more grateful for the life God had placed her in.

And if the Lord led her to a man she could love with all her heart, even better.

After gathering the last of her supplies, she penned a note to her father. The why of her sudden departure proved a bit harder to put into words.

I've gone with the Dinee traders to visit my friends in their village. I've been feeling the need to stretch my wings a bit, to see beyond the walls of Laurent, and I couldn't miss this opportunity. I'll return with some of their hunters before the Discovery Day celebration. Don't worry about me, I think the adventure will be exactly what I need.

That knot coiled in her belly again. She hated lying to her father. She'd never have imagined telling a falsehood this large before. She'd rarely gone farther than the berry patches just outside of Laurent's walls, but she had no doubt she could handle the journey to the fort since the winter snows hadn't come yet. But she couldn't let her father panic.

In the past, when any of their family or close friends had been missing outside of village walls, he'd worried and grieved and gone to dangerous lengths to bring them back. Like the time Brielle had gone looking for Marcellus in a snowstorm. No one was more capable in fierce weather than Brielle, and she'd only been gone a day and a night, but their father had gone out to search even before the storm abated. Now he was even older, his body more frail. If he came to find her, how much harder would that be on him?

She couldn't do anything to make him worry. Couldn't take even the smallest chance he would search for her. He would trust her with their Dinee friends. She'd been to their village several times with traders from Laurent, and she would be traveling with capable people now—at least, he would believe that from her note. This was the only way to keep him from intense worry and the danger that traveling through the mountains at his age would bring.

After signing the missive, she placed it on the table where he would easily see it. One more glance around the room showed nothing else she'd forgotten.

Slipping out of the gate proved as easy as Charlotte had hoped in these still-dark hours of the early morn. She avoided the camp of the Dinee traders by slipping through the trees. Laurent's hunters would set out with the first rays of daylight, so she pressed hard to cover as much ground as she could—eastward, toward the faint lightening in the sky.

The icy cold breeze tingled against her face, but she warmed soon enough with the effort of her hike. As daylight crept over the land, it didn't bring with it the warm rays of the early winter sun. Thick clouds pressed low in the sky, dulling the mood around her.

Yet she didn't let the weather dampen her spirits, even as the frigid wind swirled. She'd made the first bold decision of her life. Stepped from the shadows to choose a path for herself. She would see a world she'd never known and determine for sure whether she'd been missing anything.

She skirted the first two mountains she reached, keeping the cloud-covered sun ahead of her. But the third peak stretched wide in a range that rose so high, it would've blocked out the sun if that orb hadn't already risen to crest its zenith. There would be no way around this massive slope. Maybe a short rest and a bite of food would give her the energy to start upward.

The respite helped, but by the time she'd climbed for

another half hour, her legs had turned to pudding, and she could barely catch her breath. Sweat dripped down her back, despite the icy wind buffeting harder the higher she climbed.

Something stung her nose, but she hadn't the energy to focus on it. Then another frozen drop brushed her cheek, and one more landed on her chin.

Snow.

She pushed the last few steps to reach a boulder where she could sit and rest again. Her chest burned for air, but her frigid inhales seemed to sear all the way down. The soles of her feet ached from the rocky points that had pressed against the bottom of her moccasins. Some of those jags felt as though they'd bruised her bones.

As she stared out over the land she'd covered—not even a third of the way up the mountain—exhaustion weighed on her spirit. Could she manage two days of this? Certainty no longer strengthened her spirit.

But she wasn't locked into making the journey in two days. She could rest as she needed, even taking double the time since she'd brought enough food.

The falling snow grew thicker, cooling her more quickly than she'd expected. Her face had nearly grown numb, so she pushed to her feet and aimed herself upward again. Snow was always more likely at greater heights, but once she made it over this mountain, the weather would be better.

Wouldn't it?

⁂

Damien finished setting his last beaver snare as the first flakes fell. He'd been watching the sky grow darker all morning, the clouds pressing lower and thicker. This snow would be a big one, and he'd much rather spend it in the cave with a toasty fire than out where the wind and wet would keep him miserable.

He'd found a protected nook where Gulliver could wait out the storm and had even spread an oilskin over the area to keep the mule mostly dry. Now he just needed to get his supplies and enough firewood down into the cave. Too bad he didn't have time to hollow out a tree trunk and make a canoe to access the cave opening, like some of the voyageurs and natives did. If he stayed in this area long, he would work on the task. For now, he'd be racing against the weather to get enough supplies into the cave before his footholds iced over.

He set to work gathering firewood. He'd need enough to last a couple days, just in case. The last thing he wanted was to be iced in the cave without any firewood, and the lake not yet frozen enough to hold his weight. He wouldn't think that likely to happen with the first snowfall, but these clouds looked like they held enough icy moisture to fall for days.

He'd already used much of the dry wood in the area for his fire the night before. A recent rainfall had left the land damp, so he headed toward a group of trees where he would likely find dead wood sheltered from the rain.

It must've taken hours to gather enough logs and carry them down the cliff to the cave. Snow had covered the ground by the time he finished, piling up to cover his boots.

On his last trip to the top of the cliff, he checked on Gulliver again, taking a moment to scratch the mule's favorite itchy spot. He nuzzled Damien's side in appreciation. His one true friend. The only companion who could stand him, even on the hard days.

He patted Gulliver's woolly neck once more. "I'll be back up to check on you when I can. I think you have what you need for now."

After bidding the mule a final *au revoir*, he trudged out of the sheltered cove and to the cliff's edge. After strapping the last of his supplies to his back, he took a moment to stare out over the terrain.

The lake spread in front of him, and beyond that to the right were the woods where he'd gathered his firewood. To the left and stretching high above the trees rose a range of mountains, only a faint outline among the curtain of white. Would he eventually cross those peaks? What lay beyond? Did the village hidden in caves reside somewhere in that land?

He'd love to find it on this journey, but the chances seemed slim. Like finding a single drop in a vast ocean. He knew only that it was tucked in the mountains several days west of Fort Versailles. From what he'd heard the men at the fort say, the caves were nearly impossible to see from the outside, only discoverable if a man happened to stumble through the opening. And only a very few had managed that.

As he turned his focus away from the mountains to his immediate surroundings, a motion snagged his attention. Probably only falling snow playing tricks on his eyes. But as he squinted through the flakes, the movement became more pronounced.

An animal trudging toward the lake? It walked with a jerky step, so maybe the creature was injured. Why hadn't it taken shelter in the trees?

As he studied the figure, awareness slipped in. A person. A man trekked through this storm, half covered in snow. The fellow marched forward as though determined to reach a specific destination, though that was the most exhausted march Damien had seen in a while. More like a dragging.

Did this stranger know of the cave? Was he trying to reach it for shelter against the weather? If this was a native, maybe even one of those who'd drawn pictures on the chamber walls, that may well be the case.

When the fellow finally reached the edge of the lake, instead of skirting the edge to come around to the cliff where Damien stood, he simply dropped his pack to the ground and sagged down to sit atop it. He sank his head into his hands, as though he could no longer hold himself upright.

Something stirred inside Damien. Something too close to compassion. How many times had he wanted to slump down like that man did? He'd done exactly that more often than he could count back in the cottage he shared with Michelle, during those dark days after he lost her.

Only their parish minister's determination had pulled him from that despair. The man's strong words had forced him to get up and move on with his life—for his sister's memory, for he'd had no desire to live for himself.

Maybe helping this fellow keep going could be his one good deed. Michelle would want him to try.

Dropping his pack back to the ground, he turned and trudged around the edge of the lake. He might have to share his cave with a companion through the storm, but he could manage that if he had to.

As he neared the stranger, he made no effort to quiet his steps, though the falling snow might muffle his approach. When he was a half dozen steps away from the man, the fellow still hadn't lifted his head. Had he fallen asleep out here? He was clad in furs, so he shouldn't be cold enough to freeze to death, not since he'd been moving only minutes before.

Damien stepped around to the man's front so the fellow could catch a glimpse of him. He was about to call out when the stranger jerked upright. Wide eyes stared at him from the fur hood framing his face. Impossibly wide blue eyes.

This was no native, not fully Dinee anyway. He might be Métis, one of the children from white and native unions. The face belonged to a youth, with pale skin unlined by years.

The stranger jumped upright, stepped backward, then stumbled over the pack he'd been sitting on. Balance askew, he flailed his arms, even as he tumbled backward to the snow. The fellow tried to scramble up, but his movements were slow from exhaustion and maybe pain. He rolled onto his hands and knees, then used the pack to push himself up to standing.

Once he was back on his feet, the fellow's coat rose and fell as he took in breaths. He was winded from a tumble in the snow?

The stranger stared at him with a trace of fear illuminated in his blue eyes. Whoever this was must not be accustomed to traveling alone in this wilderness. Maybe becoming separated from his party was part of the reason for the despair he'd shown before.

Damien lifted a hand in greeting. "Name's Damien Levette." He paused to let the lad introduce himself.

The boy hesitated, then moved his gaze away as he spoke. "*Bonsoir.*"

The hesitation and the shifting eyes betrayed a lie, but as

the voice registered, Damien's mind spun a different direction. Sure, a lad's tone could range high at times, but that . . . that voice had sounded for all the world like a girl's.

He peered closer at the face. The porcelain skin, the refined features—how could he not have realized this was a woman from his very first glance?

And why was she out in this storm?

4

Damien took a step back from the woman in front of him, more on impulse than conscious intention. "Who are you, and what are you doing here?" He motioned through the falling flakes. "Where are your people?" He'd have to get her back to them, no matter how cold the temperature dropped as evening came on. Her family must be frantic.

Her chin notched up, the fear in her eyes masked by something else. Determination, maybe? That expression looked a bit too much like Michelle's form of stubbornness. "I'm Charlotte Durand. I'm on my way to Fort Versailles. Trying to cover as much ground as I can before dark."

"Alone?" The question slipped out before he had a chance to check his tone, but the idea was absurd.

Her back stiffened. "Have you come from the fort? Do you know how much farther it is?"

Yes, that was clearly stubbornness in her eyes. Stubbornness that would easily get her killed in a mountain snowstorm.

Yet a woman—any woman, but especially a young thing like her—wouldn't trust him without a little softening. He started by answering her question. "The fort is nearly two days on foot." He pointed back across the lake. "West and a little south. There's not a marked trail to it, though. I left there a couple months ago with a group of trappers, Arsenault's group. I parted ways with them only a few days ago to gather furs on my own."

He glanced at her face but didn't hold the focus long enough to make her uneasy. "This snowfall is only going to get deeper, and temperatures will drop quite a bit when darkness sets in. I found a cave across the lake with a large cavern where it shouldn't be hard to stay warm and dry. There's plenty of room for us both. You can have your own campfire, if you'd like." He'd not spoken so much at a time in weeks, but he'd likely only have one chance to set her at ease.

For a second, the determination slipped from her eyes to reveal only startled fear. She had every right to worry about taking cover with a strange man. At least that worry meant she had a shred of sense, though she couldn't possess much more than that if she was trekking to the fort on her own. The journey itself was no easy thing, but in a place like that with men of all types, she'd be wolf bait within minutes.

He could worry about that later. Right now, he had to find a way to convince her that taking shelter with him was better than staying in the elements on her own. "Tell you what. I'll take you to the cave, and if you decide you'd rather not have me there with you, I'll camp with my mule. I have him set up with cover all around, and it might be nice to stay close where I can check on him." There, that was the best he could do to set her at ease. Michelle would approve of his sacrifice, he had no doubt.

Miss Durand still hesitated, but the fear in her gaze had

turned to indecision. He waited. If he pressed any further, she might think he was trying to talk her into it for a dishonorable reason.

She glanced upward, taking in the snow that had begun to swirl instead of fall straight down. Then she eyed him again. "How far away is this cave?"

He turned and pointed across the lake again. "Just on the far bank."

When he looked back at her, she gave a single nod. "I'd like to see it."

Good. He reached for her pack, but she scooped it up before he could manage and murmured a quiet "I have it."

So he started back around the lake. By the time he got her settled, he'd have to push hard to build his own fire beside Gulliver before full dark.

After he took a few steps, a glance back showed she moved much slower than he did, so he eased his stride. Then slackened it more. She finally caught up with him, and he slowed still more so she would come alongside. At this casual pace, perhaps he could learn a bit more about her. A fresh gust of wind numbed his cheeks. "It's getting colder already. This is more snow than I expected for the first storm of the year."

She nodded and sniffed. "I had hoped it was just snowing on the mountain, that it would stop once I came down to the valley."

He turned for a glance backward. "You came over that range?"

She nodded. Her breathing had grown louder, as though toting her pack up the slight hill had worn her out. He itched to reach out for the bundle but had a feeling that would only push her away.

"You live in that direction?"

Again she nodded, but from her pinched mouth she didn't appear inclined to say more.

Perhaps she would relax if he told a bit about himself. "I started out from Fort Versailles at the end of summer with a trapping group. We went northwest first, had two different camps. When I split off from them, they were headed south."

"Why did you leave?"

Couldn't stand myself, and neither could anyone else. A pang tightened his chest. He should've known talking about himself was a bad idea. "Just . . . wanted a go at it alone."

He could feel her glance but kept his focus forward. They were nearing the last few uphill strides before reaching the cliff above the cave, so maybe they'd done enough talking.

When they stopped at his pack, snow had already formed a layer over the bundle. He brushed off the white fluff, then lifted the strap over his shoulder.

"Where's the cave?" Miss Durand looked around, and a hint of fear slipped back into her eyes.

He motioned to the cliff. "It's in the rock right below us. The climb isn't hard. I'll go first to show you where to put your hands and feet."

She took a step away from him, her blue eyes growing round. Then she shifted toward the edge, just enough to peer over. "That's straight down."

"It's not hard. Really. I've been up and down seven or eight times at least. I've stocked enough firewood that you shouldn't need to come out for a day or two, as long as you have food."

Her attention jerked to his face. "I only need a place to stay the night. I'll be on my way in the morning."

He raised his brows. "Even if it's still snowing?"

Her expression dropped to a frown, and she pulled her coat tighter around herself. "It will stop by then." Though her words weren't a question, her voice held a measure of uncertainty.

"I guess we'll see." No need to frighten her more than he'd already done. Only time would tell for sure, though from the looks of the storm, it had a long way to go before the clouds spent themselves.

He moved toward the ledge. "Watch what I do."

But he'd only turned onto his belly and dangled his feet over the edge before her shaky voice sounded above him. "Never mind. I'll find another place to camp."

He gripped a thick sapling so he could look up at her without sliding down. She'd backed three steps away and was shaking her head. "Thank you for your offer, though."

She seemed ready to turn and stride away, so he pulled a knee up onto flat ground and worked to stand. "Is it the climb down that bothers you?"

She eyed the edge of the bank. "I don't take risks like that."

This little cliff wasn't much of a risk, especially with the water below. "Would it ease your mind if we tie a rope around you, in case your foot slips?"

Her mouth thinned, and her gaze flicked from him back to the edge. "I can find other shelter."

The frustration he'd been holding back finally edged over. "Miss Durand, it's nearly dark and getting colder as we speak. You'll stay warm and dry down there. You have my word I'll get you down safely, then back up anytime you want. All you need to do is call out and I'll be here to help.

I'd rather not waste any more time. I have my own camp to set up, too."

She studied the edge of the bank, though she wasn't standing close enough to see down to the cliff or the cave. Twice she blinked. "Do you have rope?"

He eased out a breath, then lifted the pack over his shoulder. "Right here. Let's tie it around you, then I'll go down so you can see how to do it. We'll leverage the rope around this tree, and I'll hold it steady from just inside the cave."

After he handed her one end of the rope, she wrapped the braided leather around herself and attempted to tie the end. Between her thick gloves and probably cold fingers, she fumbled with the cord for a few minutes.

Finally, he slipped off one of his own gloves. "Mind if I try? We'll need that knot to be nice and tight."

She held both pieces out, and he secured a strong knot within seconds. His hand had already turned bright red and was stinging from cold as he worked his glove back on. Within another minute, he refastened his bundle so he could still wrap it around himself without the rope he'd been using as a strap.

After positioning his pack on himself, then taking on hers as well, he wound the cord around the tree he planned to use as a lever. He studied Miss Durand once more. "Ready?" A bit of that determination from before had slipped back into her eyes, making her look less like she would bolt any moment.

A tiny nod was all she offered.

He made quick work of the journey down, talking through each handhold and foothold but doing his best to make the descent sound as simple as it really was.

When he was secure at the edge of the cave, had lit a candle, and held a firm grip on the rope, he shifted his focus to the woman tied to the other end. "Lie on your belly first and let your legs hang down." He tried to soften his voice to the tone he'd always used to coax Michelle. "It'll be easier if you come before snow builds up on the footholds again. Once you lie on your belly, you don't have to look down. And I have hold of you. I'll make sure you get here safely."

She glanced at him, then squeezed her eyes shut, turned around, and dropped to her knees.

Good thing the woman wore full fur-lined pants and a thick coat, for he'd not thought about what it would be like watching from below as she descended. He did his best to focus on telling her where to place her hands and feet, not staring at any other body parts, covered though they were. He couldn't tell much through the winter clothing, but he had a feeling beneath all that fur and buckskin was a fine-looking woman.

He tightened his grip on the rope. That was the last thing he should be thinking of. And not only because the two of them were so alone out here. He needed to keep his mind on the important things.

"That's it, now you can bring your right foot all the way down to the cave floor." He kept enough tension on the rope to make her feel safe, then reached out so he could grab her if she lost balance. She'd maneuvered the climb with grace, despite all her worries.

"All right. We'll have to crawl into the cave for a ways until the ceiling gets higher." He pulled the rope down from the tree to coil it and give her freedom to move. "We'll untie you once we get in the cavern."

Crawling through this first stretch was slow, but with Miss Durand's smaller form, she was able to rise to her feet long before he could.

At last they reached the end of the passage into the wide cavern. He held the candle up, but the small light didn't allow them to see far. He motioned toward the faint rustle. "There's a little stream by that back wall, and to the right of it is where the bats leave their . . . droppings. You might want to avoid that area."

"There are bats in here?" Was it his imagination or had she edged closer to him?

"They flew out earlier when I first entered the cave. They won't hurt you. They'd rather stay far away from us." Silence filled the empty space around them. Best to get started on the fire. "Hold these, and I'll get a blaze going." He handed her the coil of rope and candle, then dropped the packs on the floor and set to work placing kindling and logs.

By the time he had the fire started, she'd untied the rope from around her and moved toward the middle of the cave to take in the room. He brushed the dirt from his hands. "Do you have food for a few days?"

She glanced back and nodded. He'd never met a woman who talked so little. Maybe all the new surroundings were what held her tongue.

She seemed to hesitate, as though she wanted to say something, so he waited. "You can camp here, too, if you think your mule won't need you nearby."

He nearly chuckled, but his face wouldn't quite form a smile. It had been too long. "Gulliver will be fine, but I don't mean to push you. If you'd be more comfortable with me out there, I have no problem camping with him."

She shook her head, the action more certain this time. "Not out in the weather."

He nodded. "Thanks."

As he turned to finish setting up camp, his mind wandered through the last year. This might be the first time some-one had actually asked for his company since Michelle. Of course, this was only sympathy from Miss Durand. And once she learned more about him, she may well send him packing, even in the snowstorm.

5

Charlotte prayed she wouldn't regret her decision.

Monsieur Levette seemed honorable, even willing to give up this dry shelter for her. Sending him back out into a snow-storm at night would have been cruel on her part. He'd of-fered separate fires, but that would be a waste of firewood. Though she would only be here til morning, he'd carried enough logs into this cavern that he must be planning to stay a while.

She had her knife, and she'd sleep lightly. She could pro-tect herself if he tried to make an advance in the night. For now, her first order of business should be to cook a warm meal for them. She had no pot, but she'd brought a metal plate that could be used in the coals near the fire.

While Monsieur Levette packed away his rope, she pulled out some bear meat she'd seasoned and roasted the day be-fore, from the same bear she'd used to make the ragoût for the returning traders. Had that only been a few days ago? It seemed years.

What were Papa and the others doing now? Did he worry about her being away from home during this first snow?

Hopefully he rested peacefully in the belief that she was safe in the Dinee village. The fact she couldn't feel her toes now made her almost wish that was where she was.

Perhaps she should have studied the weather a bit more before choosing when to leave, but she couldn't have waited around, knowing the chalice sat on the mantel in its damaged state.

As she positioned the meat on the plate to warm beside the fire, her companion rose and moved to the woodpile. "Is it all right with you if I build the other fire over there?" He motioned across the entrance to the chamber.

She shook her head. "No need. As long as you keep your sleeping pallet across the fire from mine—and stay on your side." She allowed herself a quick glance to catch the surprise in his look before turning back to the food.

"You're sure?"

She nodded. "We'll use less wood that way."

After a moment of quiet, his footsteps moved back to the woodpile, then a soft thunk sounded as he dropped his load. "I have food I'm happy to share. Nothing fresh, as I've been on the trail a couple days. But edible."

"I'm heating enough for us both. Save yours for the morning." She reached for a loaf of bread from her pack. There was plenty to share for one meal, especially if they ate from his supplies before she headed out tomorrow.

He seemed at loose ends without a task to do, laying his gloves and fur hat out to dry, stretching a blanket on the floor, then taking a log from the fire to use as a torch while he wandered around the room. His voice drifted through the quiet. "There are pictures painted here, and more on the other wall. They look like scenes of a hunting party."

She straightened and tried to see the wall where he stood, about a dozen paces away. "Were they made recently?" Did one of the Dinee tribes come here often? The two villages nearest Laurent had always been friendly and valued trading partners, but they were located in the opposite direction from this place. She had no idea which tribes came through this area . . . nor how pleased they might be to find two strangers taking up residence in a cave they might consider their own.

Just one night. She only had to keep herself safe here one night, then she'd be off again. Lord willing, by tomorrow eve, she'd be safe in Fort Versailles.

"They look to be a few years old, I think. The paint is faded, but that could be from weathering. And I'm not sure what material they used. Likely something from berries, which wouldn't last long unless they mixed it with an adhesive agent."

She shifted her gaze from the wall to the man. No mere trapper would have such knowledge of art. What had he done before coming to the mountains? He looked to be only a few years older than her, perhaps five and twenty. Maybe he'd learned this skill in the village where he'd grown up.

"Before you came to Fort Versailles, where did you live?"

He swung his focus to her, his eyes flashing with surprise for a moment before the shadows overtook him and she could no longer read their emotion. "A little village near Kingston in the Canadas." His voice came out flat, devoid of the curiosity that had been there a moment before when he spoke of the paintings.

The change gave her the feeling something had forced him to leave his home near Kingston. Did she dare ask what?

She would likely never know unless she voiced the question. "What made you leave for a fort in the mountain wilderness? For that matter, what made you leave the trapping group you were with to strike out on your own?"

His mouth tightened into a thin line. His gaze shifted from her to the fire, as though he didn't plan to answer. But then he spoke again. "What made *you* leave your home for Fort Versailles? Where are you from, anyway?"

The intrusiveness of the questions wove around her, needling her vulnerable places. But they were the same she'd asked him. No wonder he'd closed up so quickly.

Still, she should try to answer a little, without giving away her true reason for leaving. "I come from Laurent, a small village west of here." That detail should be safe to share.

Yet instead of the polite confusion she'd expected to see on his face at the name of an unknown town, intense curiosity took over his features. He moved a step toward her. "Laurent? The hidden village in caves? That's your home?" With each question, his tone took on more surprise.

Unease tightened inside her. Had telling him been a mistake? Could it somehow put her people in danger? Surely there was no way that small knowledge would harm her people, not since she was a day's trek away from Laurent's walls.

And why would this man be a danger to her village? This was simply the old fear her people had harbored that was bleeding into her new freedom. Just because one group of Englishmen had discovered their home over a decade ago with violent aims didn't mean every stranger intended harm. The council and most of their neighbors understood that now.

Still, she'd do better to proceed cautiously. "What do you know of Laurent?"

His posture relaxed a little, and he took another step closer, casting more light on his face so she could better see his expressions. "Nothing really. Only that it's a village hidden in caves that no one knew about for years. I've heard it said that sometimes two men from there show up in Fort Versailles for trading. The times the trappers have tried to follow them home to visit this town, either the men from Laurent simply disappear or those following are mysteriously injured so that they can't continue on."

She nearly smiled at the tale. How had so much intrigue come to shroud their quiet home? It sounded as though God was protecting them from strangers who would do better to mind their own affairs.

Turning back to the food, which had more than warmed, she used a stick to pull the plate from the fire. "The meal is ready if you're hungry." She reached for two strips of leather to use as plates, then loaded a goodly portion for him and a much smaller amount for herself.

He approached and took the makeshift plate she offered, then moved around to settle on the bedding he'd laid out across the fire from her. She took up her own portion and sat on her fur.

A glance around showed what she'd forgotten. "I should have melted snow for us to drink. I don't have anything to make tea, but warm water would be good with the cold."

She began to rise, but he motioned her back down. "You supplied the food. The least I can do is retrieve the drink."

Though she'd paused in getting up when he spoke, she didn't sink back to a seated position. At home, she was always the one to rise when something was needed during a meal. She liked doing for others, making sure everyone was comfortable and could enjoy the food she'd cooked.

She set her leather plate aside and pushed all the way up to her feet. "I'd like to see if it's still snowing. I'll return soon."

"At least take my pot to fill with snow." He reached into his pack and pulled out a small metal container. This would certainly hold more than the metal cup she'd planned to use.

As she made her way up the long passage, she almost turned back for a candle or torch. Through the small circle of the cave opening ahead, only white appeared. A solid curtain of snow.

As she reached the place where she had to drop to her knees to continue on, she was once more grateful for her fur leggings. The leggings were her usual outerwear when she went outside during winter but were now especially useful when crawling through caves.

At the entrance, she scooped snow from the rock crevices into the small pot. The icy wind swirled the falling crystals, benumbing her face before she finished gathering what she needed. Darkness had settled outside, but the snow glowed brightly.

When would the snow stop? With the lake below, she couldn't tell how deep the flakes might be piling. If it still fell when morning came, should she head out anyway?

But it wouldn't still be snowing by then, especially not as the day progressed. She would be able to leave here in the morning, later when the sun rose, if not at first light.

With the pot full, she turned back inside the cave and took care not to spill a single flake as she crawled forward.

Tonight, she should be thankful for the dry shelter God had led her to. Tomorrow would be a new day, hopefully with a bright sun to guide her path.

She had nothing to worry about. Except maybe the man waiting for her back at the campfire.

6

Being alone with this woman in a secluded cave didn't sit right with Damien. If this had been his sister holed up in a cave with a strange man, he'd have hunted the fellow down and strung him up the nearest tree. Even if the man hadn't done anything untoward. Just being alone with a woman in a vulnerable position was all kinds of wrong.

And as pretty as Miss Durand was . . .

Across the fire, she settled with her supplies after the meal, sorting through her pack. He rose, making his way toward the outer fringe of firelight to examine the paintings again. Anything to put space between them. Of everything in this place, the artwork had the best chance of distracting him from her presence, especially when he had his back turned to her. Not a position he usually allowed around strangers, but the more time he spent in her presence, the more she drew him.

Which meant he had to do whatever necessary not to think of her.

He scanned the less detailed set of paintings first this time. Though the outlines were rough and some of the figures not more than a single brushstroke, the three scenes told a thrilling story. A hunting party had gone out on foot, seen a group of animals on a mountain—maybe antelope or goat, it was hard to tell from the indistinct figures—and had taken large bundles of meat home to their happy families. That last scene showed women and children celebrating around the carcasses. A village of hungry people, no doubt. A much more noble reason to hunt than the uncountable number of eastern dandies willing to pay high prices for beaver hats and fashionable furs.

He pushed the thought aside and focused again on what the art told him. The hunters didn't ride horses. Miss Durand also traveled on foot. Were there not horses or mules in the area? Surely these people had some kind of mounts to make their hunting and travel easier.

He would find the chance to ask, but not now.

Moving across the cave to the other section of paintings, he allowed himself only a glimpse toward Miss Durand. She was looking at him in that same moment. Had she been watching him? He'd felt her presence so strongly, he couldn't have said whether it was her gaze that weighed so heavily or simply his need to keep from thinking about her. From wondering what she was doing. What she thought about their situation.

What she thought about *him*.

He concentrated on the paintings ahead, swallowing down the urge to look her way again. These images weren't as clearly divided into scenes as the others. The story took a moment to decipher, but this section seemed to show a single man on horseback—yes, riding—with various obstacles stretching before him. Snow covered the ground in one area, a wide river crossed his path in another, and a mountain rose up at an angle that showed a steep cliff. How had the horse managed that ascent?

Or had it? The painting only showed the traveler at the beginning of these obstacles, not having overcome them.

At the end of his journey, just past the cliff, a group of people stood with happy faces. His family? Or perhaps his village. There were a dozen figures, some of them smaller like children and one a babe cradled in the arms of a long-haired adult. The artist had added more detail to this person than the others, giving form to her face and even tucking in her clothing at the waist. The traveler's wife?

His chest tightened as he shifted his gaze back over the entire painting. He could relate to the man and his journey. All the obstacles he'd overcome. But there would be no family or village at the end of Damien's travels. No wife and babe waiting for him.

That familiar burn climbed up his throat. Michelle no longer anticipated his return. No one from their village expected him to come back. He'd cut off all ties. And the fur company certainly wouldn't miss him if he never showed up again in Fort Versailles. He was considered a free trapper, not officially in their ledgers unless he came to the fort to trade. They would never know if he disappeared into the wilderness forever.

"Do you think he made it to his people?" The soft voice behind Damien tensed all his nerves. Yet at the same time, the gentle murmur called to him, making him want to lean into the sweet tones.

He swallowed down the unwanted feeling. Forced his attention back to the painting. "I don't know." Too much emotion scraped in his voice, so he attempted to clear it away. Better to change the subject.

And put some space between them.

He moved back toward the fire, then settled on his fur. A glance around the space showed nothing he should be doing. She'd already put the food away, and he'd brought in plenty of wood for the fire. This would be a good time to work on the knife handle he'd been carving. Maybe Miss Durand would sit by the fire, and he could glean a bit more information from her.

As he chipped tiny bits of wood to form the mule's head at the bottom of the handle, she did indeed take up her place across from him. He let silence settle for a while, but the weight of her gaze on him made it impossible to relax. She didn't have any handwork to keep her busy, but she didn't seem inclined to fill the air with empty words like most women would.

If there was to be conversation, it looked like he would have to be the one to begin it. "I don't often see a woman traveling alone. Or anyone alone, really. You have business at Fort Versailles?" Perhaps he should have handled the question more tactfully, started off with small talk about the weather. But they'd already discussed the weather, and he hated coyness, both in himself and others.

A frown marked her brow. "I do have business there." Then she clamped her lips shut, the echo of stubbornness in her tone lingering in the air between them.

Perhaps he should have tried harder for subtlety. Now he'd have to work to ease her prickles. "Have you ever been there? It's not a very big place—only a trade store, the factor's house, and a few other cabins. No women at all, just a few rough men."

When he slid a glance to her, a bit of interest lit her eyes. "How far is it from here?"

Now it was his turn to frown, as the image of her trekking over the snow-covered terrain flicked through his mind. She'd been so exhausted when he'd found her by the lake. She couldn't make the rest of the journey on foot. No woman should be forced to endure that hardship. Which begged the question, why did she attempt it? What drove her through this wilderness in a snowstorm? Alone?

He tried to concentrate on her original question. "On foot, about two days. On a mount, probably a bit over a day if the weather's good. And if you don't get lost. Like I said before, there's not a road between here and there. You can't just go due east, as you have to skirt a couple mountains."

She took in his answers without showing much of her thoughts on her face. She couldn't be older than twenty, if that, yet she possessed a maturity, an intelligence, that many people twice her age couldn't boast. In his experience, that usually either came from being surrounded by wise counsel, or by simply learning wisdom the hard way, living through heartache and challenges.

He brushed the bits of wood from his design as he watched her. In truth, her beauty made studying her a pleasure. But he mostly looked for signs of her thoughts.

At last, she looked ready to speak. "You can give me directions, though?" She seemed to be attempting the shrewd look of someone negotiating, but her innocence—the sweetness cloaking her—belied the impression.

"How about if I take you there myself? My mule, Gulliver, makes a sturdy mount in the snow. That way you won't have to worry about veering off course." The trip would put him a few days behind the schedule he'd planned, but there was no way he could send this woman off on foot alone. Especially to the fort. Those rough trappers likely hadn't seen a white woman in months or years. Some might be decent to her, but others . . . He couldn't tolerate the thought.

But Miss Durand shook her head. "That won't be necessary. I'd appreciate you pointing me in the right direction and mentioning any landmarks you can remember. But if you'd rather not, I'll find my way."

He had to press his mouth shut to hold in what he wanted to say about such nonsense. He knew better than to argue with a woman who looked as stubborn as she did right now.

He held his tongue, worked a few more minutes on his carving, then added more wood to the fire and stretched out to bed down.

Tomorrow would be soon enough for the battle of wills. And knowing this wilderness as he was coming to, there might be a whole new set of challenges when they looked out the cave opening in the light of day.

Three more days until the anniversary of Michelle's death.

The reminder hit its mark before Damien even opened his eyes for the day. She'd been his first thought upon waking for a long time now, first because of her sickness, and then because the crushing weight of grief made it hard to push aside his blankets each morning.

The clink of metal against stone snapped his eyes open. In an instant, everything came back to him. The cave. The woman, who even now was nursing new flame from the coals of their campfire.

He pushed himself upright, swiping a hand down his face. He shouldn't have slept later than she did, but the darkness of the cave must have tricked his body into thinking night had lasted longer. He cleared the gravel from his throat. "Have you been outside yet?"

She shook her head. "Didn't see any light from the opening, so I thought I'd get the fire started before I retrieve snow to make water." Her voice held no remnants of sleep. How long had she been awake?

He blinked to clear the morning fog from his vision, then pushed his blankets aside and reached for the pot. "I'll get it."

Surprisingly, she allowed him. Maybe her strong will was softening.

The chill in the air as he started down the long corridor grew colder as the faint glow of morning widened in the opening ahead. When he'd crawled the final distance to stare out at the white world around them, snow blanketed the land as far as he could see, including a layer over the lake. That meant there must be ice crusting the water, though likely not thick enough to hold much weight yet.

At least no more flakes fell from above. The clouds still hung heavy and low enough that they might release another round of snowfall before the day's end. Would it be safe to start out with Miss Durand?

The cave they were in now would be the best place to wait out another snowfall, but he had a feeling Miss Durand wouldn't be willing to delay her journey.

He did his best to picture the route in his mind. He could think of no caves between here and there, but he'd only been through that territory once. He'd been part of a larger group, so he'd not paid attention to the landscape like he would when riding alone.

He leaned out the opening and peered up to the top of the cliff. He needed to check on Gulliver this morning, either way. Those hand and footholds would be icy—and cold.

After filling the pot to overflowing, he maneuvered his way back down the passage. One thing he wouldn't miss about this cave was the crawling and ducking required to traverse the tunnel.

When he reached the cavern, Miss Durand took the pot from him and nestled it by the fire. "It's not snowing any-more?" She didn't spare him a glance with the question, and her tone sounded brusque. Had he somehow already vexed her this morning?

"The snow's stopped for now, though the sky looks like it might start again any time."

Her brow wrinkled as she put something into the melting snow. "As soon as I get this cooking, I'll be heading out."

He eyed her, doing his best to think through what he'd said or done that would make her run off so quickly. It might just be her desire to get on the trail before more snow fell, but her manner gave the distinct impression he'd raised her ire. This was why he'd left Arsenault's group. He was no good for people anymore, even when he made an effort.

"Can I . . . do anything to help you?" Sometimes an offer of assistance had helped when Michelle would get in a bad mood. Though that was rare—she'd had the patience of an angel.

Miss Durand shook her head. Then, after a heartbeat, she seemed to change her mind. "The only thing I need from you is a description of the route to Fort Versailles. If you still refuse to give it, I can manage on my own."

Her words twisted into confusion in his mind. He'd not refused to give her directions; they simply hadn't finished the conversation the night before. Maybe she'd assumed that meant no.

Sinking down on his bed pallet, he let out a breath. "I didn't mean to give you the impression I wouldn't help. I thought we'd talk through the plan this morning. I can give you directions to the fort, although I've only been that route once, so I may not remember all the landmarks. I would recognize them as I go, though, even covered in snow. I need to make a trip to the fort for supplies, so we might as well travel together. There's strength in numbers, especially in this wilderness, and if we're going to the same place, it only makes sense." One could always use supplies, so his words were true enough. "Besides, the men at the fort can be a bit . . . unruly. I'm not sure it would be safe for a woman alone there."

Her mouth was still pressed into a thin line, but after a moment, she glanced at him. "I thought you said you were headed west, that you just split off from your group a few days ago." Definite suspicion in her tone, but there also seemed to be something else. Like teasing?

For the first time in a year, the corners of his mouth wanted to pull into a smile. "I'm out of coffee. That's worth a trip to the fort."

She dipped her gaze back to her work, and maybe a shadow tricked his vision, but it seemed like her mouth curved, too. "I've only had coffee once. One of our neighbors married an Englishman, and he took her to visit his family on their wedding trip. She brought back several things for us to try, including coffee. I don't know how anyone could enjoy such bitterness."

Finally, a peek into her life, however tiny. "The taste grows on you."

Silence settled again, but there seemed no animosity in her manner this time.

At last, she handed the pot to him with a spoon. "Meat porridge. My own concoction. I hope you like it."

She pushed to her feet and started to turn away, as though she didn't plan to eat with him.

"Shall I save you some, or have you already broken your fast?" He was pretty sure she hadn't since she'd been kindling the fire when he woke.

She waved the question away. "I'll eat from my pack. I'm going to see the stream once more, then I'll be ready."

As her soft footsteps faded into the darkness of the cavern, he replayed her words. Did that mean she was allowing him to travel with her? If he was ready on time, hopefully she wouldn't object. Good thing he hadn't set out traps yet.

He quickly downed half the porridge she'd cooked—a vast improvement over his regular fare—then set the pot aside for her to finish the remainder. He certainly wouldn't be eating the better food and leaving her with cold jerked meat. By the time she returned to the firelight, he had his bedding rolled and all his gear packed, except the pot.

He nodded toward the porridge. "The meal was magnificent, and I've eaten my fill. The rest is yours." He hoisted his pack over his shoulders. "I'm going up to get Gulliver ready. Come to the entrance of the cave and shout when you're ready to climb up."

She'd been eyeing the porridge as though she didn't trust it, but when he mentioned the climb, her gaze jerked up to his.

He offered an encouraging nod. "It's even easier going up than coming down, and we'll tie the rope around you again."

As he turned and strode down the cave passage, his mind played through the things he needed to accomplish before they set out. His thoughts continued to the landmarks he'd need to watch for going toward the fort.

Pain pressed in his chest. Was he really going to lead this woman into that den of raucous men? If only he knew why she traveled alone. He couldn't imagine a reason that would justify the dangers, both in the journey and the destination. If he knew how to reach Laurent, he'd take her right back there. Back to a place of safety.

If only.

7

Charlotte wouldn't have ridden the mule if her limbs didn't ache so from yesterday's trek. Gulliver seemed an obedient mount, traipsing through the snow beside Monsieur Levette. It felt wrong making him walk when the mount was his, but he'd insisted so strongly, and every part of her protested her first few steps through the snow.

Ahead, a small dark animal trotted out from the trees. Damien and the mule both saw it at the same time she did, and the mount jerked to a halt, cocking his long ears toward the newcomer.

Beside her, Damien stared at the creature, though it was far enough away she could only make out the relative size—about the height of her knees—but not what kind it might be.

"Well. My old friend." His voice held pleasure she hadn't heard in his tone. He started walking again toward the animal but didn't seem inclined to tell her what the little fellow was or how he knew it.

Gulliver kept pace beside him, and Charlotte focused on the distant creature. As they neared, she made out the shape of either a coyote or wolf. Probably the former because of its smaller size, though it could be a young wolf.

The figure stood motionless, watching their approach as they drew within twenty strides of it. Finally, Damien halted and turned to the pack he'd strapped on the mule. "Give me a minute. I have something saved for this guy."

After extracting a chunk of roasted meat, he continued walking toward the coyote. It still didn't move. Didn't look prepared to bolt. Just stood frozen, like a majestic statue, the nape at its neck rustling in the breeze.

Damien stopped about five strides away, and the two stared at each other for a long moment. There seemed almost a conversation between them, definitely a mutual respect. At last, the man tossed the food in front of the animal.

After a last look, the coyote scooped up the bite, then spun and trotted back into the trees.

As Damien turned and started back toward her, something like a smile brushed his face. His features had been handsome before, but the way his eyes brightened, that flash of white teeth against his sun-darkened skin . . . the effect on her insides was impossible to deny.

She dropped her gaze to the mule's neck before the man came close enough to see her thoughts on her face. The last thing she needed was to give him a hint she might feel some sort of attraction. Not when they traveled together with no chaperone, far from any form of civilization. Those facts alone were scandalous enough.

It was vital she keep a healthy distance between herself and this new . . . companion.

As they set off again, the chuff of the mule's hooves breaking snow blended with the lighter swish of Damien's steps. A layer of ice hadn't yet crusted the top of the snow, so both man and animal broke through the powdery flakes with each step.

Both would be exhausted within an hour. And the going would become slower and slower as they struggled.

When Damien began to show signs of weariness, falling back behind the mule, she reined Gulliver in. After sliding to the ground, she gave the animal's neck a rub. "Well done, boy." She'd had very little experience with horses, and none with mules, but this one seemed so affable that she couldn't imagine why her people hadn't gathered a whole herd of them. Finding enough food for the animals might be a challenge, but they certainly made travel easier.

Damien's breathing came hard as he approached her. "What's wrong?"

She stepped back from Gulliver. "I'll walk now to stay warm. You ride awhile."

He took in several breaths, maybe trying to catch enough air to speak. Or perhaps deciding whether to accept her offer. "Are you certain?"

She gave a sharp nod and moved to the mule's head to stroke him there. Surely this would give Damien plenty of room to mount.

He gathered the reins and swung aboard with fluid grace, despite his size and exhaustion. As he adjusted his seat, his gaze lifted to the sky above. A frown deepened his expression, and she glanced upward, too. Had those clouds darkened since they started out? Their heaviness seemed greater than before, pressing down, shrouding the air around them. As much as she wanted to deny it, he was probably right that snow would fall again soon.

She started forward. They couldn't lose a minute of travel.

Lord, please keep the snow away, at least until we stop for the night.

❧⟡❧

The snow was falling too thick to go on much farther. Damien could barely see through the swirling curtain. Every time he'd suggested a place to stop for the night, Miss Durand refused. The first two times she'd jumped off the mule and insisted he ride if he was too tired to walk.

For such a quiet woman, she possessed a stubborn streak as wide as the Lake of the Hurons. Yet not even *she* could deny it was time to make camp now.

With the sun hidden behind so many layers of clouds, he couldn't tell how late it was. Maybe around three or four in the afternoon? He could barely see his hand in front of his face, much less the landmarks he'd been watching for.

A shadow appeared through the white ahead, and he squinted to keep sight of it. The dark spot grew until it took the shape of trees.

Relief eased his insides. They would be stopping here no matter what.

Gulliver trudged along beside him, and Miss Durand didn't even question when they entered the protection of the small grove.

The curtain of white eased beneath the tree cover, but the wind still howled around them. He couldn't tell how far the woods stretched, but the trunks weren't positioned very close to one another. Staying here would be better than riding out in the worst of the storm, but he'd have to string up his oil-skins and some extra furs for protection from the elements.

At a place that seemed somewhat level, he halted. Gulliver did the same, dropping his head as he exhaled a long breath.

Damien turned to the woman. "We'll stop here. I can't see well enough in the storm to find the landmarks."

She didn't argue, just slipped down from the mule's back. She kept a hand clutched tight to the saddle even after her feet found purchase in the snow. He knew well what she must be feeling—the stinging of a hundred bees in her feet and ankles as a surge of blood rushed through them.

He moved around to untie their packs. "Let's get a fire started, then I'll tie up furs to make a shelter."

While he dug out the tinderbox and the dry wood he'd packed from the cave, Miss Durand cleared a circle of snow. There wasn't such a thick layer under the trees, but if they had to construct a fire in an area with deep-packed snow, he could teach her a trick to build it on top of the crust.

After seven tries with Miss Durand attempting to block the wind from his tinderbox, they finally fanned a flame sturdy enough to light a shaving from the dry wood. But if he pulled his arms away, the wind would whip through and kill the flame. He glanced up at the woman. "Can you protect this for a minute?"

She crouched closer, wrapping her arms around the logs as he eased away.

They may not be able to keep a fire alive out here, but he wouldn't give up until he'd given it his best effort. They both needed warmth.

He pulled out a stiff deerskin, one of his earlier attempts at scraping, when he'd still been learning the art. The hide had been too rigid to bring value in the trade room, but it made a good barrier against wet ground under his bedding.

Hopefully, this pelt would be large enough to wrap around the fire and protect it from the wind on all sides.

By the time they'd positioned the skin to guard the logs from the worst of the gales, Miss Durand had nurtured the small flame to take hold of a second log. "I'll stay with the fire." She had to raise her voice to be heard over the gusts.

Her gentle touch would likely draw out the flame better than he could do, so he turned his efforts to stretching oilskins and furs to make a shelter. Using everything he had that wouldn't be required for bedding, he strung a top and two sides for their protection. The wind still found far too many ways inside. The way the blasts swirled, the drafts seemed to come from every direction.

Straightening, he eyed the woods around them. Maybe he could find enough branches to fill in the openings. They needed firewood to dry around the edges of the blaze, too.

He turned back to Miss Durand, who still knelt by the fire, which was a decent-sized flame by now. "I'm going to gather branches and wood."

She nodded but didn't turn away from her work. Hopefully, the fire was helping warm her, as well.

Damien patted Gulliver's neck as he passed by the mule. He'd loosened the saddle but left it on to help protect the animal from the cold. Maybe he would be able to find a more sheltered place for the mount to spend the night. Good thing he still carried a bit of corn to feed him on days when there was no way to dig for fodder.

Finally, he moved deeper into the woods, searching for logs or fallen branches. Each piece he found, he leaned against a nearby tree so he could retrieve a full armload on his way back. This first trek, he needed to focus on scouting. Maybe he could find a better place for them to spend the night or, at the very least, a better area for Gulliver, since their patchy shelter would barely suffice for just the two of them.

As he walked, he kept his eye out for an ash tree. He'd not stopped to make snowshoes yet since there'd been no snow, but another day as harsh as this one would steal the last of his strength. Being able to walk atop the fluff on snowshoes would be a great improvement. Too bad he couldn't make any for the mule.

He did his best to travel in a straight line, since the snow now concealed his view of camp. He'd not found a better shelter yet, but something told him to keep going. If he could just locate a boulder or maybe a creek bed with a patch of protected ground beside the bank . . .

At last, a large outline rose in the distance. He couldn't make out its shape, but it didn't seem to be part of the trees. Maybe a massive rock? He increased his pace, renewed hope sending a fresh wave of strength through him.

His foot snagged on a branch barely poking through the snow, sending him tumbling onto his hands and knees. He scrambled back to his feet. He would come back for that branch later, but for now the hope surging inside him built with each step.

He was almost certain now—they'd found a mountain. One that would likely have boulders or cliffs to protect them far better from the growing storm.

⁖

Charlotte spun as the sound of clomping drew near, loud enough to be heard even through the wind. Damien approached in a half run, his earlier exhaustion nowhere to be seen. She tensed for whatever news he brought.

He arrived panting, but didn't stop to address her, just moved to the skins he'd tied up and began releasing the knots. "There's a mountain not far ahead. And a cave. A much better place to take shelter."

Tension coiled inside her at the thought of climbing down another cliff like the one beside the lake. Surely that wouldn't be necessary here.

Forcing her cold-numbed mind to think of what needed to be done, she eyed the fire. Could she stay by it alone? After all the work she'd put into building it, the thought of letting the blaze go out seemed a crime. Maybe she could move a few of the logs and keep them burning.

Within a few minutes, they had everything piled on the mule, and Damien carried a glowing log in each hand. He gripped each piece by the end that wasn't burning, holding them straight up like torches. That tiny flicker licking each log would be blown out by the wind soon, but she could restart the fire from the coals once they were in the cave.

She and Gulliver followed in Damien's footsteps through the trees. What little of her body that had thawed by the fire froze again with the buffeting gusts. At last, the form of a rising slope became visible through the snowfall. She tucked her chin deeper into her coat. When they left the trees and started up that mountain, the wind would blast even fiercer. Damien hadn't said how high up the cave was, but they'd traveled farther than she'd expected already. The opening must be close.

As they started up the slope, he shifted his route to the right, taking an easier path than straight uphill. At last, he pointed one of the logs toward the rock. A dark opening appeared, and relief swept through her.

Damien paused before entering, and she stepped nearer to stand beside him. The height of the entrance rose just enough for him to step through without ducking. Hopefully it would be tall enough for the mule to join them, too.

He stepped inside, and she moved in after him. The relief from the wind was immediate, and she took in a deep breath of the still air. Perhaps that was a mistake, for she nearly coughed at the pungent smell of dank animal.

Damien raised the logs, but their faint glow illuminated only a tiny space. "I'll get these lit so we can see more of the place."

He moved a few steps farther in, then dropped to his haunches and laid the wood on the stone floor.

Charlotte turned her focus to the mule, who still stood at the end of his rope outside. She gave a tug. "Come on, fella. You'll like it much better in here."

The mule didn't budge, bracing his legs instead. She leaned out into the weather to give his neck a pat. "Come, boy. The dark won't hurt you."

She eased the rope forward in a way that usually seemed to lessen the animal's resistance. But Gulliver only stretched his neck as she pulled, leaning his body backward to resist. Maybe when the fire lit the space, Gulliver would be more amenable to entering. She patted him once more. "You'll wish you came in sooner."

As much as she hated to leave the mule out in the wind, even for a few more minutes, helping Damien with the fire would expedite things. She crouched beside the man as he blew a steady breath of air over the glowing coals.

He glanced up at her. "Do you want to work on this while I get more wood?"

She nodded and leaned in to take over blowing on the coals.

He slipped out into the storm, and by the time he returned, a healthy blaze licked at the two logs. The light it cast only spread to the cave wall on one side, so she couldn't see how large this room was, or if any tunnels traveled deeper into the mountain. The place the logs sat might not be ideal for their campfire through the night. It was too close to the opening, which allowed a bit of wind inside.

Damien dropped his load of logs nearby, then scooped up two that had come from the dry pack. She raised a hand to stave him off. "Let's move the fire over a little before you add wood."

Gripping two unlit ends, she lifted them as torches like Damien had done, then turned toward the interior of the cave. "Maybe we can see how deep it goes." She moved inward, Damien close behind her. She felt like an explorer of old, trekking deep into places never before seen by humans. Perhaps this cave fit that description exactly.

A sound drifted through the air, sort of a snuffle or faint growl. With the darkness around them, it was hard to determine which direction it came from. But the noise definitely wasn't made by the man behind her. And it didn't sound like the storm.

As she took another step forward—slower this time—the back of her neck tingled. Just because she couldn't see what lay ahead in the cave didn't mean it was a threat. Straightening her shoulders, she moved forward with more confidence.

Then another noise rumbled through the space around them. Definitely a growl this time, almost a roar.

She jumped backward as a squeal slipped out, then she

reached for Damien. The pounding of her heart exploded to triple time. What would make such a ferocious sound?

The obvious answer panged through her as the clatter of wood sounded, then Damien gripped her arm and pulled her backward.

"A bear! Get out of here!"

8

Throwing the logs aside, Charlotte scrambled after Damien. His grip on her arm never loosened, propelling her forward around and ahead of him toward the daylight.

Once they were out in the swirling snow, Damien spun her and grabbed the mule's rope, then thrust the line toward her. "Take him. Get back to the trees."

Before she could answer, he slipped his rifle from the scabbard on the saddle, grabbed his shot bag, and turned back to the cave.

Another deep rumble echoed from the opening, quivering her insides. She tugged the mule's lead and started running, though the animal's lagging steps on the icy rock slowed her.

A glance backward showed Damien had only followed a short distance before he stopped and now stood with the rifle pointed toward the cave opening.

Had he lost his senses? They could give the cave over to the bear. Better they all escape far away from the creature. "Run!"

Half-turning but still running and dragging the mule, she watched to make sure Damien came.

He stood with his feet planted, rifle raised to shoot.

The bear appeared from the cave, lumbering forward on all fours. The creature was one of the largest she'd seen, the light brown color of the more dangerous breeds in the area. It paused after emerging into the white storm, then rose up on its hind legs to look around.

Its nose lifted to the air as it scanned the landscape. The moment the beast looked their way, its demeanor transformed. With a roar a hundred times greater than the rumble inside the cave, its paws swiped at air.

An explosion ricocheted off the mountainside, barely muffled by the snow and wind. Smoke or powder puffed from the rifle Damien held, even as he moved swiftly to reload.

Another thundering roar emanated from the bear. The shot seemed to have barely stunned the creature as it dropped to all fours, stumbled one step, then lumbered forward in a ground-covering run.

"Damien!" There wasn't time to say more. The bear was a half-dozen strides from him and was closing the distance fast.

Damien lifted the rifle to his shoulder again.

God, please. As she breathed the prayer, another explosion of spark and gunpowder flashed amid the falling snow.

Again the bear stumbled, this time with both front feet. One shoulder gave way, dropping to the snow. The creature's momentum cast it into a roll that threatened to tumble right into Damien.

Finally, Damien spun and ran, sprinting through the snow with long strides. She didn't wait for him to reach her and the mule, just tugged the animal and jogged as fast as Gulliver would move.

After another dozen strides, she glanced back to make sure Damien had the good sense to keep up with them.

He didn't.

He'd stopped once more and stood ten paces from the bear, reloading the rifle. The man had taken leave of his senses to stand around like that. Though the bear lay in a heap on the snow, she'd heard of such creatures resurrecting and charging the hunter again and again.

She screamed into the wind. "Damien! Run!" Surely he heard the anger giving strength to her voice. Sometimes a dozen arrows wouldn't kill these bears.

He had to run while he had the chance. Yet after raising his rifle to his shoulder once more, he stood motionless, watching the beast.

Completely ignoring her calls.

Fury steamed inside her, mixing with panic at the thought of watching that vicious creature maul him into a muddy heap. She didn't dare move closer to grab Damien's arm, but she couldn't turn and escape, either.

"Run, Damien. Now!" If he hadn't heard her anger before, there was no way to miss the fury this time.

He didn't move for a long moment, but finally his voice drifted over the wind. "It's dead. No need to worry."

He didn't lower his gun, and the urge grew strong inside her to stride forward and use the weapon to clock his witless head. She'd thought this man keen and experienced, far better at maneuvering in these mountains than she was.

Gun still in shooting position, he stepped toward the bear. She could only watch, gritting her teeth but not looking away. The heap of fur hadn't moved, so maybe the animal really was dead.

Damien's steps started out confident but grew slower as he reached the mass. Extending a foot, he lifted one of the bear's immense paws, then let it flop back down. After nudging another of the creature's body parts, he finally lowered his gun and turned to her with a nod. "It's dead."

Then he strode toward her, looking as though it didn't matter that he'd just risked his life to kill the bear when the wiser choice would have been to find a better place to camp.

As he approached, he moved to the saddle pack. "That bear had probably just begun its winter sleep. I've heard they wake easier when they've first bedded down, and they rise up with a fierce temper. I doubt anything else was in the cave with it, but let me take a candle in first before you come in."

She stood with the mule while he dug out the taper, then he turned and strode back to the cave, ducking inside. The tumult within her rivaled the swirling storm around them. She'd never been one to take unnecessary risks, and now that she'd seen the kind of danger Damien would willingly place himself in, she wasn't sure she wanted to be around him any longer. Perhaps she'd do better to find her own way to Fort Versailles.

Yet with this storm, she would be foolish not to take cover in a protected cave—as long as they were the only occupants. Could she trust that he would really make sure that was the case? Or would he only go far enough inside to glance about, then assume no other animals were there?

She would have to check every corner herself . . . once he came out and confirmed *he'd* found nothing.

As she huddled close to Gulliver, they waited for Damien's return. She would probably need to help dress the bear and smoke or roast the meat. But she couldn't bring herself to approach the creature yet. She could still picture him raised up on back legs, nose sniffing the air. Then those yawning fangs as his roar shook the mountain.

Damien finally appeared at the mouth of the cave and motioned her inside.

Gulliver seemed as suspicious of the bear carcass as she felt, so they worked their way down the slope enough to give the pile of fur a wide berth before climbing back up to the cave.

When they reached Damien, he held the lit candle in his hand and stepped backward, waving them inside. She stepped across the threshold and tugged Gulliver to follow her. He'd refused before, but maybe he'd sensed the bear inside.

He halted now but didn't seem as determined to resist. Instead, he sniffed toward the cave entrance, long ears pricked as he weighed the risk.

"Come, boy. It's better inside." She used her crooning voice and kept a steady pressure on the rope.

First one step, then another small one. The mule approached and ducked his nose inside. Another round of sniffing ensued, and she gave the fellow a pat on his neck. "This is good for you. Come on in."

At last, he seemed to finally believe her. Gulliver brought his front hoof into the cave, his hooves clacking loudly on the stone floor now that the howl of the wind was more distant.

He hesitated once more with his back half outside, and she stepped near enough to rub the spot at the base of his neck he seemed to enjoy the most. He finally blew out a long breath and dipped his head, leaning into her touch.

"There's a boy." After another moment indulging him, she gave a final pat. "Let's bring the rest of you in."

She nudged the rope forward, and this time the mule stepped in fully, then dropped his head to sniff the stone floor. "Good fella." She stroked his neck, then turned her focus to determine what needed to be done first.

Damien knelt across the cave from her, a small fire flickering from the logs in front of him. His focus was on her, though, and the light barely illuminated the curve of his mouth. "You have a way with him. I'm not sure he'd let many others coax him in with so much bear scent still lingering here. Especially not someone he'd only met this morning."

Warmth slipped through her, and she looked away to keep from showing too much of her pleasure at his words. She wasn't ready to trust this man again, and even less willing to like him.

To strengthen her resolve, she turned toward the back of the cave. The small fire didn't provide enough light for her to see the rear wall or any other tunnels. "You've searched for other animals?" She kept her focus on the darkness, straining for any sound or scent that might signal another creature.

"I did. Nothing else here except you, me, and the mule."

"How far back does it go?" Even with her eyes adjusted to the lack of light, she could make out nothing in that area.

"This room goes straight back a short distance, then a side tunnel branches off to the left. It ends at a rock wall, though. Nothing else there."

That should be easy enough to explore and check for herself. She turned toward him and the fire. "May I borrow the candle? I want to make sure it's empty."

Surprise tipped his features, but he reached for the taper, lit it in the fire, then handed the candlestick to her. "You don't believe me?" His tone sounded half-teasing, half-surprised.

She took the candle from him and shifted toward the rear of the cave. "I don't take chances." *Especially not after that bear.*

With the circle of candlelight in front of her, she traipsed up the slight incline until she reached the rear wall. This room was only about three times as deep as its width. The area at the bottom with flattened fur and other debris cluttering the floor must be where the bear had curled up for its winter sleep.

Gooseflesh rose on her arms, and she focused on the walls instead. She certainly agreed with Damien's choice to build their fire and lay out camp at the front end of the cave, far from this area.

The candlelight finally found the side tunnel he mentioned, a much smaller passage that required her to duck to enter. She hesitated at the opening. Did she really want to explore a tiny corridor?

But she had to. With the lower ceiling, Damien might have simply glanced inside and assumed nothing was there. She had to be certain.

Crouching, she extended the candle farther in front of her and stepped inside. She'd only gone five strides when the rear wall appeared ahead. After moving the light in all directions to make sure there wasn't another side tunnel, she took a final glance around the small space, then shimmied back to the bigger room.

Once she could stand up straight, she released a long breath. He'd been right. Relief sagged through her. Something about that tiny tunnel had heightened all her worries. Even the bear nest against the back wall in this main cavern now seemed easier to stomach than the smaller space.

Squaring her shoulders, she marched back up the slope

to where light from Damien's fire glowed. Had he seen her moment of fear? With the candle illuminating her face, he likely had. She would ignore that temporary weakness, and maybe he would do the same.

Damien stood as she approached, but he moved toward the mule. The animal remained where she'd left him, his silhouette outlined by the white of the snow through the entrance behind him. Perhaps he'd calmed enough to be led nearer the fire, away from the wind.

Damien stripped the saddle and packs from the animal's back and carried them to the fire. She gripped Gulliver's lead, and he obeyed her command to walk forward completely out of the wind. "Do we have anything he can eat?"

"A bit of corn. I'll pull it out in a minute." He'd untied their packs and was now unstrapping their furs.

Her heart clenched, even as she reminded herself that she'd moved the chalice from the roll of furs to her pack. And it was tucked inside the protective pouch. If he saw the chalice, would he recognize its value? Of course, in its damaged condition, the cup might not be worth taking at all.

Still, she'd best keep it hidden to eliminate any temptation. Not that she suspected Damien was the kind of man who would steal, but she couldn't risk anything else happening to this precious treasure. She had to get it to the fort, find an artisan skilled enough to repair it, then return to Laurent before the celebration. She couldn't let herself think about what she would have to do if no such metal engraver could be found at Fort Versailles.

She strode to her pack and grabbed it up, then moved around to the opposite side of the fire from Damien. She should start cooking a meal. The weather outside made it almost impossible to know what time it was, but her hungry belly rumbled at the thought of food.

While she worked, Damien brought in more logs, heaping a large pile near enough to the fire that the wood could dry from the heat. Gulliver munched the feed Damien gave him, then wandered around the small area near the entrance while Damien disappeared outside to work on the bear carcass.

At last, the meal was ready, and she called out to let Damien know. He stepped into the cave a moment later, shaking snow from his hands and coat. "Finished most of what has to be done tonight, but I'll go back out later for the rest."

As she scooped out servings of meat with savory sauce, she studied the mule from the corner of her gaze. "How long have you had Gulliver?"

Damien settled on his furs, then looked toward the animal, his gaze softening. "About six months. I bought him when I knew I planned to take up trapping full-time."

Not long, then. She'd watched man and animal interact throughout the day, and they'd developed a bond even in that short time. Damien had also earned a bit of trust from the coyote they'd met that morning.

She'd heard animals could read people better than another human could. If that was true, perhaps he was more trustworthy than this evening's events made him appear. Just because the man took unnecessary risks didn't mean he wasn't honest.

But that still didn't mean she would trust him with her own safety.

9

After Charlotte handed Damien his plate of food, she couldn't help but study him as he took his first bite. His eyes fell shut, and his face took on an expression that drew her. Pleasure. She'd not intended to continue watching him, but the curve of his mouth as his eyes opened, that glimmer of appreciation shimmering within them, those were hard to look away from.

When he finished chewing, he straightened and met her gaze. "Miss Durand, I've never met a woman who could cook fare like this over a campfire."

The warmth resonating in his voice sent a flush through her. She dropped her focus and took up her own bite. How did one answer a compliment like that? She settled for a shrug and a quiet thank-you. She was limited in supplies and cooking pots here, but she'd been cooking over a fire all her life. They'd only had a cookstove for the past two years. And part of her still preferred a simple fire.

They ate in silence for several minutes, and she could feel each time Damien settled his gaze on her. With just the two of them, she needed to accustom herself to his watching. It must be the newness of him that made her so aware of his every movement.

"You're a hard one to get to know, Miss Durand." His voice broke the silence, his words drawing her gaze up sharply.

What did he mean by that? How exactly did he want to get to know her?

His expression softened. "I only meant you're very quiet. Not talkative like most women, especially not about yourself."

She forced her shoulders to relax as her mind worked through what he might *not* be saying. Were the women in the rest of the world so forward, prattling on about whatever caught their thoughts? That image didn't appeal in the least. She did tend to be quieter than many of the other women in Laurent, but she'd found great value in listening.

Still, she didn't want to be rude to him. He'd been kind and respectful from the very beginning, far more than common decency required. She could give answers that were careful enough that she wouldn't offer information that would endanger herself or Laurent.

She kept her manner casual. "What would you wish me to talk about?"

Damien raised his brows. "I don't know. You have family back in Laurent? I'm assuming you're not married, or your husband would have never allowed you to travel unaccompanied."

Never allowed? It was a good thing she wasn't married, then, for the thought of a man forcibly commanding her actions riled. She did her best to keep her expression civil. "I have a father, an older sister and her husband, and a younger brother. Also an uncle."

Curiosity touched his features. "Your uncle lives in your father's home?"

She shook her head. "He has a room behind Papa's workshop, but he takes many of his meals with us."

"What does your father make in his workshop?"

"He's a metalworker, and he's well-known for the decorative details he adds to his pieces." As she said the words, a sudden pang twisted her insides. Had she been foolish to bring the chalice to the fort instead of seeking her father's help straightaway? He was no artist, but his talent with metals and engravings was highly respected throughout the village. If anyone could repair the damaged cup, wouldn't it be him? She took a deep breath and willed away the guilt. The artistic details on the chalice were so rich and ornate. Her father had never produced anything like it.

Perhaps Papa's abilities were average compared to those of the metalworkers at the fort. She wouldn't know until she reached that place. Her heartbeat quickened, excitement and apprehension warring inside her.

"Decorative details? Do you mean pictures or artistic touches?" The interest in Damien's voice called her back to the conversation.

"Mostly the latter." Perhaps this would be the right time to ask about his own artistic pursuits. "Are you an artist, D—" She barely stopped herself before using his given name. "Monsieur Levette?"

His eyes gentled, showing he'd caught her slip. "Please, call me Damien. I believe you already did when the bear was approaching." A twinkle entered his gaze with that last bit, and another flood of heat swept through her.

The reminder of those awful moments outside the cave

would only frustrate her, so she focused on whether she *should* call him by his given name. In truth, she'd been thinking of him that way for a while now, but speaking it broke down the barrier of decorum.

An imaginary barrier, now that she thought about it. Their current situation, traveling together in the midst of a snowstorm, didn't allow for much formality. She would be silly to require that façade.

She nodded to acknowledge his words, though she wasn't quite ready to allow the same casualness with her own name. And it was definitely time to turn the conversation back to him.

"Are you an artist, Damien?"

A frown twisted his brow, and he gave a quick shake of his head. "Not an artist."

There was something in his actions—his quick refusal, the interest he had shown in the paintings on the cave wall, the questions about her father's work—that urged her to dig deeper. "Have you done any sketches or paintings? Or engravings, maybe?"

The frown didn't leave his face, and it looked like he was trying to decide how to answer. "A few. Long ago."

As she'd expected. However long it had been since he'd taken up a brush, it seemed the love for art hadn't left him.

But he didn't seem inclined to discuss the topic further, and she wouldn't force him to speak of things he wished to avoid.

Silence settled over them again. Damien had finished eating, and she now swallowed down her last bite. The warmth of the fire had lulled away any desire to move. She needed to clean up from the meal, but the dancing flames held her captive. And the stinging in her toes had just eased.

Yet the quiet between them nudged at her. She'd told a bit about her family but knew nothing about his. She didn't lift her gaze from the fire as she spoke. "What of you? Family? A wife?"

He shook his head as he, too, stared into the fire. "A sister, but she's gone now. Our parents died years ago." A distance had slipped into his voice, leaving his words without emotion. At least one of those losses must have been within the past few years, far enough back that the wound didn't bleed still, but near and deep enough that the ache came strong.

She lifted her gaze to the man. "I'm sorry. We lost my mother when I was four. I can't imagine if I'd lost both parents and my siblings, too." And as awful as that thought was, she would still be surrounded by friends in Laurent who were as dear as family.

Damien seemed to have no one. An urge pressed inside her, the desire to be that person for him. A steadfast friend, someone he could turn to when the pain grew strongest. Someone he could depend on.

That longing was foolish, though. They would only be traveling together another day or two at the most. She would be merely a temporary companion. Yet, while she had the chance, she could be his friend.

A moment later, Damien seemed to pull himself from his thoughts. "I suppose I need to finish skinning that bear and cut the meat up before I bed down for the night."

As he pushed to his feet, Charlotte had to bite back a groan. A friend would help with such a chore. Of all things, did this first act of support have to be so much work?

Two more days until the anniversary of Michelle's death. And every part of Damien's body ached.

The thoughts came simultaneously before he opened his eyes for the day. He could almost be grateful for the pain gripping each limb, for it distracted him from the deeper ache.

A quiet clink sounded from outside his bedding, and he listened for the familiar sound of Gulliver's hooves. But then the swish of clothing slipped into his awareness, bringing back a flood of reality.

Charlotte—or rather, Miss Durand. She'd not yet given him permission to use her given name, and he had to stop thinking of her that way or the wrong version would slip out.

He pulled his furs down enough to glance out and squint at the firelight. On the other side of the flame his campmate sat, already put together for the day and stirring something in the plate she used as cookware. He sent his gaze to the cave entrance. Had he overslept again?

Only a faint glow lightened the darkness, which could either be from bright stars or the beginnings of dawn.

As much as he wanted to squeeze his eyes shut and pull the furs back over his head, he couldn't let this woman out wake him *and* outwork him. She'd stayed up as late as he had, cutting out the edible parts from the bear and wrapping them so they could freeze through the night. He would eventually need to cook the meat so he'd have fare to eat on the trail, but as long as the weather stayed so cold, that chore could wait.

Though his body protested, he pushed the furs farther down and sat up, running a hand through his unruly hair. He'd had it cut before he headed out with Arsenault, but the curly ends had grown out enough they probably stood at all angles now.

Miss Durand looked up, and when her gaze took him in, her expression softened. She was a beautiful lady at all times, but something about her now seemed to glow. Perhaps only a trick of the fire, but it stirred his insides just the same.

"Bonjour." Her soft voice warmed the cave even more than the fire.

He cleared the sleep from his throat. "Morning. Do you always get up so early after you spend half the night dressing a bear?" She'd been up early the day before, too, but he'd assumed that was because she wanted to get on the trail early. Maybe that was the case now, as well.

She glanced toward the cave opening. "The rest of my family is usually up and around by now. I try to have the morning meal ready for them."

He must be a sluggard in her eyes, then. This last year, greeting the day had been painful, so he'd found himself putting it off as long as he could. There was a time when rising hadn't been so hard, but that seemed another lifetime.

After climbing from his warm furs, he patted Gulliver on his way outside. The snow had finally stopped, and most of the wind with it. A lighter breeze stirred the frigid air, making him pull his coat tighter around himself. Dawn had just begun to break in the eastern sky, but he couldn't see the clouds well enough to know whether they portended snow again.

He had no doubt Miss Durand would want to head out this morning, either way. He'd not seen any ash trees to use for snowshoes, but maybe he should try to fashion a pair from a different type of wood. Whatever he made might not last the winter, but if they would just carry him over the fresh snowfall until they reached Fort Versailles, he'd be satisfied.

With the addition of the bear pelt, Gulliver would have more than enough work of his own today. He could probably still handle Miss Durand's slight weight, but Damien needed to stay off the poor mule's back.

The meal Miss Durand prepared was as warm and surprisingly delicious as the others she'd made. He'd been eating over a campfire for so long, he'd forgotten food could actually taste good. That a meal could be something to look forward to, full of flavor.

Somehow, she could accomplish that even over an open fire. It made him wonder what her kitchen looked like back in Laurent. Perhaps this setting was normal for her.

He found branches that could suffice for snowshoe frames, and once he'd secured the wood in an oval shape, Charlotte strapped the animal skins in place to finish the platforms. He'd not expected her help with the task, but she'd taken up the first frame when he finished it and simply begun her work. She clearly knew what she was doing—she'd probably made a dozen more pairs than he had, at the very least.

But she didn't seem to work from a desire to show her superior abilities. Since they'd talked over the evening meal last night, she appeared more relaxed in his presence. Comfortable even, as though she'd accepted him. The feeling was as foreign as . . . well, he'd certainly not felt it since he lost Michelle.

As Charlotte brought him the packs to load onto Gulliver, their supplies seemed to have doubled. When she sat the last bundle by his feet, she eyed his handiwork with a frown. "You don't expect us to ride him today. He's carrying a bear he didn't have yesterday."

Her wording brought a smile. "Not the full bear. We've

drained all the liquids and left behind the bones and organs. Gulliver's stronger than he looks. I think my weight would be too much, but he'll be fine carrying you."

She didn't lose the crease that had gathered between her brows, and when he motioned for her to mount up, she shook her head. "I'll walk until we're off the mountain."

A flare of frustration surged inside him. "I wouldn't let you hurt my mule. If I tell you he can handle your weight, it's because I'm certain he can." He should've kept his mouth shut, though, for his words only drew the stubborn jut of her chin.

"I'd rather walk."

He didn't waste his energy with an answer, just turned and tugged Gulliver forward.

As they trekked around the mountain, the usual wind whipped at them, stirring up the snow and swirling white around them. At least the gusts would die down once they reached the next valley.

In his mind, he tried to visualize the next landmark he should be watching for, then the one after that. Was it possible they might reach the fort before dark? Probably not, as slowly as they had to travel over the snow. Especially if Charlotte refused to ride at all. Then he would need to stop and make snowshoes for her, too.

That stubborn streak she possessed might be helpful at times, but there certainly were moments it worked against her—not only making her days harder, but also endangering her. Like when the bear was charging and she'd refused to take the mule and run.

If he'd been able to get a clean shot from the first, none of them would have been in danger. With the price bear hides currently brought in trade, he would've been foolish to let that opportunity go.

But when the bear sprang up again, and Charlotte refused to run, what had been a simple business decision became so much more. Instead of being able to move around and take shots from the best angle, he'd had to position himself between the beast and her. Thank God that last bullet had brought the animal down, for he'd already been imagining what a swipe from one of those powerful paws would feel like as it knocked him sideways.

And now her stubbornness to go to the fort—a woman alone in that den of iniquity—was putting her in as much danger as with that bear. Maybe worse.

Death by bear would come within minutes, no doubt. But the women-hungry men at Fort Versailles . . . there was no telling what they would put her through. Sure, there were many decent folk there, but also many who would be swept away by lust for a woman as beautiful as Miss Durand.

He sent a glance over his shoulder to where she followed in his tracks. The activity had brought a lively flush to her cheeks, brightening the porcelain of her skin. Hers was a face any artist would love, features proportioned so perfectly. How could he lead her into such danger? Even if he stayed as close as she'd allow, protected her every chance he could, her stubborn streak would likely place her in situations where he couldn't save her.

And if something happened to her—either to her life or her innocence—he couldn't live with that. A lump gathered in his throat at the thought of losing another woman who mattered to him. Charlotte wasn't like Michelle, as he'd only just met the woman two days ago, but he already felt responsible for her. More than just responsible, now that he thought about it. He *wanted* to help her. To be for her what no one else could be right now.

Not just keep her safe, but also make her happy.

Surely her family back in Laurent hadn't let her leave willingly. The way she spoke with pride of her father and with affection toward her siblings and uncle, it seemed she had people who cared about her. Maybe she would eventually trust him enough to tell him why she'd set out alone.

For now, he had to make the best decision for her that he could with the knowledge he possessed. It seemed he had three options.

He could guide her to the fort, which his mind and heart and every other part of him said was not a true option.

He could take her back to Laurent. He knew the general direction but had no idea how to find the exact mountain where the village lived. If he got her close, though, she should be able to guide them the final stretch.

Or he could wander aimlessly without telling her. That option wouldn't be possible more than a few days before she grew suspicious.

Maybe a combination of the last two would work best. He could take her in a roundabout way toward where he suspected the village to be. She probably wouldn't recognize the landmarks until they came near, so he'd have that much time to convince her the fort wasn't safe. Maybe by then she would be so cold and tired of snow, she might even be longing for home.

He glanced around again, this time seeing the landmarks from a different perspective. He would need to lead them in a wide arc as they circled back to the west. Charlotte would recognize their direction at some point—she was a savvy woman despite her stubborn streak. But the longer he could hold off her discovery, the better for her.

As much as he hated being sneaky and underhanded when she'd placed her trust in him, that very trust required him to do everything possible to keep her safe.

10

By midday, fatigue weighted Charlotte's steps. She'd given in and climbed aboard Gulliver once they reached level ground. Two days of trekking in the snow, not to mention the short night, had used up almost every bit of strength she possessed.

Damien took Gulliver to a nearby stream to crack the ice for him to drink, and she couldn't resist laying back on the fur she'd spread to sit on. Just a few minutes to rest her body might give her fresh energy for the afternoon. She wouldn't sleep, only let her eyes and body rest.

A sound pulled her from the haze her body had sunk into, and she forced her eyelids open. Damien knelt over a pile of logs in the snow, the tinderbox in his hands.

The noise came again, the scrape of flint against steel. He was building a fire?

She jerked upright, then winced at the aches shooting through her. The fur fell from around her shoulders.

The fur? Had he spread it over her like a blanket?

"What are you doing?" Her voice came out hoarse and groggy.

He glanced up, brows raised at first, then eased into a

gentle smile. "You're awake. I was worried you'd get cold, so I was starting a fire. I also thought something warm to drink might be good for us both."

She blinked. He spoke as if she'd been sleeping for hours. "I'm sorry I dozed off. I'm ready to keep going now."

He swiveled to face her, sitting on his heels. His eyes scanned her face, as though looking for something that would tell him whether she truly was ready to start out again.

She pushed the fur off and forced her aching body to stand. Damien didn't get to choose whether she was capable of traveling or not. She had to get to the fort as soon as possible, which meant she had to push through her exhaustion.

He seemed to understand, for he stood and loaded the logs back in his arms, then stowed them on Gulliver's saddle where they kept the dry wood.

As she wrapped the furs back in a bundle and tied them on the mule, a glance at the sky showed that the sun had moved much farther than she'd expected. "Was I asleep long?"

"A couple hours." Damien spoke the words casually as he pulled the strap tight on the saddle.

She nearly choked on her surprise, and the heat surging to her face warmed her better than a fire would have. "I'm . . . sorry. I didn't mean to nod off at all."

He looked at her with one of those soft expressions. "I'm glad you did. We all needed the rest."

Then he moved to hold Gulliver's bridle while she climbed aboard. She could lose herself in this man's approval, rest in his help and confidence.

But she couldn't allow herself. She had to stay focused on getting to Fort Versailles. No more time could be wasted. She'd lost so much time already.

As they traveled over the next few hours, she couldn't shake the grogginess from her nap. Thankfully, they were able to skirt the mountains in their path, keeping to valleys and small hills.

At last, they reached a river that spread wide before them. Man and mule halted together, and all three of them stared out across the expanse.

Forty strides across, at least. Snow piled in numerous drifts atop the water where the wind had blown it. That meant a layer of ice crusted the surface beneath the snow.

"Do you think the ice is strong enough to hold us?"

"Probably. The creek where I watered Gulliver at noon had ice as thick as my arm." He motioned to his forearm, no doubt full of ropey muscle that made him stronger than any ice.

Still . . . They shouldn't take chances unless there was no other option. "Perhaps there's a way around it."

He motioned toward the trees dotting the river's edge. "Let's camp here and cross in the morning."

Urgency pressed through her. "We should find a way around it tonight. Then we'll be able to start out quicker at daybreak."

He glanced toward her, his jaw tense. But as he studied her, uncertainty seeped into his gaze. Finally, his focus shifted back to the river. He stood quietly another minute before heaving a sigh. "We can check the ice. See how sturdy it is."

A knot pulled tight in her belly. "Can't we look for a way around it?"

He shook his head as he started forward. "I know this river. We'll have to cross it."

She swallowed down the fear trying to rise up, doing her

best to maintain a brave expression. When she was a young girl, one of the older lads in Laurent had fallen through thin ice. When he'd finally been pulled out, his lifeless body had already frozen. She could still remember his mother's weeping, which seemed to last for years. She couldn't do that to her own family. They would never know what had happened to her, but they would grieve.

When they reached the river's edge, she slid off the mule while Damien approached the bank. After rubbing the snow away from a spot of ice with his foot, he tapped his toe on the hard crust, then placed a tentative step on the surface.

She cringed for the splash as his foot broke through, but it didn't come. He brought his other foot forward and placed it ahead of the first, easing his weight from one to the other. "Seems sturdy enough. I'll cross over and make sure it can hold Gulliver, too."

As he took another step, the fear surged into her throat, and this time it wouldn't be swallowed down. "Wait."

He paused and looked back once more, his manner as casual as if he stood on dry ground. His raised brows said he had no idea why she would stop him.

A glance at the snow blowing across the river strengthened her resolve. They had no bodies of water this large around Laurent, only oversized streams. But she'd heard the hunters say the wider sections took longer to freeze over. A river this massive wouldn't bear the weight of a man so soon, much less a mule. "It's not safe. The snow is too new, the ice won't be strong enough in the middle of a river this wide. Isn't there a narrower place to cross?"

He shook his head. "None that would freeze as fast as

this. Too many trees coming out of the water weakens the ice. This empty stretch will be frozen. Have no fear."

Even while he still spoke, he moved out farther. She gripped Gulliver's rope as her pulse thundered through her throat. How could she stand here and watch this?

Yet she couldn't look away, cringing with each step he took. Waiting for the moment his foot broke through the surface. Surely he would have the sense to throw himself backward if that happened, and he would have to be walking slowly to manage it. His steps were measured, but his stride carried a momentum that might not allow him to grab on to safety when the ice cracked beneath him.

Lord, keep him safe. Don't let him crash through into the icy water.

If he managed to climb back out, he would take ill from the dunking. But if the ice was thin enough, it might continue to crumble until it washed him away beneath the surface. Just like that boy.

Fear pounded harder within her.

As he passed the halfway mark, she finally allowed herself to breathe once more, though she had to force each inhale. With every other thought, she lifted a prayer heavenward for his safety. Her prayer life certainly had increased since she'd met this man. Did God hear her? She'd never been certain, and she was even less so now. She'd learned the Scriptures with all the other children as part of her studies, and her father truly seemed to commune with the Lord.

She'd said her fair share of prayers, too, mostly at bedtime and when called upon at a family meal. But had God ever answered her? Sometimes the events she prayed for had happened, other times not. Could any of the answers really be ascribed to God? She usually did her best to find a way to accomplish them on her own. Was that really faith at all?

Almighty God, if you've ever thought to answer my petitions before, let this be the one.

At last, Damien reached the opposite shore, and relief nearly stole the strength from her legs. But then he turned around and started back to her side. Her breath hitched, but she forced air in and out. He'd made it once. Surely that meant he could cross safely a second time.

But with every step he progressed, a new certainty rose within her like the bear from the cave. She would not risk walking across such an expanse. She didn't take dangerous chances, and this certainly fell into that category.

There had to be a narrower stretch of river that would be safer to cross. Both for her and Gulliver.

⚬⚬⚬

Exhilaration swept through Damien as he took his last few strides to exit the ice. He'd done it.

He'd been fairly sure the ice was thick enough. No bubbles showed beneath the surface to signal weakness, and no trees or grass grew above to break the strength of the frozen expanse.

But he'd not been certain. In those steps across the deeper stretch of the river, when he'd known a break in the ice could seal his fate, that urge to embrace death had returned. A longing to be with Michelle again.

He'd not felt it since meeting Miss Durand. And this time there had been guilt interwoven with the desire. He needed to stay alive long enough to help her. Then, when his own life was all he had to consider, he could be as reckless as he wanted.

Stepping onto the snow-covered ground, he pulled his focus back to the present. But when he lifted his gaze to the woman and mule, Charlotte was turning the animal upriver.

"Where are you going? Bring him straight down." The bank wasn't steep in that spot, so Gulliver would manage it well.

But she marched forward, all signs of exhaustion gone. She also didn't appear to be planning to answer him.

Frustration swelled, but he tamped it down. "Miss Durand."

Still, she didn't answer, but her march had turned into more of a stomp along the bank.

"Charlotte." His frustration would no longer be restrained, and it turned his voice into a bark.

She spun to face him. "I'll not risk my life like you did. And I'll not let you endanger this innocent animal either. We'll find a narrower stretch to cross."

Damien strode toward her, forcing in deep breaths of the icy air to rein in his anger. Did her stubbornness know no end? There might be no narrower places safe enough to cross if she walked a long distance upstream. The only one he could remember nearby had saplings growing through the water. The ice wouldn't be as strong, though he'd been surprised how thick this section had crusted already.

He couldn't forcibly grab her to make her stop, and he'd already tried to help her see reason. He'd even shown her that his area to cross would work. All he could do now was follow along and try to keep her from doing something truly dangerous.

Onward she marched, Gulliver trudging at her side. Around a curve in the river, past a slightly narrower place where he'd worried she would make an attempt. Beyond a broader open expanse that could have served for decent crossing.

Finally, she halted at a place a bit narrower than anything they'd seen yet. Reeds pushed up through the ice on the opposite side, but they might be scant enough for the crust to still be strong.

He glanced at the woman, took in the strength of her jaw, the determination marking her face. But it was impossible not to also see the beauty of her profile, the way her nose turned up the slightest bit. She was young, maybe a full five years younger than him, but her youth was fortified by maturity. Made him want to learn everything he could about her. To really understand her.

She met his gaze, and her voice jarred him back to the present. "I can lead the mule across, unless you want to."

That reminder of their situation cleared any wistful thought from his mind. "I will. Let me cross alone first and make sure the ice is thick enough."

She raised her brows at him as her look turned incredulous. "You already did that once on a far more dangerous stretch." She moved back to where the packs were tied behind the saddle and began unfastening hers. "He's your mule, so it's your choice whether you lead him or not. I'm sufficiently certain the ice will be fine to cross here."

Pulling her pack over her shoulder, she barely spared him a glance as she turned and marched toward the river.

Troublesome woman. *She* might be sufficiently certain, but he was nothing of the kind.

The surprise in her actions stole his forward motion long enough that she reached the river's edge two strides before him. He closed that distance just as she took a tentative step onto the snow gathered at the edge of the ice.

"Charlotte, wait." He grabbed at her to stop her.

As his hand closed around her upper arm, she twisted and wrenched herself away from him. The glare she aimed his way could have melted the ice beneath her. "What?"

"The reeds on the far side of the river might have weakened the ice. Just let me check."

She glanced to the opposite bank. "It's no more than what there was where you crossed. The river's not as wide here, so the ice should be thicker."

Panic clogged his throat, maybe an unreasonable emotion since he'd only known the woman a short time. But she'd become his responsibility, just like Michelle had been.

He had to do a better job protecting this time.

11

Damien worked hard to settle both his breathing and his voice. "Please. Let me go first. It won't hurt anything if I cross over before you."

Charlotte's brows lowered, gathering into furrows. "If it's so important, go ahead. I don't think it's necessary, though."

His panic eased out, and he inhaled a deep breath to release the rest of the turmoil inside him. "Thank you." For once, her stubbornness wasn't as strong as her ability to see reason.

He motioned to the solid ground. "If you'll wait with Gulliver, I would appreciate it." The mule didn't need a guardian. He was so weary from the day's travel he stood with his head drooped. But that would give her a task to keep her out of trouble.

As she turned to walk back to the mule, he didn't miss the arch of her brows that showed she realized his ploy.

But at least she didn't argue.

Damien stepped out onto the snow-covered ice. With the trees on either bank protecting this section from the wind, a layer of white spread across the width of the river. He used a foot to brush aside some of the snow, and the ice beneath didn't appear to have bubbles. Good.

As he started forward, he tried to summon that recklessness that drove him in situations like this. Yet all he could see was an image of Charlotte breaking through the ice. Arms flailing as frigid water sucked her down.

He locked his jaw against the vision. He would make sure that didn't happen.

When he neared the far side, he skirted around the area where underbrush rose above the ice. The path he took brought him nearer to saplings growing from the water, but at least they'd be sturdier to grab onto should the surface splinter beneath his feet.

The ice stayed strong, and when he stepped onto the snowy bank, he breathed out his relief. Perhaps they would cross this river yet without a catastrophe.

He followed his tracks back across to Charlotte and the mule. Her face didn't show much of a triumphant look, mostly just the weariness from their long day.

He took Gulliver's rope from her. "Just stay on the path I took."

She nodded and started across. He gave her a few strides' lead so there wouldn't be too much weight on a single spot of the ice. Then he tugged the mule forward.

When they reached the first step onto the snow-covered ice, Gulliver hesitated, tipping his head down as he eyed the stretch ahead of them. With the snow still spread across the river, one wouldn't necessarily know at first glance that this was ice. This proved once more how the mule had an uncanny knack for sensing things. Or maybe smelling them.

He gave a pull on the rope, and after one more hesitation, Gulliver took a tentative step forward.

The ice held as Damien had expected it to in this section.

Gulliver's keen senses might give them warning if some of the frozen mass ahead was weaker. Perhaps. Damien couldn't depend on that possibility, but he'd sure appreciate if it played out.

Charlotte had gained distance from them with the mule's hesitation, and she'd now reached the center of the river. Having her so far ahead felt like her safety was out of his control, so he lengthened his strides to catch up. Gulliver refused to lengthen his, though, keeping to a plodding pace that made Damien itch to pull the animal faster.

Yet he knew better than to try to force him into anything. Mules responded much better if you eased them into doing whatever it was you needed.

He kept his gaze glued on Charlotte. Her shoulders no longer seemed tense, and her stride was more relaxed, though certainly weary. They would camp here at the river's edge no matter what. All three of them had reached their limit for the day.

He'd been guiding them southward most of the day, and tomorrow morning he would shift them to the southwest.

What should he say when she asked if they would reach the fort tomorrow? She *would* ask. She did every day. A knot tightened his throat. He hated deception, but he was fairly certain that if he told her outright he was taking her back to her village, she would leave him forthwith.

He cast his gaze to the clouds above. The expanse covered the sun but didn't have a look that portended rain or snow. More like simply a gray winter's day. If only—

A scream tore through his thoughts, jerking him to attention. A splash sounded as Charlotte's foot broke through the ice.

His pulse and body leapt to full speed as fear vaulted him forward.

Charlotte's momentum had pushed her forward into the icy water, but as her body sank down, her hands scrambled to find purchase on the snowy surface. She hooked her elbows on one edge, then a loud crack sounded as the chunk she leaned on gave way.

He'd nearly reached her as she grabbed for reeds sticking through the ice. Reeds. How had she shifted off course?

There was no time now to answer that question, and he slid to his belly so he could reach out and give her a hand to cling to. "Here! Grab my hand."

But she didn't turn to him. Didn't even acknowledge his words.

Instead, she rose up in the water, as though she'd been riding a horse submerged beneath the surface.

Then his mind finally caught up with his eyes. The water wasn't deep here. Of course it wouldn't be, so near the bank. In his panic, he'd lost sight of that fact.

"I'm all right." The water reached nearly to her waist, and she wrapped her arms around herself as she stepped toward the bank.

A new reality sank through him. He had to get away from the weak ice, then get Gulliver safely to shore. And most importantly, he had to get Charlotte warm.

In this icy temperature, life-threatening sickness wouldn't take long.

Crawling backward on his belly, he reached a spot far enough from the broken area that the ice should be strong. Then he pushed to his feet and took up the mule's rope.

Before they moved forward again, though, he mapped out

a slightly different route to the shore, staying far away from the compromised ice. The new path moved him closer to the saplings breaking through the frozen surface, but he'd have to take the chance.

When Damien tugged the rope, Gulliver plodded behind him, and he gave as much distance as he could between himself and the animal. Best to put as little weight on each spot as he could.

All went well until Damien reached the shore. Gulliver had only a single step before his front hooves found solid ground, but one of his rear feet crashed through the water near a tree.

The mule squealed as he gathered his weight on the other three legs and pulled the soaked hoof out of the water. Damien tugged hard on the rope to keep him moving forward. Though the water would be shallow, another hoof might break through any moment.

It did.

The ice under the wet leg cracked, then shattered.

"Walk on!" Damien pulled hard to get the animal the rest of the way to shore, and Gulliver did his best to obey. As one front hoof reached solid ground, the other rear hoof broke through the ice.

Gulliver squealed as he lunged forward, hopping to raise his hind legs high. Finally, he managed to get all four feet on the bank.

Damien released the rope as Gulliver dropped his head, breathing hard. Damien's own chest heaved the same way. "Good boy." He patted the mule's neck.

But he couldn't take time to rest.

Glancing around, he found Charlotte sitting on the snowy bank a few strides away, her arms wrapped around herself as she bent forward over her knees. Her entire body convulsed in shivers he could see even from this distance.

Blankets. And a fire. Something warm to drink.

He grabbed his roll of fur bedding, jerking the tie so hard he ripped off the end. In three strides, he dropped to his knees by her side and pulled the first well-used pelt around her shoulders. She clutched at the edges, pulling it tight. Her teeth chattered so forcefully that she might break a tooth if they didn't get her warm.

And much worse than that could happen.

He wrapped another fur around her shoulders, laying it atop the first. With her hands covered, she didn't grasp this one. And when he adjusted it to lay smoothly, the act felt almost intimate, her nearness rising so strong into his awareness. The next two furs he rested on her legs, which still had water dripping from her leggings. He wrapped the last fur around her shoulders once more.

She still shivered, her teeth hammering, but her eyes weren't quite as glassy as before.

"I'm going to find a place to camp around here, then I'll come get you and we'll start a fire. You'll be warm before you know it."

She flicked her gaze up to his for only a second as she nodded. Then she tucked her chin deeper in the covers.

As he stood, a glance around showed a cluster of trees downstream that might give enough cover for the night. He took up Gulliver's rope and led the mule to the spot. Once he had a fire built and Charlotte warming beside it, he'd rub down the animal's legs to help dry them. After walking in the snow all day, the dunking of his rear limbs probably hadn't added much more wetness than what was there al-

116

ready. Thankfully, Gulliver possessed a hide thick enough to shield him from most of the cold.

As soon as Damien kicked enough snow out of the way for the fire and for Charlotte to sit, he jogged back to where she waited for him. Except for shivering, she hadn't moved a hair from where he left her. Her eyelids had closed, though, and the sight sent a needle of fresh worry through him. Arsenault had spoken more than once about how sleepiness came when one grew too cold in the elements.

He dropped to his haunches beside her, resting one hand on her shoulder. "Charlotte, I found a place to camp. Can you walk there?"

For an instant, she didn't respond, and his worry turned to panic. Then her eyelids drifted halfway up, and her gaze seemed to search before it landed on him. She didn't speak.

He gave her shoulder a little shake. "Do you think you can walk?"

She stared at him through those heavy-lidded eyes for a long moment, as though trying to sort his words into meaning. "Yes." Her voice rasped as though she'd just awakened.

They didn't have time for her slow reactions. He had to get her to a fire. These wet things had to come off, and she needed warmth inside her.

"I'm going to carry you." As he slid a hand around her back and one under her legs, his fear gave him the strength to lift her as easily as he would a kitten and carry her to camp.

❦

Charlotte slipped in and out of the fog, but some of the shaking had eased from her body. She curled tighter into the warmth beside her, the body cradling her more closely than she could ever remember being held.

Then she was being lowered, seated on something hard. The warmth pulled away, and she whimpered, curling deeper into herself.

Hands rubbed her upper arms. "I'll build a fire for you." The voice rumbled near her ear, and she leaned toward it.

But then the hands left her arms and the comforting presence disappeared. She could only tuck tighter and pull the furs closer as her shoulders began to shake once more.

The movement around her faded in and out of her awareness as the aching in her entire body took over every other sensation. Her feet and legs seemed to have disappeared. When she told them to move, they did nothing she asked.

"Charlotte." The voice sounded near her ear again, warm breath tickling her nose.

She worked hard to answer, to open her eyes and respond. But that took so . . . much . . . effort.

"We have to get the wet clothing off you. Do you have something else to wear?"

She blinked, and this time managed to open her eyes and make his words penetrate her mind. Clothes. Wet. What was wet?

He was moving her furs, shifting them off her lap. When she made her eyes open, she could see him unfastening her moccasins, but couldn't feel anything he did. He was speaking aloud, though his words barely registered.

"I think you have buckskin leggings underneath these furs around your legs. Thank the Almighty. We can just take off the furs for now. The underlayer seems more dry than wet."

At last, he pulled her knees back up, the movement nearly

toppling her backward. Her legs wouldn't bend when she told them to. He wrapped an arm around her back and covered her legs and feet in layer after layer of furs.

"There. I'll add more wood to the fire, and the water should be almost warm. Once you drink that, you'll start to feel better."

The occasional sounds of his movements broke through the haze in her mind, but she didn't try to decipher what he was doing.

Finally, his hand rested on her shoulder. "Can you drink this warm water?"

Before she could bring his words into enough meaning to know how to respond, something hard touched her lips. A cup.

She parted her mouth and accepted the liquid he poured in. The warmth kept coming, and she finally shook her head.

No more. She could manage nothing else right now. Every part of her was so exhausted, she didn't have the strength to sit up.

The hand on her shoulder slid around her back, drawing her closer, giving her something solid to lay against. Finally, she could begin to relax. To give in to the yawning exhaustion that wouldn't be refused.

12

Damien held Charlotte in his arms long after he should have laid her down to sleep. She'd stopped shivering a while ago, so he was fairly certain she wasn't still suffering from the cold. She was simply exhausted.

Every part of him wanted to protect her, to give her a safe place to rest. As much as he told himself that was the only reason he sat with his arms wrapped around her, her head resting against his chest, she'd become more to him than he was ready to admit.

Such a delicate little thing in the midst of this harsh mountain wilderness. Yet time and again, she displayed a strength few women possessed. That strength might drive him to distraction at times, but he couldn't help brushing his finger down her temple now. Finally allowing himself to watch her.

Her beauty made his chest ache. That nearly porcelain skin, paler now than usual. The long lashes fanning over her cheeks.

Those lashes rose, and he stilled, barely daring to breathe. She stared forward at first, her own breathing lightened, as though she was trying to determine where she was before she reacted.

Then her head pulled away from his chest, and she lifted her gaze to his face. Wide eyes, full of worry and questions.

He needed to set her at ease. She'd been so benumbed by the cold, she might not even remember leaning against him to sleep. "Are you feeling better?"

She blinked, then her eyes returned to their rounded look, though the worry had gone. "I . . ." She pulled the furs tighter around her shoulders. She didn't seem to know how to answer.

He reached for a cup of water he'd kept warm by the fire. "Drink a little more of this. It'll heat you from the inside."

When he held it out, she removed a hand from the furs to take the mug and sip. That ability was an improvement from before.

"Do you remember what happened?"

This time when she looked at him, the real Charlotte showed in her eyes. An expression a little haggard, but also wry. "I fell through. Glad the water wasn't deep."

Did she realize she'd strayed from the path he told her to take, and that was why the ice hadn't held? A self-righteous part of him wanted to tell her, but she looked so fragile curled among the hides with her face so pale. There would be no benefit to making his point. He needed to focus on helping her recover.

After laying a few more logs on the fire, he reached for the food pack. "My meals aren't nearly as tasty as yours, but roasted meat does fill the empty places, and it will help you get your strength back."

He took the cup and handed her a chunk of meat. When

she attempted a bite, its toughness made him wish he had something better to offer. But she didn't complain, only thanked him when he gave her a second piece.

She straightened and glanced around. "Where's Gulliver? Is he well?"

The mule must have heard his name, for he stamped a hoof from where he stood just outside the light of the fire.

"He's fine. Already had his dinner and was enjoying a nap."

She looked around again, finally settling her gaze on the packs he'd placed against a tree. "I need to start cooking the bear meat."

He shook his head. "It's frozen. It'll keep for a while that way. There's nothing you need to do tonight except rest and keep yourself warm." He scanned the length of her, wrapped fully in hides. "Are any of your clothes still wet? Can you feel your legs and feet?"

She shifted the furs over her knees. "I'm warm enough." She didn't meet his gaze, though.

Did talking about clothing and body parts embarrass her? Perhaps. Or maybe something was wrong and she didn't want to tell him.

He weighed his words. He didn't want to press her to a level that made her uncomfortable, but if she didn't properly care for damaged limbs, worse could come. Finally he settled for saying, "It's important your feet and legs stay warm through the night. We may not know for a day or two if any permanent damage was done. But keeping them away from more cold might make a big difference in the outcome."

He poured another cupful of warm water and handed it

to her. "Your moccasins were wet, so I took them off. Do you want another fur to wrap around your feet?"

This time she did meet his gaze, and her eyes softened. "I'm warm, Damien. I promise. Thank you for all you've done for me, pulling me from the river and helping me get warm."

For a long moment, he searched her eyes, letting himself enjoy the connection, if only for this fleeting moment.

⸙

Charlotte still couldn't feel all her toes.

In the light of morning, she studied her feet before she pulled her moccasins on. Damien had the good sense to place the shoes by the fire the night before, so not only were they dry, but they were also soothing and warm.

He'd gone to water Gulliver, which gave her a moment to inspect whatever damage had been done in the river.

Her feet shone nearly as white as the snow around them, but she couldn't find anything different in the appearance of the toes that were still numb—two of the smaller digits on her right foot and the littlest on her left. She'd heard of people losing fingers or toes from the cold, but she'd never actually seen missing appendages.

Not from cold, anyway. An image of Hugo's knob of a finger slipped into her mind. He'd lost it in the rockslide back when he was helping build the apartment Brielle shared with her husband. If Charlotte returned to Laurent missing toes, she and Hugo would be quite the pair. Not that she would tell anyone about the loss. Perhaps she would share the news with Audrey, who still served as the village healer, in case there was something she could do to lessen further damage.

After wrapping her feet in small bits of fur to protect them, she pulled on her moccasins. Now came the real test—whether she could stand and walk without limping.

She cast a glance toward the river. Damien had taken the mule to the place she'd fallen through, probably because the ice would be easiest to break there. She would be happy if she never saw that spot again. The mule hid Damien from view, so he wouldn't be able to see her, either. She shifted to her knees, then tried to stand.

A burning sensation seared through her feet and up her legs, and she had to bite down hard to keep from crying out. Tears sprang to her eyes, but she did what she could to hold them back, staying on all fours until she'd gained control over the flow.

Her feet felt so unreliable. What parts she could feel, anyway.

She crawled on hands and knees to reach the nearest tree. She gripped the tree, slowly shifting weight onto her feet a little at a time as she straightened. Her body wobbled, and the sensation of falling swept through her. But she clung tight to the coarse bark with both hands until that feeling faded.

Her feet still burned, especially at the edges and through the toes she'd not been able to feel minutes before. If she pushed into the pain, it would probably lessen.

Still gripping the tree with one hand, she lifted her left foot and stepped forward. She had to suck in a breath with the new rush of pain as she placed her weight back on that limb. The same with the right foot. She would have to release the tree to move any farther. Though each step brought fresh fire, she should be able to balance on her own now.

Maybe.

After two achingly slow steps away from the tree, she caught a motion at the edge of her vision. Damien approached the camp with Gulliver, and he was watching her. Had he seen her first faulty steps?

She did her best to purge the pain from her face and attempt a smile. But she didn't dare take another step in front of him. He would insist she rest or some other notion that would slow them down. She'd lost so much time already— she should have arrived at the fort and found an artisan to work on the chalice by now. That familiar ball tightened in her middle.

"You're up and moving. That's a good sign." Damien's words brought a flush of heat up her neck.

She'd overslept this morning, and even once she'd awakened to find daylight, she'd had a great deal more trouble than usual forcing herself out of the warm furs. "I'll pull out food for our morning fare. Do you mind if we eat it cold today? We need to get on the trail."

She turned toward the food pack and held her breath against the pain of each careful step. When she reached her destination, she eased herself down beside the supplies. Even sitting in the snow would be better than torturing her feet any longer.

Only then did it register that Damien hadn't answered. She braved a look at him. He was watching her, brows lowered over dark eyes, so she couldn't read his thoughts. He didn't look happy, and she had a feeling she wouldn't like whatever he was considering.

At last he spoke, his tone lower than usual, almost gentle. "Charlotte . . ." His voice trailed off, as though he wasn't sure what to say.

Perhaps she should correct him for using her given name. She'd heard him speak it once or twice during the hazy hours after the river crossing. But the sound of her unique name in his deep rumble—not to mention the way it felt so natural for him to speak it—well, perhaps they knew each other well enough now to justify using Christian names. They'd certainly endured enough harrowing events.

That deep rumble broke the quiet of the morning again. "Let's take it slow today. I think we pushed too hard yesterday. We can have a hot meal here in camp, then set out when we're ready."

She shook her head before he'd finished. "I have to get to the fort. I'm already far behind schedule." She turned her attention to unfastening the pack and quickly pulled out enough food to last them the morning.

When she lifted her gaze back to Damien as she held out his portion, his lowered brows had turned to a full frown. He stepped near enough to take the food. "It's not just you I'm considering. Walking through all the snow is hard on Gulliver, too."

A pang pressed in her chest. He was right, and she'd already felt guilty about riding so much the day before. "I'll walk then. He shouldn't have to carry such a load."

A noise came from Damien—a half-grunt, half-moan she'd never heard him voice, and it drew her gaze back to his face.

His eyes flashed. "That's the last thing I want, woman. You could have frozen to death last night, and you still might have damage to your feet. I can tell walking pains you. There's no way I'll let you hike through the snow when there's a perfectly good mule to ride."

He seemed to be working to calm himself. And his voice did come out with a softer tone. "We can take some time this morning to recover. There's no sense in arriving half-dead."

Arriving? Hope surged through her. "Will we reach the fort today?" They'd been traveling long enough. If they put in a full day's journey . . .

He shook his head.

Then they needed to get going. There was much ground to cover.

But as she opened her mouth to say so, he raised a staying hand. "And killing ourselves by riding an extra hour or two won't help, either."

Frustration needled through her. Perhaps his words held some wisdom, but the heavy-handed way he spoke them made every part of her want to resist. And how could they possibly not reach the fort today? They'd been traveling for so long already.

His brows dipped in another frown. "I've been giving it a lot of thought, and going to the fort is a bad idea. You don't know how the men there are going to react to seeing you, but I do. Nothing good will come of it. I can take you back to your village. Or back to the lake so you can go on by yourself. Whichever you prefer."

Not this again. At least once a day, he'd raised the idea of her turning back. She leveled a glare on him. "Are you certain you know exactly how to reach Fort Versailles? My people are able to get there in two days. It's been three already, and you say a fourth won't even be enough?"

Albeit one of those days, they rode through a snowstorm and stopped early. But despite that, the facts stood for themselves.

Damien blinked twice, the only sign her words bothered him. In fact, his ire from moments before seemed hidden behind a careful mask. "I do know the way to the fort, and I'm certain we won't reach it tonight, no matter how hard we push." He turned toward their supplies. "I'm going to cook some of this bear meat."

If the man were closer to her, she might have shaken him. He was truly denying her request to start out now. She would leave on her own if she thought she could possibly manage it. But he was right about her pain. In all honesty, a few hours walking through the snow would likely bring her to her knees.

Though she might be dependent on him to help her travel—for now—she certainly didn't have to sit here across from him in the camp.

She used her hands to help push herself to her feet, then turned and limped through the trees. Perhaps it was her frustration that made each step more bearable than the last.

13

When Damien did something this kind, it was hard to be angry with him.

Charlotte stared at the sketch Damien had presented her when she returned to camp, taking in every remarkable detail. "It's . . . so good, Damien." Those words didn't come close to the excellence of the simple charcoal drawing. Had he done it all in the hour she sat by the river? She lifted her gaze to his face. "How did you make Gulliver look so real?"

The man only shrugged. "I suppose I've seen him often enough. Thought you might like to keep it as a memory."

Damien's embarrassment made him look adorable, brawny mountain man though he was. She hid her smile by dropping her gaze back to the sketch. Gulliver's curious face stared back at her, long ears pricked and head tipped in exactly the way she'd seen him look so many times when she greeted him.

The drawing showed only her side, and just the top half at that, stretching out her hand for the mule to sniff. Though her face was hidden by the fur of her hood, even the detail of her coat looked almost more realistic than in real life.

Once more, she raised her focus to Damien. This time she kept her commendation to herself, but she couldn't help studying him. How could a mountain man trapper possess this much skill in the finer arts? "Have you been drawing all your life?"

Again he shrugged, but this time he turned away and began placing things in his pack. "Most of it. Haven't done much lately, but I needed something to keep my hands busy while the meat cooked."

The way he nearly turned his back to her now, he clearly didn't wish to talk about it further. But she couldn't help studying the drawing once more. This wasn't the fumbling of an amateur. He possessed real talent. She had no idea whether a man could make a living selling drawings in the outside world, but her people were so hungry for new art. Most of what they had were sketches and paintings that had been in Laurent since it was settled a century ago. They would trade a great deal for a drawing with this much detail.

She would treasure this always, but how could she carry it home without damaging the paper? He'd torn it from a leather-wrapped book, so the page was thinner than the parchment her people made.

As much as she hated to give up possession of it for even a day or two, she asked, "Would you mind if I tucked it back in your book until we reach the fort? I don't want the paper bent or damaged. I can buy another book there to keep the drawing safe on my return home."

He didn't look up, just extracted the volume from his pack and held it out to her.

As she took the book and slipped her page inside the front flap, she didn't try to see what other drawings he might've done. But she didn't stop herself from glancing at the pages as the book flipped open and shut.

Blank.

As she handed it back to him, her mind mulled through that discovery. How could a man who drew with this much talent not spend a great deal of time practicing? Perhaps he'd given his other sketches away, as well. He'd said he left a larger trapping group not long ago, so maybe he'd handed out all his work there.

Except the only evidence of a torn-out page was from the image of Gulliver sniffing her hand.

As much as she longed to know his secrets, the things that made the man such a mystery, she likely wouldn't uncover them by standing here pondering. Since her packs were already bundled tight, she focused on securing the rest of the food in its wrappings, except for the bit they would want to eat on the trail.

Before long, they set off, her riding Gulliver and Damien traipsing on snowshoes beside them. She tried not to let herself think about how far into the morning the day had already progressed. More than the two hours Damien had originally insisted on.

But they were moving now, and the sun had finally broken through the clouds to cast a faint warmth on her cheeks. At last, God seemed to be helping her journey.

As the day progressed, Damien stopped more often to let Gulliver rest than he had the other days. She didn't begrudge the mule his breaks, but she couldn't help her impatience.

By midafternoon, the sun had moved to the perfect position to shine directly in her eyes. She could choose to be frustrated by the glare, especially the way the light flashed off the snow to blind her. But instead, she closed her eyes and enjoyed the warmth of it. She didn't dare stay in that position long, or she'd grow drowsy enough to fall asleep.

And that certainly wouldn't encourage Damien to continue the day's journey.

But then another thought slipped in, one that made her blink her eyes open and peer again at the sun's position. By this point in the afternoon, that big orb should be lowering to the west. Since they were traveling east, this blinding light should be at her back now.

Not directly in front.

She sorted through her memories from the morning. Had the sun shone from behind when they started out? She couldn't remember for sure, but it seemed to have been glowing mostly on the side of her face before they stopped at midday.

As she slid a glance at the man trudging beside her—the man who'd claimed so many times that he knew the way to the fort—she tried to recall an instance of him seeming uncertain which route to take.

He'd never seemed unsure. In fact, a few times over the past days, he pointed out a butte shaped in a certain way or an upcoming mountain peak as being familiar, a sign they were making progress.

Perhaps he was good at bluffing. Perhaps he was merely scrambling to find a landmark he recognized to tell them which direction to go.

Yet even *she* knew westward was the opposite of the direction they should be traveling.

Did that mean he wasn't taking her to the fort? An eerie sensation skittered up her neck, and once more, she stole a look at him. She'd decided he was trustworthy, though too reckless for her liking. But did she really know that first detail to be true?

His actions had seemed honorable, his words giving her no reason to think he might be deceiving her.

Until now.

What could she say to find out for sure if he was intentionally misguiding her? She'd never been one to jump to the worst assumptions. Maybe he really was confused about the fort's direction. She'd rather think him a bumbling fool than a deceiver.

Using as casual a tone as she could manage, she asked, "About how far away from Fort Versailles do you think we are?"

He squinted up at the sun, as though checking its position would give him an answer. If he thought that to be true, he was more a fool than she expected. "Maybe a little over a day."

Again she tried to keep her tone relaxed. "You'll likely be seeing many landmarks you recognize, then. What's coming next?"

He slid her a sideways glance, his expression almost frustrated. But then his look turned a little teasing. As much as it could with the hard breathing his trek required. "Are you getting bored up there?"

He might as well have told her she should stop talking and be thankful for her mount. Though he'd said it in a nicer way.

Still, she couldn't miss the way he'd sidestepped her question. As much as she hated to believe it, the only possible reason was that the man was intentionally taking her to a place she didn't wish to go.

Damien hated lying. And it was getting harder and harder to carry on this falsehood, especially as Charlotte asked more questions. He'd never actually said anything untrue—he formed his answers to her questions with facts, though his responses certainly alluded to something that wasn't at all true. Did she suspect he was leading her the wrong direction?

Perhaps he should simply come out and tell her what he was doing. Tell her again how unsafe it was for a lone woman to enter Fort Versailles. Tell her he was taking her back to her village where she would be safe. Maybe then he could ask why she'd set out by herself to begin with.

By now, perhaps she'd seen enough of the journey's treachery to believe what he said about the fort. And hopefully she'd also experienced enough to know better than to leave him and Gulliver to set out on her own again.

Or would her stubborn streak get the better of her good sense?

He needed to take the chance. Tonight, in camp, he would bring up the matter. He couldn't deceive her any longer. Not with the way she was coming to be more and more important to him.

Though he shouldn't crave her good opinion, he did.

This was her chance.

Charlotte's hands trembled from much more than the cold as she dug through the food pack where she'd also placed the herbs to season food and the tin of salve for injuries.

There.

She pulled out the tiny container of potion Audrey mixed for Brielle's arrows, a blend of herbs she'd developed as something of a sleeping tonic for the game Brielle shot. After being wounded with an arrow dipped in the mixture, the animal would fall asleep, which helped Brielle retrieve the body without having to track very far.

Charlotte was usually the one to apply it to Brielle's arrow tips, and she'd reached for the metal container so many times, her fingers had naturally thrown it into the satchel with the other medicines in those early morning hours when she packed. It seemed like something she might have use for at some point on this journey.

Never had she suspected how she was about to use it now.

But she had to. Not only was Damien lying to her about where he was taking her, but she'd also seen him doing something in her pack when they first made camp. She must have returned with water sooner than he expected, for he'd moved away from the satchel quickly and begun untying the tether around a bundle of his furs. She couldn't find anything missing or new that hadn't been there, so what had he been after? She'd thought she could trust him, but now . . . he'd proven untrustworthy.

She had to get away from him and finally reach the fort.

She uncapped the container but paused before pouring any into the stew boiling over the fire. Though she'd already taken out a helping for her own dinner, she couldn't risk somehow drinking the potion by pouring it into the entire pot of remaining soup. If Damien thought she'd not eaten enough, he might try to make her take more from the pot.

She'd have to pour the mixture directly onto his fare once she dished it out.

She fumbled the plate as she scooped meat and broth. The crunch of footsteps in snow sounded somewhere behind her, making her tremble even more as she tried to work fast. Damien had gone to gather firewood and was probably still searching through the trees around them.

But he could step into the firelight at any moment.

Removing the lid from the tin again, she shook a little of the sleeping tonic onto the largest piece of meat on Damien's plate. Had she used enough? Too much?

When Audrey had developed the mixture, she'd been careful to use only herbs that were edible in case the blend touched part of the meat from Brielle's catch. Twice, a human had been struck with an arrow dipped in the tonic—Brielle's and Audrey's husbands, actually. Both men had fallen asleep within minutes of being struck, and both had awakened without permanent harm.

But no one had ever been fed the tonic directly. Would it work differently going through the stomach? Would the effect be stronger or weaker?

Some of the mixture might be diluted before it reached his bloodstream, so perhaps she'd better add a bit more to his food. She couldn't risk him sleeping lightly or awakening too soon after she left.

He would go after her, she was almost certain. If only she knew why he was deceiving her, taking her to a place opposite from where she wanted to go.

After dowsing the meat a final time, she replaced the lid on the container and slipped it back in the pack with the other seasonings. A glance at the sky showed full darkness would be on them soon. The clouds smothered the stars, but the sliver of moon already revealed itself.

Now was the time she needed snow to fall, but none appeared imminent. How could she cover her tracks so Damien couldn't come after her when he awoke?

Before she could ponder that line of thought, his footsteps sounded close behind. She turned and worked for a smile. At least her hands weren't shaking now.

He dropped his load of firewood to the ground, then began positioning the pieces around the blaze so the heat could dry them. He moved with an easy grace she could watch for hours. He must have felt her stare, for he glanced up and met her gaze. The way his mouth tipped at one corner and his eyes softened made something in her belly flip. How could any woman not be affected by his handsome features? And those eyes . . .

To distract herself, she lifted his plate. "Are you hungry?" She had to remember he was not as he seemed. She'd been wary at first, as she should have been. But the more she'd come to know him . . . He'd really seemed like a gentleman. Someone she could trust.

But his actions today showed that he wasn't.

"The food looks good." He moved the last two logs, then took the plate from her and settled on the fur she'd laid out for him.

To keep herself from being too obvious as she watched his every bite, she reached for her own serving. She needed to have her food eaten by the time he grew drowsy. She'd have no time to waste, and her journey would require all the energy she could muster.

She did her best to answer the few questions Damien

asked as he ate, but the bites she took dried in her mouth and threatened to clog her throat. Was she doing the wrong thing? How could she poison a man on purpose?

It wasn't poison, though. Only a simple tonic that wouldn't cause lasting harm. She had to keep in mind what *he* planned to do to *her*.

Which she didn't know. But his duplicity didn't bode well.

As much as she tried to summon anger, though, only dread twisted in her belly.

The potion was already beginning to set in by the time he finished his food, though he'd eaten quickly. He must have been famished.

His eyelids drooped halfway closed, then farther down. He jerked them up, raising his chin, and it looked as though he was trying to focus on her. She kept herself perfectly still.

But then his eyelids dropped all the way shut. He swayed like he might fall over, then his eyes shot wide again. He would fight this as long as he could. That shouldn't surprise her. Damien's strength and perseverance had already showed itself in his willingness to walk long days on snowshoes while she rode Gulliver. He never complained, just kept going.

The tightness in her chest squeezed. She shouldn't have pushed so hard to start out early that morning. He probably needed the extra rest as much as she and the mule did.

But the delay might also have been part of whatever scheme he had planned. She had to keep reminding herself of that important fact. Had to harden her heart.

Just then, he slumped to the side, his body finally giving in to the power of the sleeping tonic.

She rose and moved to his side, helping position him more

comfortably. Reaching for the furs Damien used as covers, she laid out several atop him. She didn't want him to grow too cold while he slept.

After snatching up her pack and roll of bedding, she glanced around the campsite once more. She'd made sure to pack only what she brought, nothing that belonged to him.

Except the drawing. It still lay tucked in his book inside his satchel. She couldn't go through his things, not with him lying unconscious from her own doing. Her chest ached at the thought of leaving the drawing behind, but perhaps it would be best not to take any memories from their time together.

Would she ever see him again? Her gaze landed on the man, covered by furs from his mouth down. Even in sleep, sadness cloaked the lines around his eyes. She'd seen that shadow of melancholy a great deal more at the beginning. It seemed to have lifted some each day.

Her feet carried her toward him, and she dropped to her knees by his head. "I'm sorry, Damien." She kept her words to a whisper, though it wasn't likely she would wake him. "I wish it could have been different."

The ache pushed up to her eyes, tears stinging, though she held them back. What would have happened if they'd met under different circumstances? Would they still have been friends? She would still admire him, she knew that without a doubt. That is, she would admire the man she'd come to know.

A flicker of doubt ignited in her. Could there possibly be a good reason why he'd lied to her?

Steeling her resolve, she pushed to her feet and turned toward the darkness. Even if he had an honorable reason for his actions, she would do better on her own—as she should have stayed from the very beginning.

Slipping from camp, she stayed in the trees for as long as she could, stepping in existing tracks or barren patches where possible. *Cover my trail, Lord. Hide my route so he can't find it.*

As the night grew thicker around her, she kept her feet aimed toward the east—and Fort Versailles.

14

Damien woke to roiling in his belly so fierce that he curled around his middle to escape the agony. What had he eaten to bring this on? His foggy mind wouldn't recall anything from his last meal.

The churning increased, and he sucked in deep breaths to keep his insides from surging upward. Bile tickled his throat, and his stomach spasmed. *No.*

He scrambled onto his hands and knees as his accounts spewed out into the snow beside his bed in one convulsion after another. By the time the last one faded, his strength seeped away with it. He dropped back, resting his head on his fur pallet. Whatever meat they'd eaten in the last meal had to be thrown out. Maybe he'd purged the worst of it from his belly now.

Charlotte. Was she sick, too?

He lifted his aching head to search their camp for her. The fire burned low, but a few small flames still flickered. Darkness seemed thick outside the fringe of light.

He focused on the place where Charlotte should be

sleeping. She wasn't there, not even a covering. Had she moved her bedroll?

Shifting his head to better see around the fire, he squinted to make out what he might be missing. She didn't seem to be anywhere.

Bracing his hand on his own pallet, he pushed himself up to sitting. The movement made his head swim. Once upright, he blinked to clear his vision and searched the area once more. "Charlotte?" The word came out shaky. He worked to settle his insides and raised his voice louder. "Charlotte?"

No answer came, and his mind finally came to life. His pulse trotted faster as he pushed up to his feet, stumbling two steps before he caught his balance.

From that position, he surveyed the camp once more. She definitely wasn't here, and her bedding wasn't even laid out. In fact . . .

He moved to the pile of packs. Hers were gone completely. The only items remaining were Gulliver's saddle, his furs, and his packs and other supplies. Nothing remained that belonged to her.

His heartbeat raced to a full gallop, bringing blessed clarity to his mind. She'd left. But why? How long had she been gone? Had someone taken her captive?

That thought brought a new panic, and he spun to find Gulliver. He had to get moving. Had to catch up to them.

But as he reached the mule and the animal jerked awake, his mind registered how unlikely that scenario was. For someone to come in and take Charlotte from under his very nose. To remove only her belongings and leave his.

He laid a hand on the mule's neck as he struggled to come

up with another possibility. Why would Charlotte leave, and in the middle of the night? Without saying good-bye.

Pain speared his chest, a familiar sensation that burned through him. He worked to shore up his defenses. He'd let them fall far too low where Charlotte was concerned. Had actually thought she saw the real him and accepted him despite his prickles.

It seemed he'd been wrong.

Still, he couldn't let her wander through this mountain wilderness alone, especially at night in the piercing cold. It would be a death sentence.

Giving the mule a pat, he reached for the saddle. He could leave his furs here, but he'd need to take enough bedding and supplies in case Charlotte was in a bad condition by the time he found her.

His gut tightened. So much could happen in these wilds. If by some miracle she managed to keep warm, she could be attacked by animals or fall down a cliff—the possibilities were too many to name. And each one formed a more vicious picture in his mind.

Pulling the saddle's cinch strap tight, he turned and scooped up the packs he would need, double-checking to make sure his few precious possessions were inside—a family heirloom his parents and Michelle had treasured and Michelle's Bible. The fire had dwindled to mostly coals, so he banked them to make it easier to start again when they returned.

He could only pray that wouldn't be too long.

Charlotte's tracks out of camp were easy enough to find. She was traveling east, at least when she started out. Grabbing Gulliver's rope, he towed the mule in her footsteps.

The bit of moon that showed through the clouds didn't offer much light in the shadow of the trees, but he found one of her moccasin prints often enough to stay on the right trail.

Gulliver complained every time Damien pulled him into a trot when the tree growth thinned. But the mule was so well-trained, he didn't struggle against the rope long before acceding.

Yet they still couldn't go fast enough. Charlotte might have known exactly the direction she planned to go, but he was forced to travel slowly enough to find her tracks. How much of a lead would she have on him?

He'd simply have to outlast her and not even think about the possibility that he'd find her injured or frozen body somewhere along the way. Of course the images tried to resurrect themselves with that thought, but he pressed the lid down on them.

She must be headed to the fort, since her path still aimed due east. She'd likely realized he'd been leading her the opposite direction. He hadn't turned fully west until late in the afternoon, and he'd been hoping she wasn't paying attention to the sun's position. Why had those bright rays chosen today to break through the clouds and shimmer in her eyes?

What must she think of him for deceiving her? Sorrow pressed around him like a smothering blanket, one that did nothing to relieve the cold. She would think the worst. Anyone would without knowing his true reasons. Why did he think she wouldn't realize which way they were going? He'd not credited her for the savviness he knew she possessed.

He'd been a coward. Afraid he'd lose her by telling the truth.

Now he'd lost her anyway.

Through the night they trekked, and morning's light dawned as they finally reached an open stretch of land. Every part of him ached, but now he could finally climb aboard Gulliver to give his body a rest.

The mule plunged ahead faithfully, but as they rode, Damien had to work harder and harder to keep himself alert and focused on the tracks, occasionally lifting his gaze to sweep the area around them.

When they reached the rocky incline at the base of a mountain, he slipped from the saddle and dropped to his knees beside the mule. Scooping up a double handful of snow, he pressed the icy moisture to his face, working the crystals around his neck and beneath his hood.

All his senses sprang to life, save for his mind, which still felt a bit clouded. But at least his body wouldn't be in danger of falling asleep anytime soon.

Pushing up to his feet, he looked at the path of tracks ahead. Charlotte had ascended upward around the side of this mountain. She hadn't needed to travel as high as she had to cross over. She only needed to reach halfway up to travel through the gap between this mountain and the next.

Had she climbed higher in hopes that the boulders near the top would help hide her tracks? There were areas where the slope of the rock had kept snow from accumulating. Icy, dangerous places.

Or perhaps she thought she would find a place to hide and catch a few hours' sleep. A sprig of hope rose inside him at that thought.

As he and Gulliver started forward again, his mind played through other possible scenarios. Maybe she'd walked higher to get a better view of the landscape beyond, perhaps even trying to see the fort.

She wouldn't spot it yet. Not until she reached the last range before the flat land began. From this mountain, she would likely only see a vast expanse of peaks spreading out before her. The sight was beautiful and majestic, and always reminded him how small and insignificant he was in the vastness of this land.

It also might bring despair to a young woman traveling this wilderness alone, exhausted from trudging through snow all night.

His chest struggled for air the farther up they trekked. Even Gulliver's sides heaved, despite the hearty endurance of his breed and his years of experience with these higher climes.

Damien focused on placing one foot in front of the next. Then another step, and another. When he could go no farther, he paused, giving them both a chance to catch their breath and gather strength. He lifted his gaze up the slope, trying to ignore how steep the remaining section was that he would have to climb.

He would do this for Charlotte. He had to.

He scanned the crevices and cracks between stones, searching out an opening where she might have hidden. Perhaps there were places, but he could tell nothing for sure from this distance.

Inhaling as deep a breath as he could manage, he lifted his right foot to step forward, then his left. Gulliver trudged behind him without prodding. Maybe he sensed the importance of this mission. The mule had certainly seemed to appreciate, maybe even love, Charlotte.

I know how easy that happens, boy. She'd quickly become as important—nay, more important—to Damien than any person still alive. No one would ever take the place of his twin sister, nor his parents, though it had been many years since Mum and Dad had passed.

But Charlotte—she was still alive, and he would give everything he had to keep her that way.

Farther. Higher. His vision honed to only the snow in front of him. To Charlotte's next track, where he would also place his foot.

The wind blew harder the higher he mounted, nagging at him like a mosquito. How much farther could he manage before he had to stop for a longer rest? He'd not planned to halt until he found her, but he couldn't go much longer. His body might give out any minute.

Maybe he could at least make it down the other side of the mountain before he collapsed. Surely he could manage the easier descent. But he had to make it to the top first. He lifted his gaze to see how much farther up Charlotte's prints climbed.

His foot slipped on an icy patch, sliding out from beneath him. He scrambled to catch himself with his hands, landing on all fours. For a long moment he stayed like that, drawing in thick breaths.

Gulliver nudged him from behind, perhaps only checking on him, or maybe the mule realized he needed encouragement to stand and keep moving.

He had to keep moving.

He grabbed on to the mule to help pull himself to his feet. Every part of him had grown numb—except his lungs. His chest seared with every breath.

Once more, they started forward single file. Charlotte was clearly stronger than he'd credited her since she'd managed to make this climb after also traveling through the night. Of course, she'd been riding Gulliver the past two days, not trekking on foot. Still, she must be every bit as exhausted as he was.

Again, his foot slipped, but this time he'd stepped on a raised rock. His ankle twisted as his foot slid off the edge.

He scrambled to catch himself, but his moccasin couldn't find purchase on the slippery ground. His foot skated over icy snow, and he twisted to get his other leg beneath him. To find solid ground that would bring his sliding to a halt.

But his legs tingled beneath him, his body not doing at all what he commanded. The momentum of his efforts threw him forward, and his shoulder landed hard in the snow. The steep slope pitched him downward, rolling him. He tumbled over and over as snow wrapped him in a frigid blanket.

No matter how he tried to reach out and grasp something to stop his fall, his fingers clasped only loose snow. Any moment, his head would strike a boulder. This would be the end of him. His body would be buried in snow and ice on the side of this mountain.

At least he would finally be with Michelle.

But Charlotte . . .

His feet struck something solid, stopping his roll and jerking his upper body downward. His head dangled over empty space, and as he tried to free his hands to grab onto something, the stone released its hold on his feet, and he tumbled down.

He landed hard on his back, the thud reverberating

through him, knocking the last of the breath from his lungs. He struggled to suck in air, but his chest wouldn't rise.

Pressing his hands against the ground beneath him, he tried to sit up, tried to turn over so he could better take in breath. Though his mind knew not to panic, his body refused to listen.

At last, he inhaled a tiny dose of thin air. Closing his eyes, he focused on gathering in the next breath. A little more this time, then still more.

For long moments he stayed like that, sitting half reclined with his hands braced behind him, eyes pressed shut as he inhaled one glorious breath after another. Finally, he recovered enough to open his eyes. The rush of the wind no longer pressed against him. Maybe he'd landed beside a boulder that blocked the gusts.

But as he blinked to clear his gaze, the dim surroundings were not at all what he expected. Not a cave exactly, but something like a cleft in the rock.

His gaze caught on something moving against the rear wall. As he tried to focus, a pair of eyes stared back at him. His heart jolted.

He blinked once more to clear the mirage. She still sat there, pressed against the back wall, knees bent and hands wrapped around them. He'd *found* her.

"Charlotte?" With his face so cold-numbed, her name came out as only a mumble. Pushing to sit fully upright, he let out a long breath. He'd found her, but now he seemed to know far less than he had before. Maybe his mind was as frozen as his feet. He pressed his gloved hands to his face to try to warm his mouth enough to speak clearly.

"Are you hurt?" Her voice sounded wary, and she still

didn't move. The space was so small, only two arm lengths separated them. But at least it was protected from the wind.

He checked through each body part in his mind. "Don't . . ." He cleared his throat to try to make the words understandable. "Don't think so. Too frozen to know for sure." He scanned what he could see of her, but wrapped up in her furs, that wasn't much. "Are you all right?"

She nodded. "I'm fine." Then her gaze shifted past him. "Where's Gulliver?"

His thoughts still moved as slow as a glacier, and he had to blink to remember where he'd last seen the mule. His entire body tensed, and he struggled to move onto his hands and knees so he could stand. "On the mountain. Where I slipped." Could he get the animal down here? Not the same way Damien had come, but he could find a safer route.

"I'll get him. See if we can bring him under the shelter." Charlotte pushed up to her feet before he'd even managed to get fully on his knees.

He couldn't send her up the mountain alone. Look what had happened to him. "No, I'll do it. It's not safe."

"You're not in any condition to climb back up the slope. I'll return with him soon." She stepped out into the wind before he could manage a response.

15

Charlotte pulled her coat tighter around her as gusts whipped at her face. The mule was easy to spot, standing thirty strides up the slope, his head ducked low against the wind that tossed snowflakes through the air.

As she trudged upward, the impressions in the snow were impossible to miss—like someone had rolled all the way down to the cleft where she'd taken cover. Had Damien really tumbled so far? No wonder he'd looked like a snow creature when he dropped into her refuge.

Her exhausted limbs threatened to mutiny as she forced herself to climb the mountain that grew steeper with each step. By the time she reached the mule, she'd dropped down to all fours to help pull herself the remaining distance.

At Gulliver's side, she sat to catch her breath and gather strength. He brought his head around to nudge her shoulder, the sweet greeting he always gave her.

"Hey, fella." She lifted her face to him, and he blew against her cheek. If that wasn't incentive to stand and lead him down to shelter, she may never find it.

After struggling to her feet, she patted the mule's neck and took up his rope, then together they maneuvered the easier trail she'd spotted on her way up. Though she slipped and slid through the steeper stretches, the mule never faltered.

Damien stood at the edge of the rock shelter as she and Gulliver drew near. Perhaps he'd thought she would slip away instead of bringing the animal down. The idea hadn't occurred to her, and in truth, she had no desire to play a game of chase. He'd found her, and the fact that he'd come so far and expended so much effort meant catching up to her had been important.

Now she wanted to know why. And she wouldn't rest until she knew the truth.

He stepped back to allow her room to bring Gulliver under the rock overhang, then approached to stroke him.

She allowed herself a glance at the man's face. Deep shadows bruised the hollows under his eyes, probably similar to how she looked. She'd stopped here to sleep but had barely dozed off before Damien dropped in—quite literally.

How long had he slept under the effects of the potion? Not long, given that he'd managed to catch up with her. She'd hoped speed would be on her side, along with the fact that he'd be delayed by sleeping. Clearly that hadn't been enough.

He must've felt her gaze, for he lifted his focus to her. Tension tightened the space between them, the weight of their questions stripping the air from the small shelter.

Damien's gaze flicked to the mule. "I suspect we both need to eat. I'll loosen his saddle and get out some food for us. Then we can talk."

He stepped into motion without waiting for her agreement, and she stayed at Gulliver's head while he worked, stroking the thick fur. Damien hadn't brought his full load, only a few furs and packs. She couldn't tell for certain what all was missing, only that the usual mound piled high behind the saddle seemed half the size.

At last, he turned to her with a pack of food in one hand and some of his fur bedding in the other. She took the bundle of meat, and he spread out one of the larger pelts, then motioned for her to sit.

Once they were settled and she'd laid the food between them, Damien took up a piece of meat, and a long breath escaped him as he sank back against the rock wall. That sigh seemed to carry with it the weight of whatever emotions he'd felt since discovering she was gone.

Had he worried about her? Or simply been frustrated she'd thwarted his plans?

For several minutes, they sat quietly, eating and staring out over the snow-covered terrain. Should she begin by asking a simple question to gauge his honesty? Or jump straight into what had driven her away?

Better to get to the point. And soon. Before he spoke first.

Gathering herself, she swallowed down the dread building in her throat. "Will you tell me why you were taking me away from the fort? Why you lied about our destination?" She tried to make her voice strong, maybe even hard. But the sound came out more weak and timid, too much like she'd always been back in Laurent. Maybe that was who she really was.

He turned to face her. "Charlotte, I'm sorry. I misled you, but I did it only for your good."

His words started the ire building inside her, but he was still speaking, so she forced herself to hold her tongue.

"Fort Versailles is no place for a woman, especially traveling on her own. If you knew the kinds of men who frequent the place, you would understand. Some will be decent. Others mostly well-meaning, but they may not have seen a woman in months, maybe years. There will be some who will tell you any falsehood to lure you under their covers."

She raised her brows at him, letting her look speak for itself.

But he shook his head. "What I did was for your good, to keep you safe. Those men will be thinking of nothing but their own desires." His brows gathered. "I truly am sorry I deceived you. So many times, I thought about telling my plan, but I was afraid you would leave on your own. Then you'd be in a worse spot."

He seemed in earnest, but so many questions still stirred unrest within her. "What *was* your plan exactly?"

His mouth pressed into a sheepish expression. "I planned to take you to your home. I don't know exactly where your village is, but I thought I could get you fairly close. By then I expected you would realize where we were, and hopefully I would have talked you out of trying to get to the fort. I don't know why you left Laurent to begin with or why you're so determined to get to Fort Versailles, but you'll be so much safer with your family. Especially since I imagine you hold them in deep affection."

Indignation rose in her chest, something even stronger than the ire of moments before. "I do, but that doesn't mean I can go back there. Not yet. I have to get to the fort first. I have to see if there's—" She barely caught herself before spilling the rest of her need.

Maybe it wouldn't hurt to tell Damien she was searching for a master engraver. But she still wasn't certain she could trust him. But the confusion and curiosity on his face showed he'd noticed her slip.

He tipped his head as he studied her. "See if there's what? Perhaps I can tell you if what you seek is within fort walls."

She opened her mouth to speak of trade goods, for he likely wouldn't know exactly what supplies were on hand since he hadn't been there in months. But then the possibility in his words struck her. Perhaps he *would* know if the fort held a craftsman capable of what she needed. Could she ask without disclosing why she had to find such a man? He would never know about the chalice unless she told him.

And she wouldn't.

She studied him for another moment, searched within her spirit for any sense that she might be making a mistake in answering the simple question. Nothing rose up within her.

"I'm looking for someone who's an expert in molding metals. Not just molding, but engraving, too."

His brows rose, curiosity shifting to . . . well, something deeper. Intrigue?

"What kind of engraving? A name or verse? On what type of metal?"

She shook her head. "An image. An elaborate one. As for the metal, I believe it's brass." That should give him enough details to know whether such a man would be at Fort Versailles.

Damien's expression turned to something unreadable, and a shadow seemed to cloak his face. He was silent for long moments. Was he thinking through the skills of the people there? He seemed to be pondering, maybe even struggling within himself.

She waited. Perhaps he was debating whether to tell the

truth. If that was the case, she wanted him to reach the answer on his own, with no prodding from her. She had to be able to trust him, and he wasn't making that easy.

"I . . ." Then something like resolution settled across his features. He met her gaze, and his eyes darkened with intensity. Or maybe that was only the shadows from being tucked under the overhang. "There's not such a man at Fort Versailles. Only a blacksmith who hammers out horseshoes and makes traps on the forge. He's not very skilled at the latter. More than one man told me it was better to buy from the trade store at twice the price than from his stock. There are also men brought in to do work on the fort walls and buildings. I didn't know them long, but from what I saw, their abilities seemed a bit rougher than the blacksmith's. At least one of them was just learning how to hammer out a flat piece of metal."

Her stomach sank at his words, but she studied him. How could she know for sure whether he spoke the truth or was only trying to convince her to turn back?

He laid down the strip of meat he'd been eating and turned to face her fully. "What is it you need, Charlotte? Maybe I can find the kind of craftsman you're looking for somewhere else. Let's get you back to Laurent, then I'll seek out the right man. If he can be found anywhere, I'll locate him."

The earnestness in his voice struck a chord deep in her heart, that intensity in his gaze easing her worries. Would he really be willing to do all that? "Why? Why would you go through all that effort for me?" It didn't make sense, this willingness to expend himself for someone he'd met days before.

He pulled back the slightest bit. In fact, the movement seemed more internal than to his physical position.

Her defenses flared into anger. "Tell me, Damien. Tell me what you want from me. Why have you spent so much time and effort to *help* me?" She emphasized the word *help*, for she still wasn't sure whether that had been his motive or not. "Is it my village? You want to see Laurent? Do you have something evil planned for my people?"

Even as the words tumbled out, she could feel their unfairness. This man wasn't cruel or evil. He'd been kind and generous from their first meeting, and not just with her, but with the animals, too. Never once had she seen a sign of harshness in his actions. And traveling in these elements had pushed them all far too close to their breaking points.

But what else could be driving him?

He drew back even more, though his expression no longer seemed closed off. Shocked was a better description. His lips parted, and the surprise in his eyes mingled with something like hurt.

A pang pierced her chest, but she brushed the ache aside.

Then something shifted in his eyes. He blew out a long breath and scrubbed his hand down his face. Then his gaze lifted to hers again, his brows tenting with sorrow. "I suppose I understand why you distrust me. Why you think the worst. I really don't mean harm to your people. I'd like to see Laurent only because I've heard so much about it, but that's not why I want to take you there." He paused long enough for his throat to work in a swallow, then he seemed to be pushing himself forward.

"I have a sister—*had* a sister." Pain deepened the creases around his eyes. "Michelle. My twin. Definitely my better half. She was good—so good—and I think she was the only one who ever thought I could be that way, too. She was always pushing me to be better. To help others, even when it would be so much easier to mind my own concerns. So many times I ignored what Michelle asked of me." His gaze turned to stare out the opening ahead of them. "I wish I hadn't." His voice cracked on those words, but he pressed on. "I wish I hadn't been the one to put that disappointment in the eyes of the only person who truly loved me. Who cared enough to believe I could be better."

Silence rang between them, a quiet so laden with pain her chest ached. She wanted to reach out and close the distance between them, lay her hand on his arm. But he seemed so lost in grief. And who was she to console him anyway? She'd accused him of the very worst only moments before.

He turned to face her. Red rimmed his eyes, but determination laced them, too. "I won't make that mistake again. I may not have Michelle here to tell me what to do, but her voice lives inside me." He thumped a fist on his chest. "I knew from the moment I saw you slumped in the snow, especially when I realized you were a woman, what Michelle would have wanted. I intend to see you to safety, no matter what it takes." His chin lifted with that last bit, his gaze flaring with defiance.

He eyed her, as though daring her to refuse him. That, of course, made her own hackles rise, but she pressed them back down. Just because the man seemed to know exactly how to draw out her stronger emotions didn't mean she had to let them overcome her good sense.

Before they discussed anything further about their destination or him protecting her, though, she needed to give voice to his grief. "Your sister sounds like a wonderful woman. I'm sure she would be proud of you."

He looked toward the opening, tipping his face so she couldn't see his expression. But she didn't miss the way his throat worked. The way he seemed to struggle to rein in emotion. His grief was still so raw.

At last, he nodded, though he still didn't glance her way. "Michelle was the best. The kindest person I ever knew. The strongest. She was always my best friend, and when our parents died, she proclaimed herself my mother also." A sad chuckle lifted his chest. "She cut Mum's aprons to fit herself and would scurry around the kitchen. I told her she didn't have to work so hard. That we would take care of each other. She said I needed her, and she was doing exactly what she was supposed to do." His mouth pressed into a thin line before he continued. "She was right, I did need her. Every day since then . . ." He cut off his words, but she didn't have to guess what he would have said.

"How long has she been gone?"

What little of his expression she could see twisted with pain, even as he turned fully away. "One year. Today." He surged to his feet, keeping his head ducked under the overhang until he strode out into the bright light beyond.

The jumble of emotions he left behind made her want to stand and pace, too. How could a man be so broken—yet so good and trustworthy? Even after a year, his love for his sister came through with aching clarity. And if that love was what drove him to lie to her, could she be angry with him? *Should* she?

The chaos inside wouldn't allow her to think clearly. And she couldn't deny how the tender way he spoke of his sister made her yearn for her own family.

Perhaps returning to Laurent wouldn't be such a bad fate.

16

Damien had to get away from this smothering weight. The grief, the longing to sit across the table from Michelle once more—they were awful enough. But the fact that he'd not remembered today's anniversary . . . How could he have forgotten this day he'd been dreading for so long? He'd planned to immerse himself in memories of Michelle, to honor her. And yes, to allow himself to succumb to the grief, just for today.

But with his exhausting and desperate search for Charlotte, the anniversary date hadn't crashed over him upon awakening. He'd not actually slept through the night, so there'd been no first opening of his eyelids. He'd not had the time or energy to think about anything other than following Charlotte's tracks.

How could he have betrayed Michelle so easily?

He stomped up the mountain, pushing himself hard. Harder. Farther from the weight. He hated himself. Hated everything.

Everything that had stripped away the one good thing in his life.

He didn't regret speaking of his sister to Charlotte, though she was the first he'd been able to bring himself to tell. It seemed right to honor Michelle that way. And he'd needed Charlotte to understand his motives.

But this wrenching pain inside him . . . He had to get away from it or its pressure would smother him completely. As much as he wanted to drop to his knees and succumb, he forced himself onward. Upward. Climbing higher. Pushing himself farther.

When he reached the peak, he could go no higher, so he stumbled over the crest and started down. His vision blurred, but he ignored the tears. He could allow no weakness to stop him.

After half sliding down an icy rock, his feet found purchase in snow. On his next step, his foot glanced off something sharp hiding beneath the surface. He stumbled sideways, then caught himself on his hands and knees. Every shred of common sense told him to stop. He would break something, or worse, if he continued at this reckless pace.

But he *wanted* the worst. He'd found nothing in this life worth staying alive for, not with Michelle gone.

Charlotte.

He'd thought . . . But she would probably be better off without him, too. She wanted to do this on her own, to reach Fort Versailles. Who was he to determine what was best for her? He'd certainly never been able to protect Michelle, especially at the end.

He should let Charlotte do what she thought best. His interfering would only make things worse for her. Experience should have reminded him of that long before now.

His foot slipped on another icy rock, twisting him sideways as he scrambled for purchase. His gloved hands grabbed hold of a thick chunk of icy snow, and he gripped tight, holding himself there for long moments as he caught his breath.

The tumble, the deep inhales of frigid air, they worked to clear his mind of the turmoil. He closed his eyes, breathing in one cleansing breath after another. As much as he didn't want to go on, he had a very important reason to pull himself together and climb back over that mountain summit.

Charlotte.

She may not want him to help her, but he knew in his deepest being she needed him. Even if she could perhaps manage the men at the fort on her own—and that was quite an *if*, given how beautiful she was—traveling through these icy mountains was dangerous under any condition. So much could happen to a woman alone.

To *anyone* alone. He couldn't stand by and leave her to her own fate when he was able to help with the journey. And as much as he wanted to protect her, forcing her to return to her village against her will had been wrong. Even Michelle would have been disappointed in him.

Inhaling another deep breath to strengthen his limbs, he pushed upright and started back up the mountain.

The perk of Gulliver's ears was Charlotte's first sign of Damien's return. The mule would probably have done more than lift his head if the approaching footsteps belonged to anyone other than his master. But still, Charlotte's hand edged down to the knife handle in her moccasin.

The figure who rounded the rock and ducked into the

shelter of the overhang wore the familiar fur coat and hood. Her heart leapt at the sight of him, as it always did. This time was surely because of her concern for him.

He stopped to stroke the mule, and Gulliver turned to nuzzle Damien's hand. A depth of friendship and trust existed between them, a bond that couldn't be feigned. How could she not *also* trust this man? The story of his sister explained much about his actions, and with the strength of his emotion, it seemed impossible he would have made that up. She still didn't like his deception, but she understood his reasons. She could even think of them as noble, though that didn't help her like what he'd done any better.

At last, he turned from the mule toward her and took the last few steps to the place where he'd sat on the fur before. She let herself glance at his face as he approached. His eyes squinted enough that she couldn't tell for sure if he'd been crying, but his expression seemed to hold a bit more peace than before.

After he sat, he exhaled a long sigh. It wasn't so much the sound of it that gripped her as the feeling the act released into the air between them. He'd come to a decision and was trying to find relief in it.

A decision about what? She slid a look his way to see what she could decipher from his expression.

He met her gaze, and his mouth curved upward in what might have been a smile if his eyes didn't hold so much sadness.

She should speak. Something to break through the silence, to show she understood his grief. Something to make this better for him. She'd never been good with words, though, and nothing she found now would begin to suffice.

Thankfully, he spoke first. "I'm sorry I deceived you. I'm sorry I made the decision for you. I'm sorry I broke your trust."

Those dark eyes brimmed with an earnestness that reached in and gripped her. "Damien, I—"

He shook his head. "I just want you to know that I'll take you to the fort if you want me to. Or beyond that to find the craftsman you seek, if you're determined. I don't think it's wise. I'd rather see you safely to your village, then go find what you need and bring it back to you. But I won't take the choice away from you. I want to go along because it's safer. Traveling through this wilderness will always be safer with two. And having a man at your side in the fort will help thwart any scoundrels."

Finally he stopped talking, but he watched her, almost from the side of his gaze. As though uncertain how she would respond.

Emotion burned her throat. So much had changed this last hour. She understood a great deal more about this man, and everything she learned made her want to know more. Now he was giving her the freedom to choose for herself, giving up his concerns. Well, not giving them up exactly, but he was willing to lay them aside for her.

His sister must have been quite a woman to instill such a desire to protect. To help form him into the man who sat before her now.

She forced herself to lock her gaze with his. "I need to apologize."

His brows rose, but he said nothing.

She swallowed to bring moisture into her throat. "I . . . gave you a tonic back at the camp. That's why you slept while I left. I'm sorry I did that. I was afraid of why you were taking me away from the fort. Afraid of what you had planned. But I should have asked you about it, not run away. You've done so much to help me. I'm sorry I took the coward's way out." She could still remember the fear in her belly when she'd discovered the direction they were taking, then even more when she'd caught him riffling through her pack.

His expression had softened as he listened. Would it stir up hard feelings to ask about the last bit? She had to. "Can I ask something? When I came back into camp last night with the water, I saw you doing something with my pack."

Confusion clouded his eyes for a heartbeat. "When it fell over? The flap was loose, and some of your bundles fell out. I put everything back in."

Heat seared up her neck. She'd misjudged him even worse than she'd thought. "I'm sorry. I thought . . . after I realized you lied about the direction . . ."

He gave her a tight smile. "I guess I can understand why you tried to poison me."

She'd better set him straight on that. "It wasn't poison, not exactly. All the plants that go into it are safe to eat. It just makes you really sleepy for a while."

His brows lifted again. "Is that why I cast up my accounts the moment I woke up?"

That heat in her neck rose up to scald her ears. Now that he mentioned it, hadn't Brielle's husband, Evan, also been struck with a stomach ailment after being shot with the arrow dipped in the potion? That seemed too much of a coincidence, but she wouldn't give voice to it. She worked for a bright smile. "Glad you're feeling better now. And I am sorry."

He nodded, a relieving end to the conversation. "Any thoughts on which way you'd like to go?"

She inhaled a deep breath, then released it. She had a choice to make—return to Laurent or press on to Fort Versailles. And if no one there could accomplish what she needed, would she be willing to go farther?

"Did you speak the truth when you said there was no man at Fort Versailles skilled at fine metal engravings?" she asked.

His brows lowered in concentration, but he nodded without hesitation. "The blacksmith there is barely worthy of the title. I wouldn't trust him to make a lock for my musket, much less anything requiring real skill. I saw nothing of note in any of the new men brought in, either."

"And other forts in the area? Do you know of anyone capable there?" If a skilled craftsman might possibly be within reach . . .

His brows dipped even lower. "That's what I was trying to think of. There's a fellow who's not bad at making traps up in Fort Jarrett, but that's a special skill in itself. Just because he can twist a coil with even thickness all the way through doesn't mean he would have the artistry needed for a detailed engraving. If you want to speak with him, I can take you there. I suspect it would be at least a week's travel, though."

She pressed down her disappointment and shifted her focus to another word he'd used. *Artistry.* That sketch of Gulliver had been so intricate. So lifelike. And the glimpse she'd had of the knife handle he'd been carving that first night in the cave . . .

Even as the possibility rose with a seed of hope inside her, she tried her best to temper it. "Damien . . ." He must have caught the shift in her tone, for his brows lifted. "Do you know much about metals? Brass, especially. Could an artist and a metal craftsman work together to accomplish an engraving? Maybe one could help shape the basic form and keep the material at just the right temperature, then the artist could do the finer work."

His expression shifted, a bit of wariness slipping into his gaze. "I don't know. I suppose it would depend on the amount of detail you're talking about. And the skill of the men working on it."

The stirring of hope rose into excitement. "Have you ever drawn anything like the scene of the Lord's Last Supper?" Perhaps it was too much to think he might be able to accomplish such a masterpiece. Yet perhaps if he practiced on paper, or maybe even wood . . . and if Papa handled the preparation of the metal . . .

Now his wariness turned to suspicion. "I've never drawn anything like that. No." That wasn't a direct refusal in his tone. He spoke the words more as a statement of fact. Perhaps she could work him into the idea during the return journey to Laurent. Papa's expertise could do a great deal with the chalice, and with Damien's ability—along with having part of the scene still intact on the cup for him to study— surely they had a better chance of repairing the work than a blacksmith who could simply manage an even coil.

For the first time since she'd pulled the singed chalice from the flame—before that, even—a lightness worked its way through her. A lifting of a burden she'd not fully realized was driving her reckless desperation.

ᏩᏇᎶ

A new war waged within Damien as they set out down the mountain the next morning. They'd slept away much of their exhaustion, but he'd awakened with the things Charlotte asked pounding in his mind. Her questions wouldn't be silenced, no matter how much he tried to focus on the landscape around them.

He was no artist nor engraver. He'd attempted a bit of both, either when the urge struck him or when Michelle had pressed. But he'd only just begun carving again, and that sketch of Gulliver and Charlotte was the first drawing he had done since his sister took sick.

Nothing about his experience or skill qualified him for whatever she had in mind—a need so important she would set out alone to find a person capable. The fact that she thought she would find such a craftsman in these mountains showed her naïveté, but that didn't diminish her need.

She hadn't directly asked him for whatever it was she wanted of him. That would likely come when they reached her village and she revealed her plan. For she *had* a plan— that had been clear from the light that dawned in her eyes as she questioned him.

For now, he would be content to accompany her home. After that, he would find a way to explain how incapable he was of whatever masterpiece she needed. Maybe he would even attempt what she asked, on paper at least, where no damage could be done. One glance at his immature efforts would prove the truth with no mistake.

"How far back to the lake, do you think?"

He glanced at Charlotte, once more mounted atop Gulliver. She looked worried, though he wasn't sure if that was because of his deception before or some other reason.

Regardless, he would speak only the truth from now on. He'd already calculated the approximate time, so the answer was easy. "We'll go back by way of the campsite where you poisoned me so I can get the things I left there. That means two days to the lake, if the weather holds and we don't get more snowfall."

Disappointment clouded her expression, or perhaps worry. Did she expect the weather to hold them up? He glanced at the sky—gray, but no more so than the usual winter day. The clouds weren't the kind to bring more snow.

One more look at Charlotte's face showed what was definitely unease. "When does your family expect you back?" If she'd contemplated going on to a distant fort, they must not expect her urgently.

But the way her bottom lip slipped between her teeth made his belly tighten. And not just with longing to touch those lips himself. What had she told her family about where she was going? He still couldn't believe any decent father would allow his daughter to set out into this country alone with winter coming in earnest.

She didn't answer, but her expression turned guilty.

He tugged Gulliver to a halt so he could face Charlotte fully. The mule needed to rest anyway. "How long do they expect you to be gone?" If she snuck away without telling anyone . . .

Who knew what kind of hunt would have ensued? Despite the fact she was a woman full grown, any decent family would search for someone who went missing. Especially someone as special as Charlotte.

His chest tightened more with each second she delayed her answer.

At last, she murmured, "I said I'd be back before Discovery Day. That's when we celebrate the anniversary of when our ancestors found Laurent."

Part of his tension eased. She'd told them something at least. "And when is that?" His voice sounded calmer than he felt. Good.

"A week and a half from now." Her tone came out so small and worried, it raised up all his protective instincts.

"We should have two more days to reach the lake, and you said your village is a day beyond that, right?" They should reach her village in plenty of time.

She nodded, but apprehension still squeezed her features. "I guess I'm afraid they'll be worried. I remember how panicked my father was the time Brielle was caught in a blizzard. This isn't a blizzard, of course, but he'll still be worried."

Not an unlikely possibility. Out here, a snowstorm or animal or anything else could wipe her out in a single vicious swipe.

Her family wouldn't know Charlotte had help on her journey. They would think she traveled out here in these elements alone. On foot and carrying her pack. Any decent kin would be frantic long before now.

He tried to keep the worry from his own face and fought the urge to reach up and clasp her hand. "We'll move as quickly as we can."

She offered a tight smile—an offering of trust.

With a new determination, he turned toward the trail and nudged Gulliver forward. "Come on, fellow. We have ground to cover."

17

As much as she'd liked Damien before, this new man she was coming to know drew her so much more.

Charlotte sat in front of the campfire with only a small space between her and Damien. They'd ridden so late tonight, the only shelter they'd been able to find was the cliff wall behind them to shield some of the wind. Thus, they both huddled in front of that protection, soaking in as much warmth as the fire would provide.

Exhaustion seeped through every bone and muscle, but her mind wasn't ready for sleep yet. In truth, she wanted a little more time with the man beside her. She'd not realized how strong a barrier his deception had placed between them. He seemed lighter now, though not carefree. The weight of grief still shrouded him. But the reserve she'd felt—yet hadn't been able to name before—had slipped away.

In two days, or perhaps three, they would reach Laurent. She had a feeling everything would change—both this camaraderie between them and likely the way her family and friends viewed *her*, as well.

She didn't mean to sigh, but it slipped out as she thought of the sadness her father's face would bear. Those worry lines etched deeper each year, and she'd probably added a few more with this ill-planned trip. Hopefully her father still believed she'd gone to the Dinee camp. But if he'd found the chalice missing or simply worried too much about her, he might have sent someone after her. He might know the truth by now—at least part of it—and would be frantic.

"Are you worried?" Damien turned his gaze on her.

She glanced his way and tried for a smile, but her exhausted features wouldn't comply. "Worried about what?"

But she knew what he meant. This man's intuition continued to surprise her. Was she so easy to read, or could he see inside every person the way he did her?

"Will you be in trouble for staying gone so long?" His brows had drawn together, forming the furrows she was beginning to love. They seemed a sign of his care.

She shifted her gaze to the fire as she thought through his question. Did she dare tell him how she'd left? When he'd asked before, those details had seemed to be none of his concern. But he'd become more than a guide and traveling companion. The man beside her felt very much like a friend.

Could she trust him with her own deception?

Even as the thought settled, the similarity in their actions raised its stark head. She'd lied to her father just like Damien had lied to her. She'd written the falsehood in her note to protect her father from worrying about her, and Damien had been trying to protect her from the dangers at the fort. Neither deception was right, but the situation called to mind that very familiar verse in Matthew. *Thou hypocrite, first cast out the beam out of thine own eye.*

She and Damien had a great deal in common it seemed—
the need for grace.

And she needed to tell him all. It was time she own up to
her mistake. She would need to do that over and over once
she returned to Laurent, so this could be good practice.

But . . . she couldn't bring herself to tell him about the
chalice. Not yet. She needed to speak to her father first and
beg his forgiveness. She *could* tell Damien about her cow-
ardice in leaving the note, though.

She picked up a twig from the ground to snap between
her fingers. "I left early in the morning, before anyone else
had risen. I placed a note on the table explaining that I
was traveling with some of our Dinee friends to visit their
village. I told them not to worry, that I'd be back before
Discovery Day."

She couldn't meet his gaze as she spoke, but heat flamed
all through her. Finally, she braved a glance at him.

Damien studied her, but his dark eyes gave no sign of
what he might be thinking. Her fingers snapped the twig
into smaller pieces, moving faster as the tension inside her
built. Would he say nothing in response to her admission?

She straightened, tossing the bits of twig to the ground. "I
know lying and leaving that way was wrong. I was desperate
to get to the fort, and I knew I would worry my father if he
knew where I was really going. He would have come after
me, and he's getting older now."

His brows drew together once more. "If you'd told him,
would you have been allowed to go? Maybe with a party of
others? Or . . . is no one approved to leave without permission?"

His tone held only curiosity, and she could well imagine

how odd their situation sounded. Especially when people came and went from forts every day.

In truth, she wasn't fully sure of the answers to some of his questions. "It's not that we're not *allowed* to leave. The hunters go out all the time, and the women pick berries outside the village throughout the spring and summer. Trading parties go to the Dinee villages. We send men to Fort Versailles for trading, too."

Several beats of silence passed. "So, this is your first time leaving the village except for gathering food?" Again, surprise seemed the only decipherable emotion in his tone.

She shrugged and nodded but couldn't quite hold his gaze. How sheltered he must think her.

"Leaving took a great deal of courage, then, even slipping out the way you did." Something in his voice drew her gaze to meet his once more. His eyes looked troubled now. "I suppose that brings me back to my first question. Will you be in trouble for departing without permission? Is there a person or court responsible for such things?"

She pressed her lips together as she contemplated the question. "I suppose the council would have that authority. But I don't think there's a law saying we can't leave without approval. Audrey and her husband took a wedding trip to visit his family in England."

His brows rose again. "England, you say? I thought your village was French."

"He was an outsider. A British spy who followed Brielle's husband up from the States."

A glimmer of something like humor brushed his eyes. "Sounds like an interesting story. And he married one of your people?"

She nodded. "Audrey, one of my family's dearest friends. She's always been like a sister to me." Sometimes even more so than Brielle. Audrey had taken the time to teach her to bake all those years ago.

Damien grew silent as his gaze shifted to the leaping flames before them. Was he thinking of the people she just described? Or had his thoughts returned to whether she would be punished for leaving? She should set his mind at ease there. The council had grown a great deal more lenient in allowing trading with outsiders. And since she'd not actually met anyone on this trip except Damien, they should have no concerns that she'd bring trouble back with her.

She glanced his way again. A pensiveness guarded his expression. Then he met her gaze. "Will you tell me more about what you need engraved? You said an image of the Lord's Supper. On what? And why is it so important?"

Her breath seized. She couldn't tell him. But he'd asked the question directly. It would be rude to put him off, especially when he'd done so much for her.

She would have to be honest.

She did her best to hold his gaze. "I want to tell you. I *will* tell you. But I need to confess something to my father first. Will you be patient with me until we reach Laurent?"

He studied her. His throat worked. She couldn't breathe as she waited for his verdict. Then he nodded. "If you need me to, I'll wait."

Relief sagged through her, and she finally took in a deep breath.

Awareness slipped through her that she was touching him—or rather, her glove was touching his coat. Yet she felt the contact all the same.

He seemed to realize it at the same time, for his eyes darkened even more, taking on a charcoal hue.

She started to pull back, but he turned his arm in an easy motion, shifting his hand up to clasp hers inside his own. The smile that tugged the corners of his mouth was easy, friendly. He gave her hand a gentle squeeze, then released it. Only the touch of two friends sharing companionship. Yet the loss when he pulled away made her yearn for so much more.

She wrapped her hands around her knees to occupy them, and if a silence had stretched between them, it might have been awkward. Thankfully, he spoke right away.

"I suppose the only question that remains is what they'll think about you bringing home a stranger." A hint of teasing laced his voice, but she could well imagine that tone covered true concern. She felt him stiffen, or maybe that was only the change in the air between them.

"Or . . . maybe you'd rather not bring me into the village," he continued. "I can leave you once we're within sight." His voice had grown tight, as though with anger.

She had a feeling that wasn't his true emotion. From what he'd said of his sister, it seemed he'd not been accepted by many in his life, though she couldn't imagine why not. Likely, he thought she would shun his presence once she no longer needed him.

That couldn't be further from the truth.

She reached out and laid her hand on his arm again. "Of course I want you to come inside. You said yourself you'd like to see our village, and I need you there."

She pulled her hand back and did her best to pretend nothing worried her. Yet even as she tucked into her fur bedding, she couldn't push away the nagging question of whether she was bringing trouble to Laurent without realizing it.

But in truth, she'd already caused the trouble. She could only pray Damien would be part of the solution.

Damien stared at Charlotte's sleeping form in the gray light of early morning. Each time he looked at her, her beauty struck him anew, creating an ache in his chest and a longing in his fingers to reach out and touch her. Perhaps this was a time he could actually do that.

After all, she never slept late. This abnormal behavior might mean she was ill—feverish, even. He wouldn't know unless he brushed his fingers across her porcelain skin. She didn't seem paler than normal, and the times he'd heard her restless stirring in the night might explain why she still slept now.

He should simply speak her name and see if she awoke. But her hand on his arm last night had ignited a desire within him for more. This time without the bulky thickness of gloves.

Reaching out, he brushed the hair that framed her face. As soft as he'd expected. When his fingers moved to stroke her temple, he hovered over her skin for a moment. If she awoke and felt him touching her . . . The last thing he wanted was for her to fear him.

He shifted his hand to rest on her shoulder. "Charlotte? Charlotte, wake up."

Her eyes flickered open, and they fixed on him, though they still possessed the dreamy haze of sleep.

"It's daylight, and I thought you would want to get started

soon. You're not ill, are you?" His hand still lay on her shoulder, but he should pull it back.

When she turned under her furs, he did remove his hand. Yet the way she covered a sleepy yawn made him want to move in again. This woman ignited things in him he'd never felt toward anyone. It was a good thing they would reach her village in a couple days, for this new closeness between them was testing his self-control.

She glanced at the sky, and her eyes sharpened as though she finally realized how late it was. "I'm ready. I just need a minute to pack up."

While Charlotte slipped away from camp for her morning privacy, he rolled up her bedding and strapped it on the saddle with the rest of the gear. As she returned, he was just tightening the cinch on Gulliver. "I left some food on that rock for you. It's not the warm goodness you normally serve, but hopefully it will stick with you for a few hours." He sent her a wink, though perhaps he should have refrained.

Yet the pink that crept into her ears was too alluring not to enjoy. With the food in hand, she approached the mule and extended a hand for him to snuffle. The exact pose Damien had captured in his drawing. Maybe he would redo the sketch and include more of her than simply her hand and coat. He'd been too reluctant to capture her face or form before. That had seemed intrusive, something he'd be better off keeping only in his memory.

Or not at all.

But after what she said last night about a woman from Laurent marrying an outsider, possibility had arisen within him that he'd not been able to squelch. Not that he was ready to propose marriage, but maybe Charlotte wasn't as forbidden to him as he'd told himself from the beginning.

As she settled in Gulliver's saddle, he tightened the straps on his snowshoes. He wasn't nearly as sore as in past days, despite how long they traveled yesterday. Maybe his muscles had finally accustomed themselves to this mode of travel.

The chirp of winter birds sounded around them as they set off, and an hour or so into the ride, the sun finally broke through the haze of clouds. They spoke occasionally of things they noticed along the trail, but at least five minutes of silence had settled before Charlotte spoke up. "When did you first start drawing?"

He straightened, glancing back to her. Her sweet face held nothing but innocent curiosity, a look that meant he'd be hard-pressed to refuse anything she asked. As much as he hated talking about himself, and as hard as the memories from before were to speak of, he'd determined to do his very best to be open and honest with Charlotte. After his earlier deception, she deserved this.

Turning back to the trail ahead, he thought through his youngest memories. "I don't know. As far back as I can remember. I would go through times when I sketched everything I saw, but then I wouldn't draw again for months."

"Did you stop during hard times, or times you were busy, like with school or hunting?"

That question required a bit more thought. "I didn't draw much when we moved during my seventh summer. Nor at all for a year after my parents died." He shrugged, doing his best to keep his voice casual. Both of those had been hard seasons but were far enough in the past that he could speak of them without emotion. But this path of conversation could become far too dark if they didn't stop now.

He glanced back at her once more, making sure his tone came out light. "Any particular reason you ask? Are you studying the drawing habits of artists?" The moment that last word slipped out, he nearly bit his tongue to bring it back. "Not that I'm an artist. Far from it."

She offered a muted smile in response, its meaning impossible to decipher. "What do you think makes one an artist, Monsieur Levette?"

Though she spoke his formal name, the title seemed to ease the tension between them, not create more distance. Perhaps the softness of her voice helped, too.

Once more, he shrugged. "Someone with real talent, I suppose. Someone people recognize as an artist. A person who's paid for their work." Not a lonely boy in a small French village who needed a distraction from the rest of life.

"What are your favorite things to draw?"

Why did she press this topic so far? Her questions dug deeper than he wanted to think right now. Couldn't they just trek along in silence? Settle for pointing out unusual rock formations they passed?

But he wouldn't be rude to her. Not only did he owe her honesty, but part of him wanted her to understand, the part that wasn't too wary of diving into all these feelings.

He blew out a breath. "I suppose I like to draw life. Things I see that strike me. Memories I want to keep." Perhaps that was why he'd stopped sketching when his parents moved him away from the few friends he'd finally made, and again when Mum and Dad succumbed to the fever. And why he'd not been able to open his sketchbook this last year. Carving the knife handle had seemed less like art and more like necessity.

Then he'd met Charlotte, and taking up a pencil seemed possible again.

She was silent, and at last he braved a glance back at her. She offered him that same muted smile, though maybe it lacked the hint of sadness it held before. "I like the idea of keeping memories. I wish I could do that, too."

Part of him wanted to question the meaning behind her comment. As much as he hated talking about feelings and digging up the aches he'd buried deep, he wanted desperately to know more about Charlotte.

But out of the corner of his eye, he saw the mule's stride falter. "Ho!" Damien jerked the rope up to keep the animal from stumbling, but Gulliver had already dropped to his knees. Keeping tight pressure on the lead line helped the mule keep his head up, and with another attempt, he rose to all four feet.

Gulliver stood with hooves spread, heaving in gulps of air as though he'd just galloped up the slope. And from the angle of his legs, something looked very wrong indeed.

18

Damien's heart thundered as Charlotte slipped from Gulliver's back. "Is he hurt?" She ran her hands down the animal's shoulder and leg.

"The snow padded his fall. Not sure why he stumbled, though." As Damien's heart rate eased, he took a step back and tugged on the lead. "Come, boy. Walk on."

Charlotte moved away so Gulliver could step freely. The mule hesitated, then took a ginger stride forward. But with the second step, his head bobbed, and he nearly went down to his knees again.

"Ho. Whoa there, fella." Damien's belly formed a tight knot as he loosened the rope and stepped back to the mule's right side, where he wouldn't bear the weight. Maybe he'd picked up a pebble in the snow that packed his hoof.

Gulliver allowed him to pick up the hoof easily enough. Not a surprise, since the mule had been well trained, and lifting this hoof shouldn't pain him. He had a feeling if he tried to pick up the *other* front leg, Gulliver would struggle to shift his weight onto this one.

Chipping all the snow out of the crevices of the sole

proved the hardest part, and he only succeeded when Charlotte brought him a stick.

"There, boy. Let's see where it hurts." He pulled off his glove for this last part, for he needed better control of his fingers. The icy air stung his skin, but this sensation was better than being numb.

The moment Damien's thumb pressed on the more tender *V* in the center of the hoof, Gulliver nearly jerked the leg from his hand. "Hey there." Still holding the foot with one hand, he stroked the mule's shoulder with the other to calm him.

He needn't have bothered, for Charlotte was at the animal's head stroking and soothing in such a sweet voice that it nearly made Damien jealous.

He turned his focus back to the hoof. Using a much lighter pressure, he probed the tender flesh. There was no putrid odor or unusual coloring, and with the way the limping came on suddenly, it must be a stone bruise. He'd not scraped a stone out amid the packed snow, but Gulliver might have stepped on a sharp point hidden under the white fluff.

Easing the foot down, Damien straightened and turned to stroke the mule. What now? The injury clearly pained him. Maybe with a few minutes' rest while standing in the snow, the ache would lessen enough that they could continue. Charlotte would need to walk, but Damien had a feeling she wouldn't mind in order to help her four-legged friend.

She was watching him, brows raised. Another woman would've asked fifteen questions by now, but he loved the way Charlotte didn't need to fill the air with noise. She could say as much with her expression as another female could speak in a hundred words.

He ran his hand down the mule's neck again. "It seems like he stepped on a rock wrong and maybe bruised the hoof. Let's let him stand for a few minutes and see if he feels better after that."

Once more, her expression spoke the question. *Do you really think that will help?*

He shrugged. "It's the first thing to try. We'll see how he is from there."

The time seemed to take forever to pass, even after Charlotte pulled food from the pack and they sat on rocks to eat. There seemed nothing to speak of, nothing save the worry that hovered inside and around them both.

At last, when the sun had crossed an hour of the sky, he stood. Charlotte jerked straight at his sudden action, and even Gulliver's head rose, ears pricked toward him.

"Let's see how he's doing." Damien gentled his stride as he reached the mule's head. Taking up the rope, he nudged Gulliver forward.

The animal's reluctance was clear, and Damien had to pull harder before Gulliver finally attempted a step. The injured leg first, since that would allow him to put his weight on the hoof that didn't hurt.

The worry in Damien's gut pulled tighter as the mule hesitated once more before attempting a second step.

His head jerked nearly to the ground the moment he put weight on the right front hoof, as though trying to use his nose as a replacement limb. The act looked so painful, Damien allowed him to stop after that effort.

He stepped closer to his faithful friend and stroked the thick winter coat on his neck. "I'm sorry, fella. Let's take another look at it."

This time, he didn't have to scoop out packed ice or dirt, just brush off a light dusting of white. When his thumb brushed the spot where Gulliver had been tender before, the mule jerked back once more. If anything, the hour's rest seemed to have made the pain worse. There was still no visible damage on that spot, but the bruise must be deep.

Damien lowered the hoof gently, then straightened and turned to Charlotte. The pain on her face showed he didn't have to explain this latest update.

"Is there something more that can be done?" she asked.

He shook his head. "Rest and ice are all I know to heal it. The ice part isn't hard to accomplish." He glanced around at the surroundings. "We should look for a place to camp."

A grove of trees about thirty strides away would provide some protection and be near enough for Gulliver to reach. He could nearly feel Charlotte's sigh as they started in that direction.

Gulliver struggled with his first few steps, but seemed resigned to force himself on, even with such a violent limp. Perhaps he sensed rest would come soon.

After helping Damien scrape the bear hide all afternoon, Charlotte's arms were as weary as her mind. He'd been even more amiable than usual, keeping up conversation throughout the long hours. To distract her from worrying over the delay, no doubt. And for that, she was thankful.

At first, he'd spoken of his months with the trapping party, relaying stories that would have made her smile if she hadn't been so troubled. As he asked about her experience with scraping and preparing hides, she managed a few tales of her own, mostly involving her efforts to learn the craft. But a few included Brielle or Andre, the former as she learned to hunt, and the latter when he was too young to be of much help—yet just old enough to get in the way. There was the one time she'd found him with her freshly sharpened meat knife scraping a caribou hide—a particularly lovely one at that. Andre had pierced the skin in so many places that it was good for little except braiding into rope.

When Damien told a few stories that included his sister, she couldn't miss their significance. He mentioned Michelle's name with something almost like reverence. She could hear the grief in his voice, but she wondered if it was a relief for him to speak of her. Did he have anyone else with whom he could talk about her? Any friends who knew him well enough to be allowed into that painful place? Back in his village, there must be many. But how long since he'd been there?

Now, as they sat by the leaping flames of the campfire, darkness fully shrouding their circle of light, there was much she wanted to say. Much more to ask.

The evening meal had been eaten, plates cleaned, and plenty of firewood stacked nearby to keep the flames high throughout the night. Once more, they sat side by side, though there was no cliff wall to lean against this time to shield them from the wind. The night seemed warmer than the others, though, as warm as the camaraderie between them.

His friendship had eased the frustration of the delayed travel, but her mind had once more become fascinated with forming images of all the ways her family would be worried. All the people who might have been sent out to search for her. Were they even now huddled around a fire in a similar cluster of trees? Maybe debating where they would search on the morrow? Or maybe they'd already gone to Fort Versailles and realized she'd never reached its walls. What panic would well in Papa's mind with that knowledge?

Damien shifted beside her, reaching for his pack. From his satchel, he pulled out the book where he'd tucked the drawing of Gulliver. Next, he extracted a pencil, something her people hadn't known of until Brielle's husband first introduced it to them. As he opened the book to a blank page, she leaned in, just close enough to see but not brush against his arm.

He turned to her, brows raised. "What should I sketch? Choose the subject."

He wanted her to decide? She glanced around the area, searching for inspiration. Only the fire and the darkness and the two of them existed here. Even Gulliver stood just outside the circle of light. She didn't want a drawing of her, and the fire didn't seem interesting enough. As much as she would love a sketch of him, he may not be able to manage that without seeing his reflection in something.

A thought slipped in, bringing a smile she couldn't deny. "How about a picture of one of those stories you told me earlier, when you first learned trapping. You decide which one." But she hoped he chose the tale of the beaver that escaped from a trap right in front of Damien's eyes. He'd forgotten to set the spring fully, and when the animal scampered a dozen steps away from the iron, it turned back to eye Damien, chattering a scolding that nearly made his ears burn, or so he'd said.

Damien's brows furrowed as he studied the blank paper,

then he tipped the book away from her and brushed the pencil against the blank page. He drew for a while, which gave her the opportunity to watch his face. The intensity that marked his features as he focused sometimes gave way to other emotions. Once, his mouth tipped in the makings of a smile. Occasionally, uncertainty would crease the corners of his eyes. Several times, his gaze lifted to stare out into the darkness beyond the fire.

At last, his gaze shifted her way, and he studied her as though trying to decide something. He'd probably been drawing a half hour, but she had no sense for how long a sketch would take. He might be hesitant to reveal his art, though.

"Do I get to see it yet? It doesn't have to be finished." Whether he was finished or not, pretending he planned to work on it more might make showing his sketch easier.

His gaze sharpened, and he dipped his chin back to the drawing as he added a few more strokes with his pencil. Once more, the corner of his mouth tipped up the smallest bit.

Then he straightened and turned the book toward her. As much as she wanted to watch his face as he shared the art, she was too hungry to know what he'd drawn.

Her gaze took in the flowing water at the top of the image first, a river fading off the upper edge of the paper. Then she pulled her focus back to see the entire image.

A beaver stared at her, head cocked, its pert nose and the glint in its eye laughing at her. It held its paws together, maybe because it clutched something within them, but it seemed to be almost clapping with glee at the escape it had managed. Its flat tail was tucked underneath it.

The entire image was impossible not to smile over.

"That sneaky little thing." She raised her grin to Damien. "Is that truly how it looked when it escaped from your trap?"

He was watching her, his expression more unguarded than she'd ever seen. So vulnerable she wanted to reach out and touch him, to assure him the sketch was excellent.

He glanced down at the paper as he nodded. "That's how I remember it. I was peeved when I first looked up and saw the beaver there, but that expression on its face made it impossible to do anything but laugh. Any beaver that can best me like that deserves to run free."

A smile curved the corners of his mouth as he stared at the drawing, his eyes soft with memory. As much as she admired the strong, competent side of Damien Levette, it was this gentleness that drew her even more strongly. Made her want to reach out and touch the corner of his mouth, to connect with him through more than words.

She refocused on the sketch to push that thought away. This time, she didn't study the beaver's expression as much as she did all the other tiny details. The nuances of shadow and light in its coat, as well as the grass rising up around it. Even the river flowed with more life than she would have thought possible to portray with something as simple as a charcoal pencil.

Perhaps she spent too long staring at each detail, for when she lifted her gaze back to Damien's face, his expression had returned to that vulnerable look. Yet this time he seemed to be trying to mask it with a layer of protection.

She reached out to lay a hand on his arm. "Damien, this is remarkable. Especially in such a short amount of time. You have a rare talent." At least she assumed this ability must be rare. It was so hard to fathom how he could re-create a scene so vividly with only charcoal and paper. This sketch would be ruined by adding color.

His eyes roamed her face, as though searching for her true opinion. Maybe for a sign she didn't really feel the way she'd said. Surely he saw the depth of her appreciation.

She tightened her touch on his arm, offering a gentle squeeze. He reached over and slipped his gloved hand over hers, lifting her fingers from his arm. But then he raised them to his lips and pressed a kiss to the backs of her fingers that she felt even through the layers of leather and fur.

His eyes stayed locked with hers throughout the action, and maybe the depth of his gaze—the intimacy—was what really stole her ability to take in air. Her breath stilled even as her heart sprinted.

The rich brown of his eyes darkened to almost black, drawing her in. Would he kiss more than simply her fingers? Every part of her wanted him to. She'd come to admire this man in every way.

And then he closed the distance between them.

19

Charlotte's eyes drifted shut as Damien's breath grazed her skin, his lips brushing hers soon after. The touch sent a jolt all the way through her. Not an unpleasant shock, but a tingle that brought her closer.

He responded, his mouth caressing hers with a touch both gentle and possessing so much power it stole the strength from her body. His hand slipped up to her neck, reaching behind her head. If only so many layers of fur didn't separate them. With so much heat welling inside her, she might never be cold again.

He gentled the kiss long before she wanted him to, yet the slow give-and-take captivated her even more than the intense press of before. Did he have any idea what his touch did to her?

With a final lingering caress, he pulled back, though only far enough for their breath to mingle in the air between them. His inhales came as heavy as her own, and the sweet taste of him nearly lured her back for another kiss.

But he pulled a little farther away, enough for her gaze to focus on his entire face. His mouth danced in a smile unlike anything she'd seen on him before. His eyes lit, drawing out a giddy feeling in her chest.

His focus searched her face. "I don't know if I should apologize for that. I don't want to. But I shouldn't take advantage of being alone with you."

Her heart did another stutter at his words. Her hand still gripped his arm, but she moved it down to weave her fingers between his. "Don't apologize."

His grin widened, giving her a glimpse of what he must have looked like when he smiled before the crushing grief of losing his sister pulled him down. Now, nothing tainted the joy on his face. The warmth infusing her body spread through her heart. She'd played at least a small part in helping him find that joy.

He straightened, inhaling an audible breath then releasing it. He didn't let go of her hands as he looked around, as though trying to remember where they were and what they'd been doing.

The book still lay in her lap, though the pages had flipped to an empty section. Part of her wanted to ask him to draw something else. But if the same emotions—and other sensations—still roiling inside her matched his, it might be hard for him to produce another such masterpiece just now.

Instead, she dared to lean into him, to rest her head on his shoulder. He was the perfect height, his broad frame padded by his fur coat. If her mind were more settled, she could sleep comfortably in this position.

But she wanted more of this man. Another kiss might be too much, as inflamed as her insides were. Yet any part of him would feed her desire. "Tell me more stories from your life. Either your time trapping or before, when you were a boy."

She could feel him settling in, feel the brush of his chin on her hood. "Let's see. There was the time Michelle and I were selling produce at the village market." His voice rumbled through her ear, filling her with the most delicious sense of peace.

He followed that story with another about when Michelle nursed a neighbor through a life-threatening illness, his role being to find all the herbs and plants she needed. He seemed to have been an able assistant to his sister in all their adventures, but he always ascribed the glory to Michelle's talent or wit or sweet spirit. His sister might have been wonderful, but not any more so than this man whose every breath had now sequenced to her own.

It wasn't until they finally separated to their own bedding and she closed her eyes for the night that she thought to worry about her family. Were they tucked in their warm beds, or had they discovered her deception? Were they even now out searching for her?

Damien shifted the plate away from the fire so the meat wouldn't dry out completely. Charlotte made cooking this way look so easy, and her food always turned out moist and full of flavor. Not dry and crusty like his attempts. At least he hadn't burned it while he checked Gulliver.

He glanced at her still-sleeping form, the faint morning light casting shadows that softened her features even more than normal. She was so beautiful, his chest ached with the emotion she stirred. And that kiss . . . His blood warmed again with the memory of it. Yet as much as her beauty and her touch drew him, it was every other part of her that gave substance to the respect and admiration growing so strong inside him.

She shifted beneath her furs, and his chest tightened. He wanted her to wake, wanted to see that gentle smile she revealed more often these days.

But he wasn't ready to tell her the news. . . .

How could Gulliver not be better after a half day of rest? Perhaps the injury was much worse than a stone bruise. The poor mule could barely walk this morning, so carrying on today wouldn't be possible for him.

Which left Damien with a decision he hated. He couldn't hold Charlotte back from returning to her village. Her family must be frantic by now. If she were his, and she'd left with only a note, he'd search the entire mountain wilderness to find her. And he'd do that long before the end of the time frame she'd given for her return.

She had to travel on today. He hated the thought of sending her alone, but leaving the mule behind in this vulnerable condition also seemed cruel. He might well be sentencing the animal to death by wolf attack or by some other predator. In this weakened state, he would be easy prey.

And Charlotte had proven capable. She could manage these last two days alone, most of it over landscape she'd already traversed once. He'd watched her fortitude and ability develop more each day. He would send her with his snowshoes and enough supplies, but not so many that she was overburdened.

Yet the thought of letting her go pressed so hard on him he

could barely breathe. Would she allow him to come after her when Gulliver recovered enough to travel? His only excuse would be to make sure she'd reached her village safely. And at the rate the mule was improving, that might be long after she needed help, if anything happened to her.

And what if something *should* happen? He couldn't live with himself if he sent her off alone to her death. Better her family worry and she be safe than for them to eventually find her frozen, lifeless body.

The image that thought conjured raised bile into his throat.

"Damien?" Charlotte sat up in her bedroll, concern wrinkling her sleepy expression. She must've seen the turmoil of his thoughts on his face.

He did his best to wipe the worry from his expression, allowing the sweetness of seeing her in these morning hours to rise above everything else. "Did you sleep well?"

Perhaps that was too intimate a question, certainly nothing a gentleman should ask a lady. But no gentleman would be camping out in the elements with a lady, either. They were in this condition out of necessity, and with this new awareness between them, he had to find the right balance between propriety and practicality.

Her face took on more color. "I did." She sat fully upright and glanced around at the dawning horizon. "I'm sorry I overslept again."

"You didn't." He turned his attention to the warm water and meat by the fire. "I made the morning meal, though you may wish I hadn't."

Her focus moved from him to the fire. "Thank you. How is Gulliver?"

It seemed she wouldn't allow him to put off this hard

conversation. Gripping the cup and plate he prepared for her, he stood and stepped around to kneel beside her. She didn't even glance at the food and kept her gaze locked on his face. Searching out the truth, no doubt.

He met her look. "He doesn't seem any better. The limp appears as bad as it was yesterday." The worry that had lined her face so often yesterday now crowded back in, but it seemed to edge more toward pain and desperation this time.

She glanced toward where he'd staked Gulliver, though the morning light wasn't strong enough to see the mule from here.

For a long moment, she rolled her lips into a tight line. Probably thinking through her options. His gaze snagged on those lips, his body longing to soften them with his own. Pulling his focus away from that line of thought proved more work than it should have, but he finally succeeded just as she turned back to him.

"I need to go on this morning." Her eyes searched his, maybe seeking out whether he would argue the point.

Yet he *couldn't* argue. He understood too well. He did have concerns, but maybe they could work through some of them together.

He reached out for her, more an instinct than something planned. Her hand slipped into his, fitting there perfectly. The contact helped hone his focus. "You do need to keep going. I've been trying to think of a way I could go with you, but I can't leave Gulliver. Not injured like this and without feed."

She shook her head as he spoke, confirming that abandoning the mule was not an option for her, either.

He tightened his grip on her hand. "I'm having trouble

swallowing the thought of sending you off alone. It should only be one day to the lake, and the landmarks aren't hard to find. But you never know . . ."

She was rolling her lips again, uncertainty clouding her eyes. He'd assumed she wouldn't even blink at the thought of traveling on by herself. After all, she'd done it twice before. Maybe she finally realized how dangerous it was for a person alone in the snowy mountains. If she wasn't keen on the idea, maybe they should rethink the plan.

Then her expression turned resolved. Or maybe not *resolved* so much as earnest. "Damien." Uncertainty tinged her tone. "I can travel the rest of the way on my own. But . . . there's another reason I want you to come to Laurent."

His heart leapt, even as he commanded it to keep from jumping to conclusions. Her reason likely had nothing to do with wanting to introduce him to her family. Wanting to continue any sort of friendship—or more—after this journey ended. Would she finally tell him about the engraving project?

She nibbled the edge of her bottom lip. "Well, several reasons, actually, but there's one I need to tell you about now."

His belly clenched. It didn't look like this was a good reason. Or maybe she thought *he* wouldn't like it.

He leaned in, rubbing his thumb across the backs of her fingers. Offering what encouragement he could.

"I . . . need your drawing skills."

He raised his brows, doing his best to show only curiosity, not suspicion.

"We have a special keepsake that was handed down from the man who first helped start our village. It's something all of Laurent treasures, and it's kept in a special holder in our home. I was cleaning it and accidentally dropped it into the fire the night before I left. It's made of brass, and by the time I pulled it from the flames, the image on one side had melted."

So many questions ran through his mind, not the least of which was why such a village treasure would be kept in Charlotte's family's home. Did they hold a special position among the families? He focused on a question that might be easier for her to answer now. "What image is on this keepsake?"

Sadness tugged at her features. "The Lord's Supper. It was a beautiful rendition, so detailed. I loved to take it down and study the kindness in Jesus's eyes."

His gut roiled. Surely she didn't think he could re-create such a masterpiece. The Lord's Supper? So many human faces. He could do animals without too much trouble, but people . . .

She must have seen his reaction, for she gripped his hand with both of hers now. "My father is a master with metals. He can do all kinds of elegant scrollwork and engravings. But he's not an artist. He can't capture detail and personality the way you can. I thought maybe with the two of you working together . . ."

She looked at him with so much hope, he did his best not to show the terror her suggestion planted inside him. He'd never drawn for others. Never drawn anything that mattered. And now to attempt a repair to something the entire village treasured . . .

But . . . the Lord's Supper? His pulse quickened. Was there any chance this could be the match to his . . . Definitely not.

He closed his eyes in a desperate effort to gather his thoughts. With Charlotte staring at him with such faith, he couldn't find the clarity he needed for this decision. Too much was at stake here. Possibly her life, if he sent her on alone. Possibly anything that might continue between them if he agreed to help and his efforts ruined the project.

With a deep breath in, then out, he cleared his mind. As for the trip there, he didn't like the notion, but sending Charlotte ahead seemed the only real solution. Her family needed to know she was safe, and she would likely manage the journey as well as any female.

As for the project she asked him to help with, it seemed reasonable to agree to look at it. To speak with her father and make a decision together on what might best be done. If the man had the amount of talent she gave him credit for, he likely possessed a level head and intuition about what could be done in a situation like this. And once he saw Damien's limited ability, the man might not allow him near such a special treasure. He would have to trust the man's opinion just like Charlotte did.

Of course, she also thought Damien's skill equal to the task. She might be very mistaken on both counts.

20

Preparing to leave Damien and Gulliver was one of the hardest things Charlotte had done in a long time. Even harder than slipping out of Laurent to begin this journey, for the outcome this time seemed so much less certain.

What if he changed his mind and decided not to come after her when the mule recovered? It might be far easier for him to simply carry on with his trapping than seek out her hidden village.

That thought formed a tight knot in her chest, and she could no longer deceive herself that she only hoped he'd come to repair the chalice.

This man was so much more special than any she'd ever known—than any she could imagine. His strength, his gentleness, the way he expended everything he had for others . . . and, of course, the way his smile curled through her, bringing every part of her to life.

What if she lost him forever?

But if he was the one God intended for her, wouldn't He make sure they weren't separated forever? Still, the thought of turning over control of something so important to another—even to God—caught the breath in her throat. What if God said no to Damien as the man meant for her? The possibility made it hard to breathe.

Lord, I want to trust you. I'm not sure if I can. Give me the desire to place this in your hands.

Damien had been sketching out a map in his book for her, and now he gently tore the paper out and stood. He still studied the image as he strode to her. Her pack was ready, and they'd already strapped the snowshoes on her feet—his snowshoes. Maybe she could hold them hostage until he came to Laurent. If only snowshoes contained that power.

When he stopped in front of her, his presence felt so much larger than before. Perhaps because he came nearer than he used to. Before that kiss. A barrier between them had been broken down, allowing them to test out this new closeness. Perhaps it was best she was leaving. Even *she* knew they were playing with fire to be alone in this vast wilderness.

He extended the paper to her, his eyes finally meeting hers. "It shouldn't be hard to find your way with this. The landmarks are easy to spot." As he spoke, his throat worked, and his gaze never left hers. Maybe he was having trouble focusing on the map, too.

She took the paper and managed a thank-you, then tucked it into her coat. She would have a great deal of time to study it soon, but now might be her last chance with this man who'd so quickly won her heart.

He reached out and cupped her arms, then ran his hands down to take up her fingers. He lifted both hands and joined them at his mouth as he pressed a kiss to the backs of her gloves.

She wanted more, wanted no barrier between them. But

even this small touch brought the sting of tears once more into her eyes. She'd been holding them back the entire time she prepared to set out, but her strength was waning.

Damien's own eyes glistened, though she couldn't be sure if that was truly extra moisture or her own blurry vision. But when he spoke, his voice graveled with a gentle intensity. "Please don't take risks. If you think you're in danger or lost or if anything goes wrong, come back to me."

His words brought a smile even through the pain. "*You* tell me not to take risks? You who stand your ground as a bear charges instead of running like a sane person?"

A smile curved his mouth, though it didn't conceal the sadness in his eyes. "My life isn't worth nearly as much as yours."

Her jaw dropped open. How could he possibly think that? Not only was he created by God and cared about immeasurably, but he mattered to *her*. More than she was ready to put into words.

And since she couldn't use words, she reached up and took his face in her hands, pulling him down to show her feelings in a way that wasn't so hard to define.

He seemed as hungry for the kiss as she was, cradling her in his arms and melting their mouths together with an intensity that connected them. She could feel his fear, his craving to go with her.

She responded with her own mixture of worry and the chaos of the unknown that haunted her. If only he could come *now*.

But he couldn't. And she understood why.

At last, he pulled back far enough to rest his forehead on hers. He gripped her upper arms, a touch that both kept her from moving away and steadied her. In truth, without his solid touch, her knees would've melted during that kiss.

As their breath mingled in the icy morning air, she did her best to work up the strength to break away. If she didn't set out soon, she might never leave.

She needed one more touch, and she didn't dare another kiss, so she moved in closer and rested her head on his shoulder. As he wrapped his arms around her, surrounding her with his strength and safety and solidness, the tears finally came.

When she tore herself away, she didn't look at his face. She wouldn't have made out his features anyway through the moisture blurring her vision. She simply reached for her pack, hauled it over her shoulders, and turned toward the west.

The day proved more grueling than Charlotte expected. She'd been riding Gulliver much of the time during the past few days on the trail, so she'd forgotten how hard it was to walk through the snow. For hour upon hour.

Without Damien's map, she might never have reached the lake, and even with the clear landmarks he'd drawn, it was still well after dark before she glimpsed the familiar snow-covered waters. She could've camped before that spot, but being there made her feel more protected. She certainly didn't plan to climb down to the cave without his rope to secure her, but this place held so many memories. Its arms wrapped around her a little like home, or at least like a comfortable blanket.

Without too much effort, she found the protected area where Damien had tied the mule the last time they'd been here. This would do for shelter.

As she gathered wood for the fire and enough branches to place around her for better protection from the wind, her mind drifted to Damien as it had all day. She never would have known how to set up a suitable camp without him, especially with the ground covered in so much snow. That first night, she might have frozen to death if not for the way he insisted she come into the cave.

Looking back through their time together, he'd been so protective, so gallant, saving her even when she refused to be saved—or didn't know she needed help.

What was he doing now? Nestled beside the campfire, no doubt. Would he pull out his sketchbook and draw? Maybe since he'd begun to take up his pencil again, he might turn to that pastime once more. Would he draw another animal? Or maybe a person. Her heart skittered at the thought that he might create her likeness. But she pushed away the selfish idea.

Perhaps he'd attempt the Lord's Supper, although it seemed like a futile effort until he saw the damaged chalice. Then he would know the entire scene and could practice the details he needed to fill in.

When she'd eaten and occupied her time with everything she could think of, she curled up in her bedroll. Despite her exhaustion, sleep was long in coming.

She woke before dawn, and by the time the sun lit the snow enough for her to see the path, she'd already set out.

Damien's map ended at the lake, so she had to rely on her memories from that first day to guide her. Before she'd met this man. Another lifetime.

She reached the base of the first mountain, the tallest one she'd climbed that day. The snow had begun partway up the other side, and she foolishly thought it would end once she descended from the heights.

No snow fell this time, though the trek upward stole her breath. She had to stop more than once to find enough air and rest her weary body.

At last, she reached the peak and dropped to her knees for another much-needed break. Her pulse stuttered in her ears, and every breath burned. Her lungs couldn't drag in enough air to satisfy her aching chest. She let herself slump against a rock for long minutes, eyes closed as her mind wandered to Damien once more.

Was he still encamped in that same place, nursing Gulliver's injured hoof? Or had the mule recovered some in the day and a half since she'd seen them? Maybe they'd started out and would reach Laurent only a day or two behind her.

Lord, let that be the case. Let all be well with them.

The thought of trouble sent her mind conjuring every possible scenario. What if wolves found the mule while Damien was away from camp hunting or gathering wood? As he'd said, Gulliver was weak and an easy target in his current condition. Or a mountain lion might sniff out the two of them. She couldn't think of any other animal large enough to be a danger to the mule. As long as the bears were all hibernating.

She opened her eyes and lifted her head from the stone. She'd caught her breath enough now, so she should be ready for the downhill slope.

But as she peered over the crest, her gaze scanning to find the route she should take, a dark figure appeared on the lower part of the slope. She squinted to make out its shape. The sun hid behind the clouds, so the snow wasn't as blinding as it could have been. But the vast canvas of white often played tricks on her eyes.

That was definitely a person. Or no . . . Maybe two people. A person and an animal? Nay, two people, she was almost certain now.

They might be a search party from Laurent. Should she hurry down the mountain to meet them? The sooner she could put their worry to rest, the better.

But they might also be strangers. After all, she'd first met Damien not far from this place. She could no longer be so naïve as to think she wouldn't meet another person.

And this time, strangers might not be so respectful as Damien. They might be the rougher sort he'd feared she would meet at the fort.

She waited there, kneeling behind the sharp stone that marked the peak of the mountain. At least this would allow her a longer rest as she waited for the strangers to come near enough to make out their features.

Their climb took longer than she anticipated. Though she couldn't make out faces yet, she could determine they were white men, not any of the Dinee natives. One seemed older, for he used a walking staff and hunched more than the other. *He* wouldn't be a danger to her.

But that other fellow . . . She didn't dare make her presence known until she was certain he didn't intend harm.

More time passed, an hour maybe. Or perhaps it only felt that long. At times she rested, but her mind sank too easily into thoughts of Damien. What he might be doing. What he might want for a future between them. What it would be like to introduce him to her father. The rest of her family. The entire village.

When that line of thought churned worry inside her, she peered over the rock at the coming men. They'd reached halfway up the mountain, and she could more plainly see the facts she'd already deduced. Two men. Pale skin, though plenty tanned from the sun. One older. The other could be anywhere in his twenties or thirties from the way he moved. There was nothing unusual about him—at least, that she could tell from here.

The aged fellow . . . Something in his bearing seemed familiar. Or maybe it was simply the rounded shoulders that often developed more when a person grew older.

But the longer she studied him, the more it felt as though she knew this man well. Then he pointed at something on the mountainside, and that gesture, the lift of his face, she knew beyond a doubt.

Papa.

21

Springing to her feet, Charlotte may have squealed as she threw on her pack and scampered over the sharp rocks. Down the other slope, she slid and skidded, glancing up every so often to make sure she was staying on course toward the men.

Her father had found her. He'd come searching, which meant he'd discovered her duplicity. She had much to explain and apologize for. But seeing him here and healthy . . . Too much pleasure bounded inside her not to run to him.

Papa's voice sounded through the crisp mountain air, but she didn't slow to decipher the words. When she closed half the distance between them, she glanced up once more. She could see the other man better now.

Hugo Lemaire.

Her chest pinched. She couldn't worry about him now, wouldn't let it distract from the meeting with her father.

When she finally reached them, Papa straightened, arms out, and she stepped into his embrace. He clutched her tight, those strong arms that had wrapped around her so many times from her earliest days. They didn't seem as stout as in her memories. A fresh spear of guilt stabbed her.

"I'm sorry, Papa." She pulled back, but her father only allowed her to go far enough that he could grip her upper arms. Moisture glimmered in his eyes, and she couldn't remember the last time she'd seen that. When Mama was killed, certainly. But maybe not since those dark days of mourning.

"My Charlotte." His voice wavered a little, and his gaze searched her face, then slipped down the length of her, as though checking for injury.

"I'm all right, Papa. And I'm sorry. Have you been searching long?" She slid a glance toward Hugo, who stood back, allowing them a private moment. She offered what she hoped would pass as a smile of greeting, then turned her focus back to her father.

"Brielle went after you the day you left." His eyes took on a bit of reproof, and she fought the urge to duck her head under the weight of his disappointment that she'd worked so hard all her life to avoid. "When she caught up with the Dinee party and learned you weren't with them, we found your tracks coming this way. We lost them at the base of this mountain, though." Then his gaze turned sad, a soul-deep disappointment that made tears burn her eyes. "Why did you lie? What did you need to do so badly that you couldn't have told me?"

She swallowed the knot in her throat so she could speak. "I'm sorry. I had to get to the fort, and I knew you'd worry if I told you where I was going. I meant only to protect you." Yet she'd done the very opposite. And the new lines carving his face showed just how much he'd suffered during her absence.

She gripped his arms more securely. "I'll tell you every-

216

thing when we get back home. Just know I'm so sorry I worried you. Are others out searching?"

Papa nodded. "Your Uncle Carter and Levi took a route farther south. Brielle and Evan are to the north."

Her insides tightened. Three groups looking for her. The people she cared most about—well, them and Hugo.

She turned to that man. "Is there a way to let them know you found me?"

His face took on a troubled expression. "We set up a whistle to alert one another. They might be too far away, but I'll try it."

He loosed a piercing whistle, one nearly as familiar as her father's form had been. The signal that someone approached the gates of Laurent in peace—the indication that all was well.

The meaning of the sound raised a sting in her throat. She needed this reminder of her people, of home. That she was still a part of the whole.

They all stood motionless, listening for the response that the guards always gave, signaling they heard and understood. After a few heartbeats, that sound drifted up from the south.

Her mouth curled into a smile. Uncle Carter had a lusty whistle, one full of body and vigor.

No answer came from the north, though, so Hugo cupped his hands around his mouth and faced that direction as he sounded the call again.

Twice more he whistled, and she was preparing to set out in that direction when the return signal finally sounded.

She pressed a thankful hand to her chest. "They'll come this way, then?"

Papa nodded. "We agreed the whistle would be a call, so they should come find us. Let's find a place to sit, then you have time to tell us exactly what you've been up to."

❧

At last, Gulliver seemed to be healing. A full day had passed since Charlotte set out—a full day Damien had worried and paced and done everything he could think of to keep himself busy instead of setting off after her.

When he'd checked the mule last night, the animal seemed to be walking a little better. He tried not to let himself hope too much.

But now, the lessening of the limp was clear. Each step no longer looked like torture. Would it be acceptable to start out with him healed this much? Or would walking at this point simply make the mule worse again right away?

As much as he wanted to leave, though, he couldn't risk another setback. He'd promised Charlotte he would come as soon as Gulliver could travel, and that's what he would do. Perhaps giving her a bit of time to explain his presence to her people would be better for them all.

That familiar pressure tightened his chest. Would her family be angry with him for keeping her away? He'd actually been doing the opposite, trying to return her. But would they understand that, or would they simply see a man who traveled with Charlotte alone for a week? Their Charlotte.

Yet in his mind, she'd become *his* Charlotte, too.

He fed the mule an extra ration at noon, then tested his stride again to see if he could spot more improvement.

Yes. Gulliver's gait was stiff, but nothing like the excruciating limp from yesterday. He patted the animal's neck. "Good boy. Well done. Think we're ready to catch up to Charlotte?"

The mule nudged his arm in the same way he did with Charlotte, almost like a hug.

"Fine, then. Let's pack up and set off."

He disassembled camp faster than he'd ever done, strapping only the saddle onto Gulliver. The packs he would carry himself, even the impossibly heavy bear skin. If it came down to it, he could shed the furs, maybe tuck them in a tree where he could come back and retrieve them later. The six dollars he could get in trade for that grizzly hide seemed like pittance compared to reaching Charlotte.

They moved far slower than Damien would've liked, both because of Gulliver's stilted gait and his own weakness under the load of the packs and furs. If he were the only one slowing them down, he would've pushed harder or unloaded some weight. But he couldn't risk Gulliver worsening.

At this rate, there was no way they would come near the lake until several hours after dark. If Gulliver could manage it, they would reach the water before resting a few hours.

Then they could push farther. He wouldn't stop until they found Charlotte.

"I need to go back and make sure they're all right." Charlotte studied her father as she waited for his answer. They'd stepped away from the rest of the group—Brielle, Evan, Levi, and Uncle Carter. And Hugo.

She'd planned to accompany them all home, but as she relayed her tale to her father, a worry had slipped in, settling deep. Perhaps this was simply her longing not to lose Damien, but the feeling seemed like more. When she thought of walking toward the village, away from where she left him, panic welled inside her that couldn't be from simple longing.

Something was wrong. Maybe with Gulliver. Perhaps with Damien. She couldn't turn away and leave them behind.

Her father didn't look certain, though. "We don't even know this man, Charlotte. Besides, if he's as capable as you say, he'll have no problem finding Laurent after his animal is recovered." His eyes held a bit of reproof when he spoke of Damien finding Laurent. As though she shouldn't have given directions to an outsider.

Regarding anyone else, she would agree with him. More and more, though, she was having trouble thinking of Damien as an outsider. He certainly didn't possess that title in her own life. And *she* was part of Laurent.

Even more, she wanted him to see that part of her. To meet her family, experience the village that had formed her life.

But before that could happen, she had to make sure he arrived, and an inner warning told her he needed help. She simply had to convince her father.

She pressed a hand to her chest. "Something's wrong. I feel it here, and I can't ignore it. I'm going back to find him and do what I can to help. I know the way to Laurent. I'll be home as soon as we can get there."

Papa studied her with eyes that seemed older than his years. The last thing she wanted was to put this worry on him. She was his youngest daughter, and he was accustomed to protecting her, even if she didn't need as much oversight now.

She softened her voice. "I'll see if Brielle and Evan will

go with me. The rest of you can return home and rest." The search had clearly worn him out, giving him a haggard look that hadn't been there before.

But her father straightened. "I'll come with you. Brielle and Evan, too, if they want to accompany us. The others can go back to tell everyone you're safe." His look turned pointed. "Andre is nearly beside himself. Especially when I wouldn't let him come along this time."

Her heart clutched at the thought of her baby brother worrying. She'd been both sister and mother to him since Mama died when he was too young to remember. She should have thought what her sudden leaving would do to Andre.

She could remedy that later. For now, there was no time to lose. She looked past her father to the rest of the group. "Do you want to tell them or should I?"

⚜

Damien shouldn't have pushed Gulliver so far.

They'd trudged hours into the night—he lost track of how much time. But he was determined to reach the lake before stopping. That last half hour turned out to be the mule's un-doing. There was nothing very different in the terrain, except that it grew hillier as they skirted the base of a mountain.

Yet by the time they reached the creek that fed into the lake, the mule's limp had grown decidedly stronger.

"Just a little farther, fella." He patted his faithful companion's neck. "At least it's not as cold as it has been." After dark fell, a warm wind had begun to blow. A blessed relief, though he'd been sweating under his load for a while now.

At last, they reached the hollow where he'd staked Gulliver

the last time they came through here. He dropped his pack with a thud and sank down to sit on it. "We made it." He could hobble Gulliver here again, then climb down to the cave. He wanted to see it once more, sure, but a bigger part of him wanted to relive those memories of his early days with Charlotte. She'd been such a slight, skittish thing, making him want to do everything in his power to ease her fears and protect her.

That last part hadn't changed, but in only a few days she'd gone from timid to seasoned. Charlotte Durand truly was remarkable.

After unsaddling and feeding the mule, then securing him for the night, he gave the animal a final pat and turned to his own bundle. Trying to climb down the cliff wall to the cave with this massive load rising high above his head would throw off his balance. Better to leave the furs in the crook of a tree.

Once he'd secured them, he turned his exhausted self toward the lake. The moonlight shone across the expanse of snow that had layered over the ice. At least the tall bank around three sides of the lake would make it clear to new-comers that ice and water lay underneath the layers of pris-tine white.

When he dropped to his knees and peered over the cliff, he spotted the hand and footholds he'd used before. A layer of snow covered them, but that would be easy enough to brush off.

He lowered to his belly and swung his legs down the cliff, searching for those perches that had been so familiar only a week ago.

There. His left foot found a slot, then his right. The holds were still icy, though he'd expected them to have melted with this warm wind. He managed to kick off the slippery covering.

One by one, he maneuvered down from grip to grip. Almost to the cave. He reached with his right foot to knock the snow off the crevice he needed to place his toe in, but his boot slipped on the icy stone.

He gripped hard to keep from falling, even as his body swung right with the momentum of his slide. He struggled to stretch far enough for his foot to land on the cave floor. He could manage it, just barely.

But the stretch shoved his other foot out of its hold, his boot slipping along the icy stone wall. His body nearly rent in two, and a cry slipped out as pain coursed through him. He pushed against the rock, doing his best to swing over into the cave opening. But his fingers were losing their grip.

He couldn't stop the fall, but at least the snow below would give a gentle landing on the ice. He released the cliff completely and pushed away so he wasn't scraped on his way down. He did his best to brace for the landing.

The drop into the snow wrapped frozen fluff around him, then his hip hit hard against the ice. A soft whoosh sounded again as the solid shelf beneath him gave way.

Confusion swam in his foggy, exhausted mind. Then a single detail registered with aching clarity.

Water.

And cold.

Frigid cold that burned everywhere it touched.

22

Damien's mind still tried to make sense of what was happening. How could there be water on top of the ice?

As his body dropped farther, reality finally became clear. The ice had cracked under his weight, and the lake water now surged up to his shoulders. He scrambled for the solid edge of the ice.

He had to get out of here. If he stayed in this water long . . .

Liquid had seeped into his clothing and coat, pulling him down. He fought hard against the weight, finally gripping something strong enough to hold him up. The ice felt thick within his grip, but he knew well enough it could break off if he pulled his full weight on it.

He had to work up onto the ice slowly, then roll away from this broken area. But what if other sections had weakened, too? His body could barely hang on as it was; if he fell again, he may not have the strength to climb back out.

He raised an arm over the ice, stretching as far as he could to spread his weight. The water pulled him down too much. He wouldn't be able to lift himself up, not with as numb as parts of him had gone.

Something tugged him backward. His coat. Maybe removing the fur would help lighten him enough to climb out of the water.

Even allowing the wet pelt to slide off his body took almost all his energy, as he had to switch the arm gripping the ice. Thank God the edge hadn't broken any farther yet.

Thank God. It had been so long since he'd ascribed anything good to the Almighty. But if He was up there and cared at all, Damien needed Him now.

He worked a foot up onto a different section of ice. The frozen surface cracked under his weight, dropping his lower body back into the water.

God, please. Help me get out of here. Alive, *if you can manage it.*

What if he never saw Charlotte again? Would she think he'd chosen not to come? Chosen not to help her?

The thought gave him the strength he needed to try once more, bracing his foot in a different area. The ice seemed stronger there, and by stiffening his body, he managed to lift up out of the water.

He did his best to use the momentum to roll away from the edge. A mound of snow stopped him, and he had to climb up over it. No matter what, he had to find solid ice.

Or rather, had to get off the ice completely.

His body had turned so numb he wasn't entirely sure his arms and legs did what he commanded. Racking shivers shook him, making his movements even harder to control. But he would get to shore.

He had to get to shore.

As he looked up to find the shortest way to the bank, darkness shrouded every direction. Even the snow seemed nearly black. He blinked, trying to clear the haze from his vision. The snow should glow in the moonlight. Yet he could make out no looming shadows that might be the edge of the lake.

God, please. Help!

Why should the Almighty help him now, after Damien had so resolutely turned his back on Him?

I'm sorry for that. For blaming you for Michelle's death. I understand if you'd rather let me die out here. But if you'd help me make it alive, to Charlotte . . .

His mind couldn't find words after that. He'd never been one to bargain with God, had always felt the Lord deserved more respect than that. But if he could only make it out of this alive, he'd like to open communication between them again. Real conversation—not this desperate plea to save a dying man.

He squeezed his eyes shut, then summoned more strength and lifted his head, peering at the landscape around him. The snow seemed whiter now, though there must not be enough moonlight to shimmer off it. He still couldn't find a dark mound that would signal a bank, but he had to start crawling. If he lay here much longer, the cold from the icy water would consume him.

His knees buckled more than once as he crawled. Convulsions shook his entire body, but he focused on the darkness ahead. There must be land there somewhere.

Get me there, God. Get me there.

He crawled for hours—or at least it felt that way. Squeezing his eyes shut was the only way he could keep going. He would know when he reached land, he simply had to force himself onward.

At last, the surface beneath his hands changed. Not the icy crunch of snow, but the tangle of vines.

He forced his eyes open, but the way his head rattled from the shivers, he couldn't focus on what he was seeing. This must be land, though. It had to be land. The last of his strength gave out, and he rolled onto his side.

As the darkness closed around him, the only sound he heard was the howl of a wolf.

❦

Why did Charlotte's heart race the nearer they drew to the lake? It wasn't because she feared introducing her family to Damien. If they took any effort to get to know him, they would quickly see past the solemn façade to the caring man beneath.

It would be another day before they reached the place where she'd left Damien and Gulliver, anyway. She'd insisted they push on to the lake, though night had fallen many hours ago. The nook where she'd spent the night before was by far the best shelter around.

An eerie howl rose into the darkness, raising gooseflesh on her arms and sending her pulse skittering a little faster. They'd been hearing the wolf calls since dusk, but this was definitely nearer. Maybe the noise echoed more off the snow, but it sounded like the creatures were just on the lake ahead. If darkness didn't shroud everything in shadows, she should be able to see the snow-covered ice in the distance.

"They're coming closer." Brielle kept her voice quiet beside Charlotte, but the words confirmed what she feared.

Charlotte pushed harder, lengthening her stride despite the weight of the snowshoes. Brielle matched her pace, and neither of them glanced back to see if Papa and Evan kept up. Wolf howls usually meant the pack was hungry, searching for food. What if they'd already spotted their prey?

It was unlikely Damien and Gulliver would have reached this place yet. But if they had . . .

At last, the flat surface of the lake appeared ahead. As she kept moving, she scanned what parts of the bank she could see. She must be near the area where she'd first seen Damien. She'd been at the end of her strength that day, frozen and exhausted. He'd appeared seemingly from nowhere, giving her enough fear to resurrect a bit of energy. Now, she couldn't be more thankful he'd found her.

She refocused her attention on the terrain ahead—and covering it as quickly as possible. A sound drifted from the distance. Something like a snarl, but maybe her imagination had distorted the noise.

Still, she charged forward. What if the wolf pack had found that scrawny coyote Damien made friends with? Seeing the animal's trust of him had been one of her first inklings of his true heart.

Lord, don't let that innocent coyote be the victim this night.

They maneuvered a quarter of the way around the lake, which meant in another quarter, they would reach the cave and the area where she planned to make camp. The sounds seemed to be coming from that direction, too.

"Charlotte."

She nearly jumped at Brielle's hissed word. Though she turned to see what her sister wanted, she didn't slow her pace. At least, not until she realized Brielle had stepped off the path. She was peering at something on the lake, though the underbrush must make it hard to see.

"What is it? I think the wolves might have something pinned up there." She sent a glance forward as another snarl sounded, this one too guttural and ferocious to be mistaken.

But when she took a step toward the animal noises, Brielle's words gave her pause again. "Something's here."

Charlotte's heart stuttered. "An animal?" Maybe the wolves had already attacked the coyote, then moved on to new prey. But there must be hundreds of animals living in this area. Chances of this being Damien's little friend were unlikely.

"A person." Brielle plunged through the brush, and her words made Charlotte's breath stall.

A person? Who would be out here? Had this become someone's frozen grave? The men caught up to them as Charlotte crowded behind her sister. Brielle dropped to her knees beside a figure covered in snow, with only a few dark patches of fur showing at each end.

"I think he's still alive." Brielle pressed a hand to one of those dark patches.

Charlotte sucked in a breath as she moved to a place where she could kneel beside her sister. Only then did she get a clear view of the strip of face peering through snow and fur.

Damien.

A cry slipped out as she reached for him. How could he be here? Like this?

She slid her fingers across his brow—cold, but not so much that death had already taken over. *Lord, don't let him . . .*

She scraped the snow from his short beard, her movements turning frantic as she struggled to get the icy powder off him. Brielle did the same for his shoulders, and when she finished his face, Charlotte reached toward an arm that poked up from the snow. As she scrubbed the snow off, she struggled to imagine why he would be out here at the edge of the lake, nearly dead. *Lord, don't let him be past recovery.*

It didn't look as though fresh snow had fallen over his body—more like he'd rolled in the powder. But the ice crystals hanging from every part of him . . . Why would they have gathered, especially with this warm wind? And where was his coat?

Evan had moved to Damien's feet and was working to clear the snow there, while Brielle kept scrubbing at his shirt. Charlotte refocused her attention on Damien's face, turning his head so she could place her hands on both cheeks. "Wake up, my love. Wake up."

His skin felt so cold. Was he really still alive, or did the heat take time to leave his lifeless body? The thought welled panic inside her, and she tapped his cheeks. "Wake up, Damien. You have to wake up."

His mouth parted. Was that because she'd jarred his head, or had he moved consciously?

She leaned closer. "Damien, please. Wake up. We're going to get you warm."

The others buzzed around her, adjusting his tunic and adding layers on top of him. But she couldn't pull her focus from his face.

She had to get him warm. Had to wake him up.

Somewhere in the distance, awful sounds rose. Barking, growling, the ferocious howls of a canine battle . . . then the terrified bray of a mule.

Charlotte jerked her head up, a new panic rising inside her. "Gulliver. The mule." With Damien here somehow, Gulliver must be nearby. If only she'd found them sooner.

Before the wolves.

Brielle leapt to her feet and sprinted toward the sounds. But Charlotte couldn't move. She couldn't leave Damien, not until he awoke and they got him warm.

Evan ran in his wife's footsteps, easing the knot of fear in Charlotte's belly a tiny bit. The two of them could handle the wolves. *Please, Lord.*

Her father moved in beside her. "Let's get him warm, daughter. These wet things have to come off first. Looks like he's had a drenching."

She turned her full attention back to Damien and focused on working the buttons of his tunic. Papa was prying off the boots and could handle the rest of what was needed in that area.

Had Damien gotten completely wet? How? There had been no rain, and this short stretch of warmth hadn't melted the ice covering the lake so quickly.

But when she pulled his tunic back, the shirt underneath was soaked. The buckskin would've protected him from rain, so he must have been submerged in the lake. At least the warm air had kept the undershirt from freezing into a crisp layer of ice. But how long had he been lying here, drenched and coated in snow?

She worked his arms out of the buckskin, then reached for one of the layers they'd piled on top of him before she pried off his shirt. She would need to slip this dry garment on him the moment she had the wet off.

Perhaps it was unseemly for her to remove his shirt, but they had no time for propriety. Getting Damien warm was the only way they could save his life.

As she tugged the soaked shirt over his head, a moan

slipped from him. *Thank you, Lord.* Maybe there was hope yet.

Through the commotion in the distance, a few shouts rose. Brielle would know better than anyone how to quell the wolf attack, and with Evan at her side, Gulliver had the best chance of survival. She'd never been so grateful to have her family nearby as in this moment.

When she managed to wrap the coat around Damien and button it across his front, her father motioned her away. "See if you can build a fire while I strip the rest of his wet things off."

Though she hated to leave Damien's side, her father spoke wisdom. A fire would be the next step to warm him, first on the outside, then with a warm drink for his insides.

She stood and turned away, working to unscramble her thoughts and focus on how to start a flame. They had no dry wood—her family hadn't tucked any in their packs. There might be some in the cave. Did she dare attempt to climb down without Damien's rope securing her against a fall?

He would have dry wood in the pack on Gulliver's saddle. That might be the easiest way right now. And though the thought of seeing the mule battered and bloodied made bile rise in her throat, she needed to know how Gulliver fared.

23

With her back to Damien and her father, Charlotte bent down and untied the laces from her snowshoes. They'd helped with travel over long distances, but just now, the encumbrance would only slow her down—and she needed all the speed she could manage.

Running in Brielle's tracks, she found her way to the attack site far sooner than she was ready to arrive. The wolves had attacked in the gulley where she'd slept only the night before. Blood littered the snow, and even in the dim light of the night, she could make out three carcasses—all wolves, as best she could tell.

Brielle and Evan knelt over another form, its larger shape and brown hair proclaiming what she already knew.

Gulliver.

The mule lay on his side, and with the two people leaning over him, she couldn't tell if he lived or not.

She took a step toward them but couldn't bring herself to take a second stride. "How is he?"

Brielle jerked her head around, took in Charlotte, then refocused on the mule. "He has several gashes, but if we can get them to stop bleeding, I think he'll recover well."

Recover. The word seemed impossibly sweet. And not at all likely.

But it gave her courage to step forward and kneel down at the mule's head. She stroked his jaw, and he snuffled a greeting. When she moved her hand down to his muzzle, he nudged her as he always did.

Sweet friend.

Brielle was working on his chest, packing snow that quickly turned dark when she placed it on the animal's hide. "They went for his neck and hindquarters like they usually do. Got a few good licks on his chest before we arrived. This one is the only one I can't get to stop bleeding."

"Shall I try?" Tending wounds was more often her responsibility than Brielle's, at least when Audrey wasn't around. She usually had the benefit of many herbs and bandages, but she could apply ice and pressure as well as her sister.

But Brielle didn't move aside. "How is the man?"

The reminder jolted her. "Papa's changing him out of his wet clothing. He must have fallen through the ice in the lake. I came to find dry firewood and his pack."

Brielle glanced up at her, the gentleness in her eyes matching her voice. "Go build the fire and tend him. I'll take care of things here."

Whether from the words or the reminder that she had help now, Charlotte's spirit eased. She inhaled a deep breath to steady herself, then released it. "Call if you need anything." She glanced between Brielle and Evan, sending her quiet thanks to them both.

Evan stood as she did. "I'll be more help with the wood and the fire than I am here."

She turned to scan the area for Damien's packs, doing

her best to avoid glimpsing the wolf carcasses. The saddle lay a short distance away, but the bundles had already been removed. Had Damien planned to sleep in the cave? Possibly. The climb down the cliff never seemed to bother him.

She strode that direction, sweeping her gaze across the path in case she found his things along the way. There, on the ground above the cliff wall, lay the thick roll of furs. Another pack perched beside it, the one that would contain firewood. Damien must have left them both here on purpose, maybe while he scouted the cave.

She took up the smaller satchel. "All of these might be helpful." Some of the furs hadn't been scraped yet, but they would do for warmth.

By the time they reached her father and Damien, Papa had him bundled in all the dry furs and clothing at hand, including Papa's own coat, which was what she'd fastened around Damien's upper body.

Her father motioned her toward Damien's still form. "Come sit with him while I help Evan set up camp."

She dropped to her knees by Damien's head.

Her father groaned as he pushed up to his feet. "He's made a few noises, but I haven't seen him open his eyes yet. Maybe rub his arms to get the blood flowing."

She could certainly do that, but first she cupped her hands to his face, then leaned close so her words carried only to him. "Can you wake up now, my love? I need you to wake up." His skin felt a little warmer beneath her touch. She prayed he would come back to awareness soon.

She moved her hands down to rub his arms as her father suggested, scrubbing vigorously over the furs that covered him. After working in that spot for several minutes, she moved down to his legs and feet. Would he lose fingers and toes from being frozen? Or even hands or feet? She couldn't let herself contemplate anything worse than that.

As she rubbed his legs, his limbs began to tremble. Was that a good sign? Maybe his body was working to return to a normal temperature.

She shifted back up to his shoulders and rubbed his upper arms as she studied his face. Still so pale, but his lips had now turned a bright red. A shiver slipped through her own body. If only he would wake up so she would know for sure he was recovering and not taking a turn for the worse.

Her father and Evan approached, Evan moving to Damien's head. "Let's get him to the fire now."

She stood and backed away as they carried him toward the orange flames flickering a few strides away. Damien's head rolled to the side as his body hung between them. The sight made him look too much like a corpse.

Lord, please bring him back. Please don't let me lose him. Having him come to Laurent for his art skills no longer carried any weight in her mind. She couldn't lose him—this man who'd come to mean so much to her in such a short time.

Once they'd positioned Damien's body as near the fire as they dared, Evan left to check on Brielle and the mule. Papa motioned toward Damien. "Find a place beside him and keep rubbing his limbs. I'll get water heating."

She should be the one attending the fire and heating water, but maybe her father knew she wouldn't want to stray far from Damien's side.

As she continued rubbing warmth back into his body, her mind recalled the time she'd fallen through the ice of the river they crossed. When she'd awakened from her frozen stupor, she'd been tucked into the crook of Damien's arm. No place could have been warmer.

She couldn't do the same for him, though. His larger bulk would be impossible for her to sit upright, even with her father's help.

This was the best she could manage. This, and prayer.

❧❧❧

Every part of Damien ached. The parts he could feel, at least.

His lower legs didn't seem connected to his body any longer. When he tried to move them, he couldn't tell if anything shifted.

Someone else was hovering over him, rubbing his arms enough to make them burn. He couldn't quite remember what had happened, but surely the hands scrubbing his arms were trying to help. He didn't have the energy to make them stop anyway.

He told his eyes to open, but they only obeyed in small slits. Even then, the world looked mostly dark. Shadowy forms moved around him, and he worked to decipher the outlines. The one nearest, the one scrubbing his arms, seemed familiar. He forced his eyes open farther, letting in more light.

Charlotte.

Her outline was unmistakable, but he couldn't make out the features of her face. Still, her presence eased through him like warm coffee on a cold morning. Comforting. Invigorating. Returning strength to his limbs.

He tried to raise a hand, but something held him down.

"Damien?" She must've seen his movement. "Thanks be to God." Her hands shifted to his face, one palm cradling his cheek and the other stroking his brow.

He leaned in to the touch, even as his mind struggled to place where he was and why he felt so weak. He'd been crawling . . . or swimming. Either way, he'd been clawing through the thickness that restrained him.

"What happened, Damien?" Charlotte spoke again.

As he opened his mouth to respond, a flash of memory lit his mind. "I fell, and the ice broke through." His voice rasped like he'd lived a hundred years, and a shiver slipped through him.

"Here's warm water to drink. It will help." A male voice spoke the words, and he struggled to determine if he knew the tone. The man was older, but with the firelight behind him, Damien could only make out a profile.

Charlotte took the cup and slipped a hand behind Damien's head. As she touched the metal to his mouth, she spoke. "This is my father, Henri Durand."

Damien's gaze shot to the man again, though he couldn't stop sipping lest he choke as Charlotte steadily poured the liquid in his mouth. He still couldn't see the fellow well, but his eyes were adjusting to the shadows shrouding his face. This was not the way he'd planned to make a good impression.

When Charlotte finally pulled the cup away, Damien cleared his throat and worked for a clearer voice. "It's a pleasure to meet you, sir."

The man's head dipped in a nod. "Glad you're warming up. See if you can drink the rest of that. I have more heating."

Damien obeyed as Charlotte raised the cup to his mouth again. What he wanted more than this hot water was to sit up. If they'd unwrap these furs binding him, he should be able to handle the cup himself.

At last, she pulled the drink away and helped him free his hands. "You should keep these furs over you, though."

"I will. Just let me sit up." Though the night air was warm, when its fingers slipped through his protective coverings, his skin prickled.

After struggling through the effort to sit up, he could finally make his hands and fingers work the way he told them to. His feet still wouldn't comply, and he reached down to massage the muscles below his knees, beginning with his left leg.

Monsieur Durand shifted to Damien's feet and began rubbing the right. The last thing Damien wanted was this man thinking him weak and in need of . . . well, coddling. But he might consider it rude if Damien told him to stop such an act of kindness. So he took the opportunity with the firelight brushing Durand's side to sneak a glance at him.

The fellow wore the lines of age, maybe thirty years or more older than Charlotte, though that might be a trick of the firelight. How had he come to be in this place with her?

"I found my father and others from our village earlier today." Charlotte's voice slipped in to answer the question he hadn't yet put words to. "A few went back, but my father, sister, and her husband came with me to find you."

Once more, his gaze jerked to her face. "Your sister is here?"

Charlotte's focus lifted into the darkness on the other side of the fire, and he turned that way, too. "She and Evan are with Gulliver."

Something in her tone clenched a knot in his chest. He studied her face, the way lines had tightened under her eyes. "Where is he? What's wrong?"

Her lips pressed together as she stared a moment longer into the darkness. Then she dropped her gaze to him. "Wolves. We heard them attack just as we found you. Brielle and Evan fought them off and have been tending Gulliver while Papa and I focused on you."

He pulled his legs beneath him and prepared to rise. He had to get to his old friend, see if anything could be done to help him. But his legs refused to obey. His knees bent on command, but the feet wouldn't straighten beneath him.

"Hold on there, lad. You're not ready to sprint off yet." Monsieur Durand laid a staying hand across Damien's calves, then pulled the legs straight again.

"Brielle is tending him, Damien. She had almost all the bleeding stopped when I checked on them. She thinks Gulliver should be fine." Charlotte's voice didn't soothe as much as it had before. Though she probably meant her words to lessen his worry, they painted a picture that accelerated his pulse.

Almost all the bleeding stopped. *Should* be fine. That meant there was still a question. Still a chance he could lose the animal who'd stayed by Damien's side despite his worst moods. Had carried him over terrain he never should have been asked to maneuver.

"I need to help him." This time, instead of relying on his feet to obey, he shifted onto his hands and knees. He'd still need his feet to bear his weight, but this way he could ease onto them.

"Stop. Damien." Charlotte gripped his shoulder, but he could easily pull away from her slight restraint. Once he got on his feet, he could make her see why he had to help the mule. She probably understood already but was simply worried about him. He would show her he could manage.

He did succeed in placing one foot flat underneath him,

but he still couldn't feel the appendage, and when he tried to put weight on that leg, the knee buckled forward. The numb parts of Damien's feet simply wouldn't do as he commanded.

"Damien." Charlotte sounded more than frustrated now.

Braced on one knee with his hands pressed to the snowy ground, he teetered on the edge of losing his balance. His body seemed determined to betray him.

She moved in front and dropped to her knees. "I'll go see how Gulliver is doing. If he's up and walking, we'll bring him to you." She took his face in her hands and lifted his gaze to hers. The earnestness there, something like love that glimmered in her eyes . . . they arrested his heart. How could he worry her, even for Gulliver?

He nodded, and Charlotte helped him ease back down to sitting. "I'll return soon."

As she disappeared into the darkness, silence settled over them. Her father still knelt in the same place he'd been as he rubbed Damien's foot. What did he think of Damien's stubbornness? Perhaps the man assumed his mind was also still numb from the cold—too numb to reason properly.

He dared a glance at Durand. Some of the shadows had cleared from his face, allowing a better view of his expression. Still, his mood was hard to read. He certainly studied Damien. With consternation? Distrust?

Damien should be the first to speak, attempt to explain why seeing the mule for himself was so important. He cleared his throat. "He's been a good friend to me, my mule. Willing, even when I asked much of him. It's only right that I care for him in return."

Durand's chin dipped. "I understand."

Yet his tone didn't sound convincing. Pacifying, perhaps? Maybe better for Damien to simply take the words at face value, or he might drive himself truly mad. He'd so wanted to make a good impression on Charlotte's father, and none of this had gone as he planned.

The older man reached for one of the furs Damien had shucked off when he tried to stand. "Let's get you bundled back up. See if you can slip your arms in this. You're broader through the shoulders than I am, but I think it will fit well enough."

For the first time, Damien took a better look at the fellow. He wore no coat, nor gloves, nor hat. Though the warm chinook wind made the night's temperature mild, the snow must chill him. He tried to slip out of the man's coat, which was around him. "I'm better now. You wear it."

Durand held up a hand to stop him. "I'm not the one who fell into a lake. If I don't do all in my power to keep you from taking ill, I'll have my daughter to face. I just found her; I don't plan to lose her again so soon."

What did he mean by that? Had Charlotte already spoken to her father about Damien and what had grown between them? Either that or her father assumed. If forced to make a choice, would Charlotte choose a life with Damien over her father?

The thought should give him hope, but in truth, he didn't *want* her to have to choose. He wanted her to be surrounded by everyone she loved—and he couldn't help the longing for that to include him. To be part of her community, to be accepted by them, maybe even be a permanent part of her life . . . The more he thought about it, the more he craved that possibility.

Was this the time to tell her father he needn't worry? He nearly opened his mouth to do so, then caught himself. With the voices drifting across the snowy darkness, it sounded like they wouldn't be alone much longer.

Charlotte's tone was easy to pick out, and the man's baritone must belong to her brother-in-law. He strained to make out any other sounds—namely, the pained grunt of a mule. Or maybe limping hoof steps, though they would be hard to hear through the snow.

But he could decipher neither, and even the voices dropped away to leave only the quiet swish of snow.

Then, from the darkness, shadows emerged. First, the broad frame of a man, then Charlotte, and the sight of her eased the tightness in his chest. Beside her appeared the unmistakable blaze and floppy ears of his faithful companion.

Gulliver limped slowly, but that could be as much from his previously injured hoof as from the wolf attack. The mule crowded close to Charlotte, as though leaning against her for comfort.

I know the feeling, friend.

Damien started to push up to his feet, but the numbness in his legs stopped him once more. Besides, he'd all but promised Charlotte he would stay put.

He didn't take his focus from the woman and mule as they approached. In his periphery, he registered another person on the other side of Gulliver, but he'd much rather look at Charlotte than her sister.

She led the mule all the way to him, and Gulliver dipped his muzzle to sniff Damien's outstretched hand. He rubbed the side of the animal's nose. "How are you, fella? Looks like you're healing faster than me." Gulliver dropped his head lower for Damien to run his palm up the mule's forehead, just like he'd done hundreds of times before.

At last, Damien shifted his focus farther back on the animal, and the gash across his chest made Damien's own belly cramp. The wolves had gone for the kill veins, but if Gulliver still lived—and lived enough to walk—they'd not succeeded.

Shadows hid the animal's hindquarters, so he couldn't tell if the damage continued farther back. He sought Charlotte's gaze as he nodded toward Gulliver's chest. "Are these the worst wounds?"

She looked over at her sister. "Brielle has done most of the tending."

The other woman stepped farther into the light, coming alongside Gulliver's head. She wore a noble, confident look. A person accustomed to taking charge. "He lost a great deal of blood, but he's a strong one. He'd already slain one of the wolves when I reached them, and he fought valiantly, despite his injuries."

Damien turned his focus back to the mule, stroking Gulliver's muzzle as he snuffled Damien's face. "You're a strong one, eh?"

As the animal blew a string of slobber on him, tugging a chuckle from Charlotte, Damien finally let himself rest in the faith that things really might turn out well for them all.

24

Charlotte itched to finish the final leg of their journey. Now that she was safely back with Damien and had her father, Brielle, and Evan around her, her spirit craved to set out on the final trek that would return them to Laurent.

Yet Damien would need at least this day to rest, and they still hadn't seen for sure whether his feet would bear his weight again. Lulled by the warm drink her father prepared and the furs they heaped over him, he'd fallen asleep not long after he'd seen for himself that Gulliver would recover.

The mule also needed this extra day of rest to heal from both the bruised hoof and the gashes caused by the wolf pack. Once Damien could walk, they'd all agreed to move slowly, most likely dividing this last stretch into two days.

Or longer, if need be.

She studied the top half of the sleeping face belonging to the man who held her heart. Even with lines around his eyes that revealed the harrowing event his body still healed from, she'd never seen a man so handsome.

Yet it was his inner strength and character that drew her even more than his attractive exterior. She could imagine herself growing old beside him, raising a home full of children together—boys with the same breadth of shoulder as their father, and girls with the same striking dark hair and eyes. With this man guiding them, raising them to be strong of character and full of kindness, could she ask for a better life? Maybe it was too soon to be picturing such a scene, but the thoughts had taken hold anyway.

But would he be accepted in Laurent? Though both Evan and Levi had been held with suspicion when they'd arrived in Laurent, each man had shown his willingness to embrace the life there. They'd also shared knowledge and connections to help their new neighbors.

Damien would do the same, she had no doubt.

Would he be happy in such a remote, quiet village? He was used to a trapper's life and was more than willing to take risks in the wilderness. Could he be content with a life lived in one location?

Or could she leave her home, her people, to be with him? Could she be happy with the life of a wanderer? A trapper's wife?

Her brow furrowed at the thought. When a trapper married, did his wife even travel with him? Or was the woman set up in a home somewhere, waiting weeks or months for her man to return? She'd much rather trek through the snow with Damien, as long as she could be by his side.

Of course, she'd be certain to make sure they thoroughly investigated every cave before they set up camp within. No more bear attacks if she could prevent them.

The furs covering Damien stirred, and his eyelids flickered open. His gaze met hers, as though he'd known she would be sitting exactly in that place, staring at him.

She smiled to cover the warmth creeping up her neck. "Bonjour."

He shifted the furs down to reveal one of those sleepy half smiles that curled her insides, heating her in a way that had nothing to do with embarrassment. "Good morning."

His focus lingered on her face for another moment, then swept around the campsite. "Where is everyone?"

She reached for the pot of tea she'd kept warming by the fire and poured him a cup. "My father went for a walk, and Brielle and Evan are exploring the cave. I told them about the paintings inside, and Brielle had to see them. I think Evan went along to make sure she didn't fall from the cliff or find some other danger."

Damien's smile deepened. "I get the feeling she's as strong-willed as you are."

She raised her brows at him. "I'm nothing like my sister. I've always been the quiet one in the family."

Damien studied her, his dark eyes piercing deeper than usual. If he thought he saw a likeness in personality between her and Brielle, he was quite mistaken. No one had even hinted that she might have Brielle's charisma and leadership abilities, that strength that attracted people to her.

Charlotte moved to his side with the cup as she scrambled for a new topic to speak of.

Damien sat up as she approached and reached out for the drink. His hands took hers, though, instead of the mug, forcing her attention to his face. He gave her that searching look once more, but this time its intensity was eased by the warmth in his gaze. "You are quiet. Your thoughtfulness is one of the things that intrigued me from the very beginning." One corner of his mouth tipped up. "One of the many things."

That one-sided roguish grin tugged a smile from her own mouth.

But his expression grew serious again, even more earnest than before. "I don't know your sister yet, but I do know you. I know how deep your strength runs. How beautiful your heart shines. How stubborn you can be when you're certain what must be done. You're tenacious, yet gentle. The perfect blend."

His words brought an ache in her chest that rose up to steam her eyes and clog her throat. No one had ever complimented her so thoroughly. Did he really mean those words?

Before she could gather her wits to answer, footsteps sounded in the snow. She glanced over to see her father approaching, a load of firewood in his arms.

Damien took the cup from her, and she pulled her hands back, though she made sure nothing was rushed in the action. She was pretty sure Papa suspected her feelings for Damien, but if not, he would realize soon enough. And the last thing she wanted was for him to think she was trying to cover up something untoward.

"How are those legs feeling?" Her father's voice sounded chipper. He looked refreshed and invigorated from his walk.

His question was one she should have already asked, but she'd been too caught up in the man and the things he'd said. It seemed too wonderful to think he truly meant them.

Damien set the mug to the side and pulled off his remaining covers. "I have more feeling in my feet, so I should be able to walk now." All pleasure had slipped from his expression, and twin lines formed between his brows as he pulled on his boots, then positioned his feet. He used his hands to place them flat on the ground. That didn't seem good.

Then he shifted onto his hands and knees. Charlotte rose to stand on one side as her father positioned himself on Damien's other. If he fell or simply needed extra balance, they would be there. But she had a feeling he'd rather do this on his own.

He managed to get his feet underneath him and rise partway with them bearing his weight—far more than he could do the night before. But halfway to standing, he began to wobble.

As he pitched forward, she grabbed for his hand. She barely gripped his arm in time to catch him, but thankfully her father managed a firmer hold. Papa slipped himself under Damien's shoulder, propping him up and helping him stand the rest of the way. She did the same on her side, but she could tell Damien rested more of his weight on her father.

For a moment, they stood in that position, then Damien eased out a long breath that seemed to come from his deepest insides.

"Can you feel your toes?" Her father's voice stayed low.

Damien hesitated before answering. "Some of them."

"You're making progress. We'll do another rubdown soon. For now, let's see if we can take a few steps. That will help bring the blood flowing."

She remained silent as her father guided Damien. His easy tone made his instructions far more palatable, no doubt. Her father had been chief of Laurent since before she was born, and he possessed a special way with people. A manner of interacting that didn't feel domineering or heavy-handed. He made you want to do as he asked simply out of respect for his good opinion.

Damien struggled through his first few steps, and she

stayed by his side, his arm wrapped around her shoulders. The touch didn't feel as much like she was supporting him as he was tucking her close. She loved the connection, but she wanted to be a help to him, not just someone he felt obligated to protect.

"That's enough for now, I think." Papa's voice broke through her rather selfish line of thought. "Let's get you back to the blankets, and I'll work on those toes more. Have you broken your fast yet?"

"I've a stew keeping warm for you," Charlotte said quickly. She should have already offered that to him. But at least it was ready.

"How is Gulliver today?" Damien seemed to be walking more steadily now, though his labored words showed his breaths came harder. He nodded toward the mule grazing near the lake's edge.

"He's enjoying the grass Evan uncovered for him. This warm chinook wind is already starting to melt snow."

"I appreciate you all taking such good care of him." Though Damien seemed to be trying to conceal his pain, when he lowered to his furs, a grunt slipped out.

Once he was finally seated, his gaze met her father's first, then shifted to hers. "I'll be ready to move on tomorrow, as long as Gulliver is well enough."

His words matched their own plan, but her father didn't speak up to agree. That probably meant he held concerns about how recovered Damien would be by then. He would wait until he had more details before making a decision. Papa always thought through every matter thoroughly.

Yet she had a feeling Damien wouldn't bide quietly if her father suggested they wait.

25

Would it always be this way?

Charlotte had been watching Damien throughout the day's trek, doing her best not to fret. Her father clearly felt they shouldn't have set out yet, that Damien needed at least one more day of rest before hiking through the snow.

But Damien had insisted.

As much as she disliked knowing the two men she loved weren't in agreement, her greater worry for Damien overwhelmed every other thought. They'd nearly reached the top of the first peak, the place she'd hid only two days before as she watched her father and Hugo climb the opposite side.

Though they'd only covered half the ground they could in a normal day's journey, Damien's every breath rasped through the air as he pushed one foot up, then the next. Her heart ached to help him, or better yet, stop and make camp here on the mountainside. To prepare a hearty meal that would give him strength, then watch his exhausted body rest deeply enough to recover.

He possessed grit and determination. He'd proven that all day, though she'd known it from the other days they traveled together. But watching those qualities push him harder and farther than was good for his body made her want to beg him to stop.

At least he had one hand propped on Gulliver's back for support. The day of rest seemed to have helped the mule a great deal, and likely the slower pace today aided, too.

Finally, they reached the peak, and she half expected Damien to drop to his knees as she had the other day—exhausted and too weary to do anything but rest until he regained some strength.

But he didn't. Man and mule stood at the pinnacle of the mountain, staring out at the vast expanse beyond. The usual wind whipped at them, still warm from the chinook, flapping the loose tendrils of his hair and drying the sweat-dampened locks.

She stood a step away and a little behind, letting herself admire the strength and intense handsomeness of the picture he formed. Yet it wasn't just attraction that made her heart yearn so. It was longing and respect and the desire to reach out and touch him. In truth, she couldn't put into words the emotions clogging inside her, other than to say she'd never known how rich and deep love could feel.

She moved alongside him. The others had lined up along the peak on the other side of Gulliver, and the view before them might well occupy a quarter hour at least.

Damien glanced over at her, and the warmth in his smile covered most of the exhaustion lining his face. He reached out and tucked his arm around her shoulders, pulling her into his side. She slipped into a place so comfortable, so natural, she let her eyes drift shut just to relish it for a moment.

When she opened them, she rested her head against his

shoulder. From this perspective, the landscape around them took on a new look, as though she saw the expanse of snowy mountains through unsullied eyes. No longer was this sight the same boulder-strewn slopes that she'd seen her entire life.

The majesty of mountain upon mountain, spreading as far as her gaze could reach . . . the glory of it all surged through her. She'd heard of places without these peaks, flat and covered with endless grass. Perhaps that landscape held its own appeal, but her heart came alive as she soaked in the world around her. God had loved her enough to plant her among grandeur only He could imagine and create.

She squeezed her eyes shut as the depth of that love filled her, stinging with its power. *Thank you, Lord.* The words were so paltry, but she meant them with everything inside her. His plan for her life, even down to the place she grew up, was far more perfect than anything she could orchestrate.

As though he felt the richness of her emotions, Damien pulled her a little closer, and she nestled deeper into his side.

Far too soon, her father's voice drifted from the other side of the mule. "That group of boulders would make a good place to camp for the night. If we tie up some furs, we'll have a nice windbreak."

The rocks her father pointed to were only thirty strides down the slope. She wouldn't have thought it wise to camp so near the peak, but he was right. They would be able to block most of the wind. A glance at the darkening sky showed they had only another hour or two before dusk settled.

Not even Damien argued to push past the place, and within an hour they were settled into a cozy camp. They'd stretched furs to cover most of the gaps between the boulders, creating a space large enough for even Gulliver to inhabit.

When the fire grew hot enough, it didn't take long for her to warm the stew she'd prepared that morning. But the group took even less time scraping the pot clean. Even the shorter trek had created hungry bellies, and she allowed herself a moment to watch the way her preparations satisfied and delighted. Perhaps *delighted* was too strong a word for a simple campfire stew, but each expression around the circle had brightened by the time they finished the meal. She would never tire of bringing pleasure to those she loved.

Evan was the first to break the lull that fell during the meal. "I'll gather more wood to carry us through the night. I saw some fallen branches around the slope there." He pointed toward the west.

"I can help carry them." Brielle gave her husband the gentle smile reserved only for him. No doubt the two craved a quiet moment alone as much as they felt the need for more firewood.

That thought no longer brought a yearning for her own love like that. No longer ached the way it had weeks ago. The man who sat beside her now satisfied the longing that had grown more with each of these last years.

Damien sat with his back against one of the boulders, and though darkness hadn't yet settled over them, his eyes had drifted nearly shut. Now that his belly was full, he needed to sleep as long as he could manage.

She rose quietly and moved to where he'd piled his packs. It didn't take long to find the furs he normally used for bedding, and she carried them over to crouch beside him.

He lifted his eyelids, but they still looked impossibly heavy. "I'm sorry. I should be helping."

Exhaustion must be clouding his mind. "There's nothing left to do. Lie down." She used a voice stern enough that he wouldn't argue, though his compliance might have more to do with exhaustion. He simply took the covers and attempted to spread them over himself. He was too weary to even accomplish that, so she made sure they were tucked around his feet so no cold could creep in.

When she was satisfied he would stay warm through the night, she turned toward the fire and the dishes waiting for her. She'd already filled the pot with snow, which had melted into wash water. As she reached to gather the plates, her father shifted across from the fire. His scrutinizing gaze showed he'd been watching her for a while. Watching her ministrations with Damien, no doubt.

Heat crept up her neck, though she had nothing to be embarrassed about. She met his gaze with as natural a smile as she could muster. "Would you like me to warm some water for tea?" Papa always enjoyed a cup before bed.

He shook his head, the intensity of his gaze softening a little. "I have all I need." His gaze lifted into the distance, and he didn't appear as though he planned to say anything else.

She turned her attention back to cleaning up from the meal. But as she worked, she sent regular glances toward her father, and it didn't surprise her that his focus settled on Damien's sleeping form. She sent her own gaze that direction, just to see what her father saw. Damien's shoulders rose and fell in steady rhythm, only his closed eyelids visible among his fur coverings. Even in sleep, she could watch him for hours.

"What are his plans after he and his animal are recovered?"

She didn't turn to her father. Not yet. Not when her eyes might give away too much of her thoughts. In truth, she didn't know exactly what Damien's plans were. She knew what she *wanted* them to be. She'd let herself hope, and even entertained the possibility that he wanted to explore what more could grow between them.

But all she really knew was that he'd agreed to help with the project she hadn't yet fully told him about. At least, she'd not shown him the chalice. She'd not enlisted her father's assistance yet either. Not even confessed and asked his forgiveness. She would do that when they were back home. When no one was around to interrupt or overhear the conversation. Even now, she could hear the voices of her sister and brother-in-law coming their way.

She turned to meet her father's gaze. "There's something I need his help with in Laurent. I'd appreciate your assistance, too. If you'd be willing."

His brows shot high. "I'm always happy to help. Will you tell what this something is?"

A shot of fear slipped through her. She would have to overcome that anxiety, and soon.

* * *

"There it is."

It took everything Damien had left to keep one foot in front of the other, but at the excitement in Charlotte's voice, he forced the effort to lift his gaze and take in the secret village of Laurent.

He squinted, trying to find the homes hidden among the smattering of mountains and low peaks around them. The people lived in caves, but he expected to see a sign of openings and the evidence of a population. Trampled snow, or perhaps some livestock. Children playing outside, even.

Perhaps they weren't close enough to the village yet. He refocused his effort on the path directly in front. Charlotte had taken over leading Gulliver, but Damien walked on the mule's other side so he could use the animal for support. His feet still burned with a searing ache, and his lungs raged with every breath, as though a fire smoldered in his chest. He'd long ago stopped trying to hide the rasp of each inhale.

They kept on for another hour, or at least it felt that long. Damien gave up watching for signs of the village, his focus honing to only the snow ahead. He leaned more heavily on Gulliver than he should, but at least the mule's limp had grown much better.

A shrill whistle sounded around him, and the murmurs of his companions hummed like a shroud of fog. He didn't have the strength to decipher the voices, much less their words.

One step. Another.

A boulder appeared ahead of him. Or perhaps that was the base of a mountain. Mayhap, a stone wall. An opening appeared beside them, and Charlotte turned Gulliver into it.

People crowded around, voices clamoring. More than he could take in.

He squeezed his eyes shut and inhaled a breath to gather the last of his strength. Then he opened his eyes and lifted his head.

Perhaps thirty strangers, or maybe more, were gathered around them. Children, women, men of all ages.

For the most part, the crowd gave them space to continue walking, though a few approached Charlotte and Monsieur Durand. A young man, perhaps fourteen or fifteen, walked between father and daughter, and Charlotte had her arm wrapped around the lad's waist.

Her brother.

With the haze lacing Damien's mind, he couldn't remember the boy's name. But from the endearing way Charlotte had spoken of him, Damien had expected him to be a bit younger. Not this lanky young man who already topped his sister in height.

A woman had been speaking to Brielle and now moved in front of Gulliver to greet Charlotte. She seemed about Brielle's age, and genuine pleasure shone on her face as she wrapped Charlotte in an embrace.

When Charlotte stepped back, she motioned toward Damien. "Audrey, I have someone for you to meet. Damien Levette has been . . . Well, I wouldn't have made it home without him."

Damien worked for a smile to greet the woman, but the feat proved impossible. His weary face refused to comply.

The pleasure slipped from the woman's expression as her brows drew together in concern. "You're exhausted." She strode back around Gulliver's head to reach Damien, and from there, everything faded to a blur.

As Audrey took charge, Gulliver's sturdy frame disappeared from beside him, and a strange man took his place, supporting Damien. Charlotte slipped under his other side, her presence easing the worry that tried to press into his chest.

"We're going to get you to bed. You can sleep as long as you need to. Audrey will know what to do." Her gentle murmur was the only thing that penetrated the fog in his mind.

He did his best not to stumble as they led him through a doorway, into a darker room with a stone floor. Then the bed appeared in the thin circle of his vision. The man who'd helped prop him up now turned him, and Damien let his body sink onto the cot.

As hands worked around him, lifting his feet and straightening his body, his eyes refused to see anything except darkness. In the morning, he would have the strength to face all these people. To meet Charlotte's family and friends.

Maybe he would even manage an earnest conversation with her father. He could finally speak with the man as an equal and make the kind of impression he'd hoped to from the beginning.

26

"He's still not awake." Charlotte motioned Audrey inside their apartment and reached for the carafe in her hands.

Audrey glanced toward the bed Damien had occupied for over a full day now, a frown gathering her brows. "The sleep should be healing for him. Is there fever?"

They both placed their loads on the table, and Charlotte motioned for Audrey to precede her toward the sleeping man. "Not that I can tell. He's barely moved, though." She'd crept over more times than she could count to make sure he still breathed, and each time the steady rise and fall of his chest was her only relief.

Audrey rested a hand on Damien's brow and studied him for a long moment, her expression intense. If Damien fought a deeper illness, Audrey's skills as a healer would enable her to detect it.

When she turned away from Damien, her expression softened into a gentle smile. "Rest is what he needs. I'll sit with him to give you a break."

Charlotte shook her head. "I'll stay here." She didn't want him to awaken to a stranger in this unknown place. And if he grew feverish or restless in his sleep, she needed to be here for him. Besides, she'd underestimated the comfort of being back within these familiar walls. She could be content for days here, with only an occasional trip outside.

A stirring on the bed tugged her notice. Perhaps it was only a shifting of the covers, for Damien's eyes still remained shut. But his expression had tightened, losing the serene, almost-lifeless appearance his features had held since yesterday.

Audrey stepped back, allowing Charlotte to move closer and seat herself in the chair she'd placed by his side. As she sank down, his eyelids flickered, then opened. Relief washed through her, and she perched on the edge of the chair as she waited for him to come fully awake.

As awareness lit his gaze, he turned his head and found her. Her own smile was impossible to contain. "You're finally awake."

He blinked, then glanced around, maybe looking for a window. "How long did I sleep?" His focus halted on Audrey, and his brows lowered as though he was trying to place her.

"We arrived yesterday afternoon, and it's evening now." Charlotte motioned to the woman standing beside her. "You were so tired, you might not remember meeting Audrey Masters. She's a good friend and the village healer."

Comprehension settled in his gaze, and his chin dipped in a nod. "It's a pleasure to meet you, Mrs. Masters. Charlotte spoke highly of you."

Warmth spread through her chest. She had mentioned Audrey a number of times, and he'd remembered. How could Audrey not be charmed with such a greeting?

Charlotte refocused on Damien. "How do you feel? Audrey brought medicines to help you recover."

Once more, his gaze flicked to Audrey, this time a hint of wariness in his eyes. His hands slid up to tuck the covering tighter around him. "I'm recovered. Just needed that sleep, though I didn't intend so much of it. I'm ready to be up and about."

"Good to hear." Audrey's voice held a hint of mirth. "Charlotte told us of your dunking in the icy lake. Might I take a quick look at your hands and feet?"

The wariness didn't leave his expression, but he extracted his hands from the covers. Charlotte shifted her chair to move out of Audrey's way so she could inspect each of the fingers. She murmured a series of questions about whether Damien could feel her pressure and any pain or numbness. She seemed satisfied with his answers, then moved to the end of the bed and lifted the covers off his feet.

They'd removed his boots and wrapped warm cloths around his feet yesterday when they first arrived, and Audrey unwound the fabric now. Her expression remained focused as she went through the same round of questions. Nothing in her demeanor had changed, but tension hung in the air that hadn't been there moments before.

When she finished her scrutiny, she lifted her focus to meet Damien's gaze. "A few of these toes don't look well. The three on this right foot, and the two smallest on the left. I brought an oil that needs to be rubbed into the skin several times a day. We may save them yet."

He nodded, a tightness pulling at his expression.

Audrey rose and moved to the table, then returned with a cup of tea and a metal cannister. "Charlotte and I will be next door for a while. There's a chamber pot under your bed."

Damien's expression eased, flooding Charlotte with guilt. After sleeping so long, he would need such a necessity. Leave it to Audrey to think of it.

When the two of them stepped into the hallway, Audrey spoke first. "Your father and brother are visiting with my menfolk. We can give your Monsieur Levette a bit of time to gather himself."

Before Audrey could open the door to her own chamber, Charlotte grabbed her arm. The torches in the corridor cast shadows on her friend's face, making it hard to read. And Charlotte had to know. "Will he be well? Recover fully?"

Audrey placed her hand over Charlotte's, her voice softening. "Only God holds our times in His hand, but I don't see anything that makes me fear your friend might grow worse. He may lose some of those toes, but there's a chance we can save them. As for the rest, he seems a remarkable man to have endured so much."

Charlotte soaked in the words as she eased out a breath, pleasure coiling through her. A remarkable man, indeed. Audrey didn't know the half. Though with her perceptiveness, she might suspect more than she let on.

When they stepped into the chamber Audrey and her husband shared with her father, both men were settled at the table, Charlotte's father and brother with them.

Audrey approached and stopped behind Levi's chair, her hand resting on her husband's shoulder. "My, you all look like you could be plotting trouble."

He reached up and covered her hand with his own, sending her a wink. "Only the best kind." Levi's British accent had become more familiar, but after having not heard it for over a week, Charlotte was struck anew by the cadence. The pair had been married for almost two years, but they still seemed to swoon in each other's presence.

"How is our patient?" Charlotte's father propped an arm on the back of his chair as he turned to her. "If you've left his side, does that mean he's awakened?"

Heat slipped up to her cheeks, and she nodded. She'd wanted to make her feelings plain about this man, and clearly she'd done just that. But this might be a good time to focus on the facts. "He seems much recovered. Audrey brought a tea for him and an oil for his feet. Hopefully he need only regain his strength now."

Her father nodded. "Glad to hear it. Is he up for a visitor?"

Charlotte glanced to Audrey, but her friend was looking at her. In fact, the entire group seemed to be waiting for Charlotte to answer. Damien might appreciate a bit of company, and it was time he get to know the people of Laurent. Her father would be a comfortable place to start, since they'd already spent several days together.

She nodded. "We're giving him a few minutes to see to personal matters, then I'm sure he'd welcome company." And the longer her father stayed busy with other matters, the less likely that he'd notice the chalice missing from their mantel. She had to face him soon to discuss the matter. Perhaps tomorrow when Damien was up and around, she could find a private moment with Papa. She was being a coward. Her father had always been fair and forgiving. *Lord, give me strength. Please.*

But perhaps Damien should be part of the conversation, too. Maybe she should bring him in right after she'd confessed privately to her father?

Both options sat heavy in her belly.

The men took a few more minutes to finish the conversation, then her father rose. "It's been a pleasure, as always." He tapped Andre's shoulder. "Son, you can stay for a few more of Levi's stories while I check on our guest."

Her father rested a hand on Charlotte's back as though to guide her toward the corridor with him. She'd planned to accompany him to their quarters and see what she could do to help Damien, but the strength in his touch made her suspect he had more in mind than a visit.

Did he plan to confront Damien about his intentions once he recovered? Her father usually kept a level head, and surely he wouldn't be rude to Damien. Yet she couldn't help the worry niggling in her midsection.

She tapped on the rear door to their chamber and cracked it enough for her voice to carry inside. "It's me, Damien. And my father."

"Enter, of course." His voice sounded stronger than before, more like the man she'd known through most of their travels.

She pushed the door wide and stepped inside, her father following behind her. Damien sat on the edge of his cot, lacing one of his boots. He looked up to offer one of those warm smiles to her and a pleasant nod to her father. "Sir. Good to see you again. I'm sorry for sleeping so long."

Damien started to rise, but her father waved him down as he pulled a chair over from their table. "Make yourself comfortable. I'm grateful you're looking much heartier than when we arrived yesterday."

Damien nodded as her father motioned for Charlotte to sit in her usual chair by the bed. With the three of them settled, Papa leaned back in his chair, his hands clasped over his middle. His gaze flicked from Damien to her, and if it weren't for the hint of a smile at his mouth, her own would have gone impossibly dry. What exactly did her father plan to say?

He leveled his focus on her. "Charlotte. You've had my curiosity piqued for days now. Are you ready to tell us what you need our help with?"

That dryness in her mouth took over now. This was the moment. With both men watching her, she had to tell all.

"I . . ." She scrambled for how best to begin. "Let me show you." The few moments it took to stand and retrieve the damaged chalice from her pack were far too short a reprieve.

When she returned to her seat, the bronze cup cradled in her hands, her father looked from her face to the heirloom, then back to her eyes. No surprise marked his expression. In fact, she couldn't tell exactly what emotion showed there. His drawn brows revealed intensity, but little more.

She'd been holding the chalice with only a little of the damage facing upward, but now she lifted it to her father, turning the cup so the melted side glared up at him. "I dropped it in the fire. By the time I realized where it was, the damage had been done. I'm so sorry." A knot pulled in her throat to match the one cinching her belly. Tears sprang up to her eyes, but she forced them back. "I tried to take it to Fort Versailles to see if anyone there might have the skill to repair it."

She glanced at Damien, whose eyes had grown wide as he took in the awful condition of the cup. "I didn't make it to the fort, as you know. But along the way, I learned Damien has incredible skill as an artist. I thought perhaps between your abilities with metal and his talent with artistic detail . . ."

She couldn't finish the idea. As capable as these two were, how could anyone—or any two—match the skill of the great Titus Trouvé, who had first cast this chalice?

Her father had remained silent throughout her explanation, and when she finally ceased speaking, she could feel his sigh all the way through her. He lifted his gaze from the chalice in her hands to meet her eyes. "I assumed something had happened to it, since it disappeared the same time you did. I wish you'd told me. Given me the chance to help you from the beginning."

Those tears she'd been holding back would no longer comply. Hot moisture rushed her eyes, blurring her vision. "I'm sorry." She could say no more as her voice cracked.

Beside her, Damien's throat cleared. The sound brought a welcome distraction, as they both glanced his way. Did he think her foolish to imagine he and her father could repair such a treasure?

But he was motioning toward something on the floor by her chair. "Could you hand me that pack, please?" A touch of something odd sounded in his voice. Not quite excitement, but close. Were his fingers itching to sketch the scene on the cup?

He took the satchel from her hand, then flipped it open and rummaged inside. Instead of pulling out the leather book with the blank pages, he extracted a small cloth bag. His fingers took an impossibly long time to unfasten the strings, but when he finished, the glimmer of metal inside made her catch her breath.

As he removed a bronze chalice from the wrapping, the world seemed to grow hazy around her. How had their village treasure gotten into his pack? But it wasn't theirs.

She still held the damaged chalice. Yet the cup in Damien's hands—the one he now held out to Papa—looked identical.

Her father's sharp inhale finally brought her vision into focus, clearing her mind. Could Damien's possibly be . . . ?

She leaned closer and made out the figure of Jesus with a child perched on each leg. The detail was exquisite, showing such an expression of love on the Savior's face. Few artists could achieve such a feat.

Her father lifted his gaze to meet hers, the awe on his face matching what thrummed through her body. "It's the pair." Then he shifted his focus to Damien. "It seems we have much to discuss."

27

As much as Damien loved having Charlotte at his side, he was grateful she'd left him to work with her father alone. This project was too important for his focus to be distracted.

And she provided too alluring a distraction.

"I've recast the cup to make a smooth curve. As we suspected, we lost more of the image in that process." Chief Durand held out the chalice for Damien to study. Being in this man's presence was even harder now that he knew he was the chief of Laurent, basically governor of the entire village. Why had Charlotte never mentioned that in all the times she spoke of her father?

Damien took the cup and studied the smoothness of what had so recently been wrinkled, distorted metal. He ran several fingers over the surface, searching for any flat spot or sharper curve that would distort the image he engraved. His touch found nothing but perfection.

He lifted his gaze to the chief with a nod of appreciation. "It seems flawless."

The older man's gaze softened. "I hope so."

Now the weight of the project's success pressed on Damien's

shoulders. He opened his sketchbook and withdrew several pages he'd already torn out. "I think this one turned out best. I also sketched the other image several times, the one of Jesus with the children. I wanted to get a better feel for the artist's style." He laid all the pages on the worktable, including both scenes. "I think part of what made him such a master is that he used the chisel at different depths in the model to create shading. That's what makes each expression come alive."

Chief Durand lifted his gaze to Damien, brows rising. "Interesting. Do you think you can mimic that technique?"

His voice didn't sound skeptical, just questioning. Yet the inquiry didn't help the ball tightening in Damien's gut. "I've been practicing." For many days, though only during daylight hours. He'd not allowed himself to work late into the night, for he needed his senses and reflexes to be as sharp as possible for this project.

The chief nodded. "All we can do is our best." He motioned toward the sketches. "From these, I'd say you've mastered the style and images." Then the man turned his focus fully to Damien. "I appreciate your efforts to help restore this chalice to its original condition. It means a lot to our people. We have so little that connects us to our heritage before our ancestors established Laurent. We've treasured this piece."

Damien nodded. He could understand their desire, though he'd focused more on things that would connect him to his more recent heritage—Michelle and his parents.

"Do you know the full story behind the chalices?" The chief eyed him, pleasure curving his mouth.

"I remember my father saying it was handed down from his father, who received it from his grandfather. Two cups were given, one to him and one to his brother, part of a set engraved by the great Titus Trouvé. The one belonging to our family has been passed down the male line. Michelle, my sister, safeguarded ours after our parents died."

He'd had no idea what a treasure they possessed. Michelle may not even have fully understood. The cup symbolized the gift of connection—of family, no matter how far separated. These people seemed to realize that. And now he was being tasked with the job of restoring the symbol of that connection to its original glory.

"There's one thing I'd like you to remember as you're working."

Damien cringed at the chief's words. Not one more layer of pressure being added to this already impossible task. But he forced himself to meet the man's gaze. "Yes, sir?"

"No matter how well you duplicate the original etching, this will never again be an exact Trouvé work of art." His dark eyes grew darker, as though he were trying to emphasize the importance of what he just said.

Was he so angry still about the damage Charlotte had inflicted? Damien had watched the chief's response when Charlotte first revealed the damaged chalice—at least, until he'd realized exactly what the treasure she held out was. He'd not recognized any harsh anger in the man's expression, only sadness. And disappointment when her father spoke of wishing she'd come to him first.

Damien swallowed, trying to force down the lump that had now risen into his throat. This had been an accident, and he would do everything he could to protect Charlotte from any recourse. "Sir, I know Charlotte never meant for this to happen. It was an accident, and I'm sure if she had it to do over again—"

Durand raised his hand to halt Damien. A hint of humor glimmered in his gaze. "You don't need to defend my daughter to me, son. What I meant to say was that the final version of this chalice, after you're finished with it, will no longer be only the work of Trouvé. It will also bear your own signature. A hint of your own style, even as you try to mimic another's. As much as we want it to look like the original chalice, I have no doubt what you add will make the original even better."

The knot in Damien's throat melted, burning on its way down as he took in the man's words. The faith he showed so freely. Only Michelle had ever believed in him so strongly. Well, and perhaps Charlotte.

He managed only a nod in response.

Chief Durand took the chalice and locked it in the brace he'd prepared for it. Damien positioned his pencils, chisels, and hammer so he'd have access to each as he needed them.

Then, with a deep breath and a heartfelt prayer, he set to work.

Damien had not expected the project to take this long, but as he tapped his smallest chisel into the edge of Jesus's robe on the third day, he couldn't deny the sense of satisfaction at each scrape that pierced exactly where and how deeply it needed to.

Nor could he deny the sharp ache in his shoulder after so many days of exacting work. Setting down his tools, he straightened slowly, easing his body out of the bent position.

"Shall I go get more salve for your neck?" Charlotte

glanced up from the mending she stitched, concern marking her features.

He shook his head, then tried to still his wince at the pain that shot up his spine. "I have some left from what you brought before."

She set aside the garment and stood. "The least I can do is rub out that knot again. You're doing all the hard work to fix my blunder."

Perhaps he should protest, but as her strong fingers worked in the salve and kneaded the pains in his neck and shoulders, he could only slump forward in a heavenly stupor. He should take more care with Charlotte's reputation, perhaps not allow her to touch him like this, especially when they were alone.

He knew beyond a doubt she was the match God had created for him. How soon before he could speak those words aloud? They'd known each other for such a short time. She deserved to be courted properly, and that meant speaking to her father.

"Well." Chief Durand's voice rang across the workroom, as though summoned by Damien's thoughts alone.

Damien jerked his head up, checking the man's face for signs of anger at seeing them so near each other. Especially when he should be at work on the chalice. But amusement seemed the primary emotion in his expression.

Charlotte didn't cease her efforts with his neck, though his own enjoyment of it wasn't quite as intense with her father approaching them.

"Do you bring good news?" Her voice sounded hopeful.

"I do." The chief stopped across the worktable from them and leaned closer to study Damien's progress on the cup. "It's coming along faster than I expected."

Thankfully, Charlotte ceased her ministrations and moved back to her sewing as her father raised his gaze to Damien.

Damien stood and worked to regather his composure as he nodded. "I'd hoped to finish it yesterday, but I suspect I'll need through tomorrow, as well. I keep having to re-sketch the sections where my fingers rub off the pencil marks."

The corners of the chief's mouth twitched. "I know that frustration well. You'll be more familiar with each line by the time you begin to chisel it, though."

"What's the news?" Charlotte's impatient tone broke in.

Her father straightened. "The council was as surprised and overjoyed as we were to find the great-great-grandson of Pierre Curtois." Chief Durand's focus honed on Damien. "Our Discovery Day feast is in three days' time. Our people want to focus the celebration on welcoming you to Laurent. Perhaps you can tell any stories you've heard of our ancestors. If this chalice is ready by then, both cups can be displayed—reunited once more."

Damien had backed up a step before he realized it. "Me?" He'd never been the cause for feasting and rejoicing, and the thought of being the central focus of all those people . . . He didn't even know how many villagers lived in Laurent, but he couldn't stand before so many. He'd never be able to find the right words.

Charlotte stepped to his side, her hand resting on his back, providing a solidness that helped anchor the chaos inside him. "Our feasts are wonderful times. An opportunity for neighbors and friends to visit without the encumbrance of work. They'll love you, there's no doubt in my mind."

He possessed enough doubt for them both, but as he

glanced from Charlotte to her father, their hope-filled expressions were impossible to deny. "Good."

Charlotte squeezed his arm. "I should begin preparations. I think I'll need to send Brielle out hunting." She left her father's workshop with a lift in her step, and the silence in her wake felt deeper than before.

Durand's chuckle filled the stillness. "There's nothing these women like more than preparing for a feast."

Damien nodded, though his belly still clenched at the thought of all those people focused on him.

Perhaps the other man could read his thoughts in his expression. "Don't let yourself worry over it. There will be so much food and frivolity, you'll simply be one of the many. And I doubt my daughter will stray far from your side, so you needn't worry about facing it all alone."

The man's voice seemed to grow serious with that last statement, and Damien sharpened his focus on the chief's face. They'd not discussed Charlotte yet. Her father hadn't seemed wary of Damien, so that might be a mark in his favor. Perhaps this was his chance to ask that question he'd been pondering.

He swallowed to bring moisture back into his dry mouth. "Sir, I . . ." He should have thought through how to say this before beginning to speak.

He'd never been eloquent with words. That had been Michelle's talent, among many others. He knew what he wanted to say, though, and perhaps straightforward would be the best approach. It was certainly the manner he preferred. "Sir, I'd like to ask your permission to court your daughter. She's a remarkable woman, a woman I didn't believe existed. Far above my station, I know, but I can't help but think God brought us together. You haven't known me long, but I hope with time you'll approve."

He kept his gaze locked with Durand's, despite the challenge of doing so. And now, he didn't miss the raising of the man's brows. "Do you intend to stay with us in Laurent for a while, or would you come and go with your trapping work?"

Heat flushed up Damien's neck. He should have spoken of the logistics before now. In truth, he'd held too much fear they wouldn't allow him to stay. "I suppose that's up to you and the rest of Laurent. I'd be honored to stay on longer if you'll allow it. Though I would need to do some trapping to earn my keep. I'd happily camp outside of village walls if you permit."

Durand's brows lowered, and Damien couldn't tell if it was from the intensity of his thoughts or from displeasure. The tightening within him pressed harder as he waited.

Then the man's expression cleared, turning earnest as his gaze searched Damien's face. "You're welcome to stay in our village as long as it suits. Perhaps Carter might have an extra bed you can use." He glanced toward the door at the rear of the workshop, the one leading to the apartment where Charlotte's uncle lived. But then his gaze locked on Damien's once more. "I can tell my daughter is impressed with you, and I look forward to knowing you better. If she agrees to a courtship, you have my permission."

Those were the words he'd been hoping for, but the chief's manner showed he had more to say. His pause made it hard to know whether Damien should answer or wait.

At last, the man let out a sigh, his eyes crinkling at the edges in a look so fatherly, it made Damien want to lean in. "Son, I try not to give advice unless it's requested, but there's one thing that strikes me every time we talk. I don't know much about your growing-up years. But I'm not sure you fully understand your value in God's eyes. Before you were formed in your mother's womb, He knew you. He planned every part of your personality and all the rest of you.

"And the best part . . . He loves how you turned out. You are exactly the outcome He hoped for. We're all impacted by the things that happen to us; they mold our personalities and attitudes. It's up to us how we let them develop our character. But the core of you—your talents, mannerisms, even the color of your eyes—was perfectly designed by Him. When He looks at you, He's pleased. And because of that, you are not second best to any other. Your Father is delighted in you. You needn't fear the opinion of anyone else."

He straightened, patting the worktable between them. "I don't normally sermonize, but something told me you needed to hear that." The lines at his eyes finally smiled as he stood. "You can speak with Charlotte when you're ready. In the meantime, I'll leave you to work in peace."

28

An entire day had passed since the conversation with Chief Durand, and his words seemed to grow stronger in Damien's mind with each passing hour. They certainly didn't allow him peace, especially as he tapped stroke after stroke to finish the chalice.

Charlotte had been called to help Mrs. Masters attend a birthing, so he didn't even have her quiet presence nearby to distract his thoughts.

"Your Father is delighted in you. You needn't fear the opinion of anyone else." Did Damien really fear what others thought of him? He'd always avoided considering opinions, if at all possible. Most people left him alone, and he returned the favor. That was as he liked it.

Had it always been like that? Even when he and Michelle were on their own, when they'd seen neighbors on the road or gone to the village for trading, people spoke to Michelle. He stayed in the background, as her protector, there for whatever she might need. But she was the one with the outgoing manner, the one who could so easily converse with others.

And people loved her. Who couldn't love Michelle, with

her kindness and endlessly giving spirit? She blessed all who knew her, but no one more than him.

So, *did* he fear what others thought of him? Perhaps he harbored a bit of concern over what the people of Laurent would think. They were Charlotte's family and friends, after all. Their opinion might determine his future with the woman who had quickly come to mean more to him than anyone else.

You needn't fear the opinion of anyone else. . . . Your Father is delighted in you.

If he were ousted by the people of Laurent, his chance with Charlotte gone forever, could having God's good opinion make up for that loss? The thought seemed laughable. He'd been estranged from God for so long, even before Michelle's death, if he were honest. Charlotte's presence in his life had helped so much, easing the numbing grief that choked his spirit before he met her.

But even now that he'd found her, there was still something yearning deep in his spirit. A longing. He'd ascribed it to the fact that she still wasn't fully his—he still had to win over her family and convince her to wed him.

But could that longing be for something altogether different?

His gaze blurred, and he placed his tools on the table. Less than an hour and he would be finished with the image, save one more thorough examination and a few final touches.

But the weight pressing on his chest wouldn't let him continue. Would barely allow him to breathe.

He dropped his head, squeezing his eyes shut against the moisture threatening. "What is it you want from me?" His words sounded loud in the workshop, though he spoke them quietly.

Your Father is delighted in you. Chief Durand had meant God, but Damien had always had trouble thinking of the Almighty as a Father. Ever since his own parents died, he'd not had a father. Not needed one.

He'd taken care of Michelle, and they'd been just fine.

He'd refused to acknowledge any void in their lives. But when Michelle died, the hole had been impossible to ignore. He'd been so angry with God for taking her. There was no way he would consider giving the Almighty a place in his life.

Did he want to allow that now? Could God truly look at him with anything other than disgust or disappointment?

He raised his gaze to the ceiling, the rough stone a better fit for him than any cathedral. He swallowed down a lump. Straightforward had worked in the conversation with Durand. Would it be too disrespectful in speaking to the Almighty? It was the best he had to offer.

"I know I said if you'd get me out of the lake and let me help Charlotte, we'd have more regular conversations. I haven't kept up my end of the bargain. I'm sorry for that." The words came easier than he'd expected, rolling out of him. And the strange thing was they didn't seem to be bouncing off the rock. It was as though God leaned close, listening. What did He think?

A new burning stung his eyes as realization swept through him. "Durand is right that I've been afraid of what people think. But maybe I've also been afraid of what you might think of me. It's hard to believe you could delight in me. Most days, it's hard to believe you can *tolerate* me." The way he'd deceived Charlotte about their route was a good example. Shame slipped through him afresh.

But he'd begun this conversation, and he would finish it. "I don't get things right. But the truth is, I want to. I want to be a good man, maybe even the one you planned when you first formed me. Will you help? Show me what that looks like, give me strength to walk in your steps for my life. Help me be the man you want me to be. The man Charlotte needs."

With each word, the struggle inside him seemed to ease. The turmoil slipped away, and a peace settled somewhere in the vicinity of that longing he'd been fighting for so long.

With a deep breath in, he pulled in the comfort, the strength he'd just asked for. *Thank you . . . Father. Help me be the son you want me to be.*

⚬⚮⚬

Excitement thrummed in the air. Not just in their apartment, but down the main corridor and buzzing through every voice as people carried food toward the assembly room.

Charlotte glanced back at Damien as they followed the stream of neighbors that direction. He gave her enough of a smile that she could still spot his nerves, but he was intent on seeing the feast through.

If she could have, she would have slowed enough for him to come alongside, for her to slip her arm in the crook of his. But there were too many people around to allow the space. Besides, they both carried baskets of food.

As they stepped into the large high-ceilinged room where every major gathering was held, she was pretty sure she heard Damien's inhale. She could definitely feel his awe as he slowed to take in the expanse.

She stepped back against the wall so they could pause and allow him a moment to take it all in. He leaned close enough for her to hear amid the voices around them. "Did your people cut this room out of the mountain?"

She stared up at the dome, attempting to see it as a new-comer. "Our ancestors discovered this room mostly as it is. They also found a few other smaller chambers that they cut larger into apartments, but I think the group lived in this room for a while until homes were made for all."

He met her gaze, his eyes shining. "If only my great-great-grandfather had been as brave as yours, my ancestors might have camped here, too. I might have been part of Laurent."

She chuckled. "Brave or stubborn. Perhaps a bit of both." She leaned her upper arm against his, stretching up so her breath brushed his ear. "Besides, there's more than one way to become part of Laurent."

He met her gaze, his eyes darkening as the corners of his lips tipped. The look reminded her of the rogue she'd first thought him to be. And when his focus slipped to her mouth, she could taste the kisses they'd shared. Her entire body yearned to repeat that sensation, here and now.

They'd not kissed since she left him and Gulliver on the trail, all those days ago. Even in the long hours when she sat nearby while he worked on the chalice, she'd been careful not to distract him from his focus.

Yet now, the etching was finished—masterfully completed. If only all these people didn't surround them.

Damien's eyes crinkled as a deeper smile played at his lips. *Later*, his gaze seemed to say.

And she would hold him to that promise.

"Charlotte, I've saved us a table." Brielle's hand on her arm nearly made Charlotte jump.

She turned to her sister, and Brielle's raised brows said she'd noticed at least a little of what passed. She didn't say anything about it, so Charlotte merely nodded.

Once they were settled at the table with Brielle, Evan, and Uncle Carter on one side, she tucked Damien between herself and Andre, then began passing out food.

"Will your father join us?"

She glanced up and followed Damien's gaze to where Papa greeted Monsieur and Madame Thayer. "He'll try to sit with us at some point, but someone always comes to speak with him or needs him to attend to a matter of business. He tries to make the rounds before he settles in to eat, but that doesn't usually help." It used to bother her that he never had a chance to eat the feast she prepared, but she couldn't blame the others for seeking his company. Their family was blessed with his presence most other days, so she could freely share with the village on feast days.

She uncovered the last of the pastry baskets and placed them in the center of the table, but it appeared she'd forgotten the berry pudding. "I need to get one more thing from our apartment. I'll be only a minute." She sent Damien an encouraging smile, then turned and slipped through the crowd toward the doors.

Only a few people still strode through the corridor, and she stepped close to the wall to allow two youngsters to dart past toward the feast. Perhaps they'd been sent on an errand to retrieve something their mother forgot.

Her family's apartment was one of the first past the hall

that led outside, but as she reached the door, she glanced at a figure approaching from farther down the corridor.

Hugo.

Her chest tightened at the sight of him. She owed him an explanation. And more.

She waited for him to reach her, and he slowed as he neared. When he passed near one of the torches that lit the hallway, the light showed a hint of wariness in his expression. Had she hurt him by not returning his affections? Had he truly *felt* affection for her, or had he been simply going along with her father's suggestions? She needed to be careful with this conversation, just in case.

She made sure her voice held a gentle smile. "Hello, Hugo."

He stopped several steps away from her. "Mademoiselle Durand." He'd not been so formal with her in a long time, but she didn't blame him.

"I wanted to say . . . thank you. For searching for me. For helping my father while I was gone." She swallowed. This was every bit as hard as she'd expected, but she couldn't stop until she'd said everything. "You're a good man. My father respects you, and he values you—your friendship, your opinion. I know he wanted . . . something . . . between us. But I'm not the one God has planned for you. I know He'll give you someone far better when the time is right. But thank you for all you've done for my father. For us all."

Hugo stood stiffly through her entire speech, and he still didn't move for a long moment after she stopped. Part of her itched to fill the silence. But what more could she say? Perhaps she'd missed something, but the way he studied her had begun to muddle her mind.

At last, he nodded. "I respect you father a great deal. It's an honor to work with him."

That seemed all he planned to say, so she did her best to offer a smile. "I know he feels the same way."

Hugo stepped forward and to the side, as though trying to edge around her. That was it, then.

She moved into their apartment doorway to allow him to pass. "Enjoy the feast."

As the sound of his footsteps faded down the hallway, she inhaled a steadying breath. It would take time for things to smooth over between them, but she would do her best for her father, and because Hugo had proven himself a good friend. And friends should be cherished.

When she returned to the celebration, other friends had already begun crowding their own table. With Damien spending most of his time in the workshop since his recovery, most of the villagers hadn't met him yet. Some had only caught that first glimpse as he stumbled across the courtyard on the day of their arrival, too exhausted to be aware of those around him.

Marcellus appeared first, with his father in the wheeled chair that helped him maneuver, despite being paralyzed from the waist down. To no one's surprise, Marcellus greeted Damien with warm enthusiasm. His mind may not have developed as much as other men his age, but he brought a joy everywhere he went, making him a favorite of the entire village.

The Chapuis family came next, with little Jacques sitting on his papa's shoulders as they welcomed Damien. The lad possessed more energy than anyone should be allowed, but being placed up high seemed to contain him better.

In families or groups, the visitors continued, and she kept an eye on Damien's expression to watch for overwhelm. He seemed content, though, responding with politeness to each person.

Partway through the parade of friends, she found Damien's hand under the table and wove her fingers through his. A simple reminder that he wasn't alone.

He slipped a glance her way, the lines at the corners of his eyes deepening in a look just for her.

Finally, her father called for silence in the room and opened the feast with a prayer of thanks, not just for the bounty they shared on the tables, but for the way only God could have brought Damien to them, reuniting what had been separated over a century before.

The words coursed warmth through her, even more so when Damien gave her hand a gentle squeeze under the table.

As she suspected, Papa attempted to join them for the meal. He managed a bowl of stew and part of a *galette* before one of the council members came to seek his advice on resolving a matter before the next meeting.

As her father followed Erik away from their table, Damien found her gaze, his raised brows saying she'd been right in foretelling that event.

Watching him interact with her family eased her angst. He seemed more comfortable around them, drawing out Andre's talkative side and even chatting with Uncle Carter, who usually preferred to blend into the background.

At last, Papa appeared at their table again. His gaze and tone stayed relaxed as he addressed Damien. "Would you like to come up and join me as we share the story of the chalices?"

As Damien rose and followed her father toward the front

of the room, Charlotte's chest tightened. She shouldn't be nervous for him. He was a grown man, after all. Perhaps a bit of her unrest stemmed from the part she'd played in damaging Laurent's chalice.

Yet without that accident, she would never have gone out seeking an artisan for the repairs. She never would have met Damien. Never would have begged him to come back to the village with her.

God's hand had woven their paths seamlessly, beginning with their ancestors and all the way to this present day. What would He do in their future?

As her father introduced Damien to the crowd, she couldn't have been prouder of both men. Damien stood tall and broad-shouldered, his appearance causing a swell in her chest as it always did. Papa's shoulders stooped more, but he still possessed that bearing that drew others to him—a natural leader.

It was Damien who told the story of his great-great-grandfather Pierre Curtois, brother to Louis, the man who led the pilgrims to discover Laurent. When Louis and his group set off for the west to find a quieter place to live, far from the unrest of New France, the chalices they had been gifted were separated, as were the brothers.

Now, the collection was complete again, the offspring reunited. Damien was the last of his line, as far as he knew. But Louis's blood ran in many a family in Laurent, as the generations married among each other.

By the time he finished the tale and the chalices were lifted for display, the room full of villagers had turned almost unruly with their cheers. The musicians struck up a lively tune, and Papa escorted Damien back to their table. Embarrassment marked his handsome features when he met her gaze, and he slipped into his seat beside her without a word. But when his hand found hers, his fingers weaving between her own, she settled against the warmth of his arm.

At last, she could allow herself to enjoy the festivities, the pleasure of friends and family, content beside the man she loved.

EPILOGUE

Charlotte lifted her gaze from the fur she was scraping as a familiar whistle sounded—the high-low-high-low-low tones that signaled one of Laurent's own approached the gate in peace. That was Damien's tone, she was almost certain of it. Three hunters had also gone out that morning, but he'd left the day before to check his trap lines and planned to be out only one night.

She dipped her hands in the bucket of wash water she'd placed by the stoop, frigid though it was in the icy air. Perhaps she should remain with her work and wait for Damien to enter the gate and come to her. Or at the very least, make sure this newcomer was him and not the hunting party.

But she knew that whistle, and the excitement within her wouldn't wait.

She started toward the gate, wiping her wet hands on her skirt. With each step, her stride grew faster. Longer. With the weak winter sun shining this afternoon, several other women also worked outside their doors. She didn't slow to call greetings, just kept her focus on the opening in the wall.

There. That familiar outline, those broad shoulders, the brindle color of his coat, even the way he walked in his snowshoes. Her heart leapt and her feet shifted into a run to match her pulse.

She closed the last ten strides between them as Damien led Gulliver through the gate, then turned to her. His white teeth flashed in a grin as he strode forward and swept her into the hug she'd been longing for all day.

He wrapped her tight, tucking his face into the crook of her neck. "My Charlotte."

She clung to him as he held her. Thankfully, he seemed reluctant to release her. She breathed in the scent of him that he always carried when he came in from his traps—something wild and manly, fully unique to him.

Too soon, his arms around her loosened and he pulled back, moving his hands up to cradle her face. Her hair must have been a mess, for he smoothed strands back from her cheeks, then kept his hands cupped there. She drank him in, the same way his gaze roamed over her.

"I can't do these overnight trips anymore. I miss you too much."

As much as she loved those words, she had to fight the urge to reach up and grab his coat, then pull his mouth down for a kiss. Why did he hold back?

Perhaps he was concerned about the onlookers, though their nearest audience worked thirty strides away. Besides, everyone knew they were courting. The last four months, Damien had been a permanent fixture in the midst of their family, sleeping on an extra cot in Uncle Carter's apartment, but taking most of his meals in the Durand home, just as her uncle did.

He still studied her, as though he'd not seen her face in weeks, maybe months. Perhaps she really should initiate the kiss.

But before she could act, he lowered his hands from her cheeks and ran them down her arms to take her fingers in his. As he lifted them in his own gloved hands, pressing a kiss to the back of one hand, then the other, she squeezed his fingers. Her skin was bright red from working in the cold without gloves, certainly not a flattering appearance. But at least he wasn't looking at her hands. His gaze stayed locked on her face.

"Charlotte, this may be too soon, but I've never been good with patience. We can wait as long as you wish, but say you'll marry me. Please. You're the one who completes me. God's perfect match for me. And being apart from you is far too hard."

Tears sprang to her eyes, her heart brimming with so much emotion she couldn't find the words at first. She'd hoped this was coming. Courtship was intended to grow toward marriage, after all. But hearing the words on Damien's lips . . . the fulfillment of what she'd been longing for . . .

She moved her hands to his chest, pressing them flat against his coat, his fingers still wrapped around hers. She needed that strong contact as she met his gaze. "I would be honored to marry you. The way God brought our paths together, the certainty in my spirit as I pray for you—for us—I don't doubt for a minute you're the man He planned for me. He's brought us together through one miracle after another, and I can't wait to see what else is in store. I'll go with you wherever you want."

Those beautiful creases at the corners of his eyes deepened as his mouth widened in a smile that lit her all the way through. "Good. You name the day, and I'll have a home ready for us. If you want to go anywhere else at any time, just let me know."

A home ready? They'd not talked about where they might live. In truth, this was the first time they'd spoken of marriage at all. Did he plan to set her up in a cabin somewhere as he'd said other trappers built, either for their belongings or their women?

She softened her words with a smile that came so easily. "I don't want us to be separated, Damien. I'll go where you go, I'll help with your traps and your skins and whatever else you need. I don't want to be left behind."

He moved his hands back to her face, cupping her cheeks and ears. "I'd like that. A lot. We'll make our home here, but I'd rather not spend another night by myself once we wed. I'd miss you too much."

Surprise jolted through her. "Here? In Laurent?"

He nodded, something mischievous slipping into his gaze. "Your father mentioned the Rochettes' apartment might be available since they'll be moving into the bigger new home with their daughter's family. I plan to speak with Monsieur Rochette today to see if we might use it."

Hope surged in her chest. "But is that possible? With your trapping? Don't you need to set up quarters closer to a fort?"

His delicious lips twitched. "I might make an occasional trip to the fort for trading. Your father also mentioned that the council plans to send another trading party or two each year. If your people have been able to thrive a hundred years without living near the fort, I'm hoping we'll be able to do the same."

Then a bit of seriousness slipped into his expression. "Charlotte, I'll take you wherever you want to go. If you wish to see the world, all you have to do is tell me. But your family is important to you. They're important to me, too. I won't separate you from them, not when this is your home. Our home."

She could stand it no longer. Gripping his coat, she pulled this wonderful man close enough to draw his lips to hers. No matter what lay ahead, God had brought the perfect match for her.

And she would cling to them both for the rest of her days.

USA Today bestselling author **Misty M. Beller** writes romantic mountain stories set on the 1800s frontier and woven with the truth of God's love. She was raised on a farm in South Carolina, so her Southern roots run deep. Growing up, her family was close, and they continue to maintain those ties today. Her husband and children now add another dimension to her life, keeping her both grounded and crazy. God has placed a desire in Misty's heart to combine her love for Christian fiction and the simpler ranch life, writing historical novels that display God's abundant love through the twists and turns in the lives of her characters. Learn more and see Misty's other books at MistyMBeller.com.

Sign Up for Misty's Newsletter

Keep up to date with Misty's news on book releases and events by signing up for her email list at mistymbeller.com.

More from Misty M. Beller

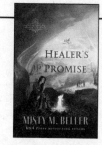

British spy Levi Masters is captured while investigating a discovery that could give America an upper hand in future conflicts. Village healer Audrey Moreau is drawn to the captive's commitment to honesty and is compelled to help him escape. But when he faces a severe injury, they are forced to decide how far they'll go to ensure the other's safety.

A Healer's Promise • BRIDES OF LAURENT #2

BETHANYHOUSE

You May Also Like . . .

On assignment to help America win the War of 1812, Evan MacManus is taken prisoner by Brielle Durand—the key defender of her people's secret French settlement in the Canadian Rocky Mountains. But when his mission becomes at odds with his growing appreciation of Brielle and the villagers, does he dare take a risk on the path his heart tells him is right?

A Warrior's Heart by Misty M. Beller
BRIDES OF LAURENT #1
mistymbeller.com

Nate Long has always watched over his twin, even if it's led him to be an outlaw. When his brother is wounded in a shootout, it's their former prisoner, Laura, who ends up nursing his wounds at Settler's Fort. She knows Nate wants a fresh start, but struggles with how his devotion blinds him. Do the futures they seek include love, or is too much in the way?

Faith's Mountain Home by Misty M. Beller
HEARTS OF MONTANA #3
mistymbeller.com

After her son goes missing, Joanna Watson enlists Isaac Bowen—a man she prays has enough experience in the rugged country—to help. As they press on against the elements, they find encouragement in the tentative trust that grows between them, but whether it can withstand the danger and coming confrontation is far from certain in this wild, unpredictable land.

Love's Mountain Quest by Misty M. Beller
HEARTS OF MONTANA #2
mistymbeller.com

◆ BETHANYHOUSE

More from Bethany House

On her way to deliver vaccines to a mining town in the Montana Territory, Ingrid Chastain never anticipated a terrible accident would leave her alone and badly injured in the wilderness. When rescue comes in the form of a mysterious mountain man, she's hesitant to trust him, but the journey ahead will change their lives more than they could have known.

Hope's Highest Mountain by Misty M. Beller
HEARTS OF MONTANA #1
mistymbeller.com

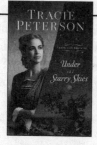

When an accident leaves Cassandra Barton incapacitated, she spends her time compiling a book of stories about the men working on the Santa Fe Railroad. But worry grows as revolutionaries set out to destroy the railroad. As the danger intensifies, Cassie and her longtime friend Brandon must rely on their faith to overcome the obstacles that stand in the way.

Under the Starry Skies by Tracie Peterson
LOVE ON THE SANTA FE
traciepeterson.com

Longing for a fresh start, Julia Schultz takes a job as a Harvey Girl at the El Tovar Hotel, where she's challenged to be her true self. United by the discovery of a legendary treasure, Julia and master jeweler Christopher Miller find hope in each other. But when Julia's past catches up with her, will she lose everyone's trust?

A Gem of Truth by Kimberley Woodhouse
SECRETS OF THE CANYON #2
kimberleywoodhouse.com

BETHANYHOUSE